JOE BARRETT

SEMI-GLOSS

Black Rose Writing | Texas

©2023 by Joe Barrett
All rights reserved. No part of this book may be reproduced, stored in a retrieval system or transmitted in any form or by any means without the prior written permission of the publishers, except by a reviewer who may quote brief passages in a review to be printed in a newspaper, magazine or journal.

The author grants the final approval for this literary material.

First printing

This is a work of fiction. Names, characters, businesses, places, events, and incidents are either the products of the author's imagination or used in a fictitious manner. Any resemblance to actual persons, living or dead, or actual events is purely coincidental.

ISBN: 978-1-68513-182-1
PUBLISHED BY BLACK ROSE WRITING
www.blackrosewriting.com

Printed in the United States of America
Suggested Retail Price (SRP) $21.95

Semi-Gloss is printed in Minion Pro

*As a planet-friendly publisher, Black Rose Writing does its best to eliminate unnecessary waste to reduce paper usage and energy costs, while never compromising the reading experience. As a result, the final word count vs. page count may not meet common expectations.

SEMI-GLOSS

SAMMY

"Nine-one-one, what's your emergency?"

"Hey, there. Uh, yeah. I don't know if I'd call it an actual emergency, like, at this point."

"This line is reserved for actual emergencies, sir."

"Well, this definitely was an emergency, not too long ago."

"Is it an emergency now?"

"See, I'm not really sure if you'd quantify it as an emergency, right this minute."

"We have to keep this line open for emergencies, sir."

"Okay," I say, "so, can you tell me…um, hello?"

Rude.

I totally should have shut down this thing with Janice weeks ago.

I Google "what to do when you wake up next to a dead girl" and Google tells me to call nine-one-one, so that's no help. And now I've got a sick feeling in my gut that this whole dead-Janice-in-my-bed thing is going to make me miss brunch. I know that sounds shallow, but Saturday brunch, like, only happens once a week.

Screw it. I pay taxes.

"Nine-one-one, what's your emergency?"

"There's a dead girl in my bed." Probably what I should have said first time around.

"Alright, sir. I need you to calm down." I glance at my iWatch. My heart rate a steady sixty-two beats per minute. The operator is reading from a script. But the clock's ticking on brunch, so I just get on with it.

"Right, fine. Calm. What do I do about the dead girl?"

"Okay, okay. So first, let's just make sure she's really dead."

"Beg pardon?" That doesn't seem right.

"The girl. We need to make sure she's really dead."

"Whatever." Sigh. What kind of logic is this? "So should I, like, stuff a pillow on her face and hold it there for a few minutes?"

"What? No! What are you talking about?!"

"What are you talking about? You said we needed to make sure she's really dead."

"I need you to *check again* to see if she's really dead!"

"Ah…" That makes more sense. I glance at the bed. "She's dead."

"You're absolutely certain."

"Pretty sure. I mean, I'm not a doctor or anything, but she hasn't taken a breath since I woke up. And she's cold to touch. And she, um, you know, messed up the bed."

"Messed up the bed?"

"Number two." Sigh.

"Sir?"

"She had a bowel movement in my bed, okay? And I just washed the sheets, like, four days ago." Probably didn't need to share that last part. Makes me sound petty.

Finally the operator takes my information, tells me she's sending a car.

I hang up. Take a beat. Try to think about Janice instead of brunch, which is hard because I'm super hungry. But I've got to wait for nine-one-one to send some kind of body-removal crew, anyway. So I try to forget about Belgian waffles and spend a few minutes thinking about Janice. Seems like the right thing to do.

She was an okay girl, that Janice. Always said she liked my eyes. "Pretty green eyes" she would say, and I would smile and say "Thanks." It occurs to me, most of our conversations were that short. Wonder if

English was her second language. Anyway, she picked a totally inconvenient time to die, but she was an okay girl, that Janice.

I'm thinking about Belgian waffles when I'm startled by loud knocks a few moments later.

"Whoa." I pull open the door of my place, two of Tampa's finest on the front steps. This just keeps getting weirder and weirder. "Uh, is there a problem, officers?"

"Someone placed a nine-one-one call from this address about a dead body?"

"Oh, yeah. That's right."

"I'm Officer Kundy. This is Officer Brady."

"Hey, guys."

"Can we come in?"

"For sure. Sorry." I step back from the door, more than a little surprised. "Nine-one-one sent the cops?"

"Exactly who did you think nine-one-one would send?"

"Don't know, maybe someone from the morgue? I mean, she's already dead, so…"

"Can you show us the body, please?"

"Yeah, sure. She's right back there. In the bedroom." Officer Kundy walks down the hall, sticks his head into the open door of my bathroom. "No, on the right. Sorry, it's kind of a mess. Wasn't expecting company."

Officer Brady just stands there, looking at me.

"Do you guys want a cup of coffee or anything? I've got a Keurig."

"No, thank you." Officer Brady, curt.

It suddenly occurs to me that these guys might be just as put out by this whole dead-Janice-in-my-bed thing as I am. Probably were expecting to be out fighting crime today. Or driving around eating donuts. Don't really know what cops do. But instead, a sucky job like taking away a dead body. This is a hassle, all around.

I wonder if these guys have to clean up my apartment, too? Can't picture the cops doing my laundry in their starchy uniforms, so figure they just hire a service or something. How ever they do it, would be awesome if they can get this place cleaned up while I'm still out at brunch. I love the idea of coming home to a freshly serviced apartment…like when you go to breakfast at a nice hotel and by the time you get back the maids have already cleaned your room. Nice way to start the day.

"So, you guys get a lot of calls like this?" I try to make conversation, pass the time.

"No, we don't."

"Really? I read somewhere every twelve seconds someone in the United States dies. Never occurred to me that picking up the bodies is something cops do." Officer Brady just looks at me. "So, anyway, you got this covered or do you need me to stick around?"

"Excuse me?" He speaks slowly, like he spends his days talking to little kids or something.

"I was hoping to head out and grab some brunch."

"You'll need to stay here until the medical examiner and detectives arrive. In the meantime, why don't we take a seat and you can give me your statement."

"My statement?" I upturn palms, shrug my shoulders. "I woke up. She was dead."

"Yeah, well," Officer Brady in that same slow voice. He walks into my kitchen, sits down like he owns the place. "We're going to need a little more information than that, sir."

Five minutes later and we're just getting to the dead-Janice-in-my-bed part.

"So, you didn't go out last night with Miss…"

"Janice." This could get a little embarrassing, right here.

"Her full name?"

"Yeah. We weren't really on, like, a full name basis."

"You don't know her last name? And how long did you say you knew her?"

"I didn't. But it was, like, three or four weeks. Maybe a month, max. Definitely not more than a month."

"And you were seeing her the whole time? Dating, I mean."

"Well, I wouldn't exactly call it dating. I mean, I didn't even know her last name." A helpful point, I think, for Officer Brady to depth-gauge my relationship with the deceased.

"But you were intimate," Officer Brady, flat tone.

"Oh, sure. Physically, yeah."

"How often did you see her?"

"Couple, two or three times a week over the past month, I guess."

"And you didn't start the evening with Miss…with Janice, last night?"

"I never started the evening with Janice. She would just show up."

"And then go home with you?"

"Well, drink furiously, then go home with me. Janice drank like a fish."

"So she would be intoxicated when she went home with you."

"That part I can only assume, as I was always intoxicated when she went home with me. But I think it's a fair assumption, yeah."

"And in the mornings, you guys didn't…"

"Gone in the morning. Every time. Before I even woke up. And that's why it was so strange, her still in bed when I woke up today. Until I figured out she was dead. Cleared up that particular mystery on the quick."

"So, this morning," Brady continues, disapproving look, "when you noticed she was still in the bed with you…"

"When I smelled her…it."

"It?"

"What do you want me to say? She had a bowel movement in my bed and the smell woke me up. Don't look at me like that…it's the truth."

"Fine. And then?"

"And then I immediately got the hell out of bed. What'd you think, I was going to spoon with her or something? It freaked me out."

"And that's when you realized she was dead."

"No. At first I just thought she had really bad manners. I didn't realize she was dead until I poked her with a broom."

"You poked her with a broom? Why?"

"Because she wasn't moving. She didn't move when I freaked out."

"You freaked out because you thought she was dead?"

"I freaked out because she had a bowel movement in my bed! Are you kidding with that look? Put yourself in my position. It was a difficult moment."

"You're talking about the bowel movement, not the fact that you woke up next to a dead woman."

"Take your pick. Anyway, when she didn't move, I poked her with a broom. To try and wake her up."

"A broom? Why not just shake her shoulder or something?"

"I wasn't going to touch her."

"Because you thought she was..." I pull an exasperated face. "Right. Got it. You didn't want to touch her because she had a bowel movement in your bed."

"Bingo."

"Johnny!" Officer Brady calls over my shoulder. "Check the shoulders, back and neck for bruising. Like from a broom handle!"

"I didn't poke her with the handle. I poked her with the sweep-end. She might have a tiny bit of brush-burn, but probably no bruising."

"And then you called nine-one-one."

"Yeah. I mean, sequentially, I called nine-one-one after I realized she wasn't moving. Like, not long after."

"How long after?"

"I don't know exactly. I mean, I was still way hung over, you know? Maybe an hour. Not more than an hour and a half."

"Son, what the hell were you doing for an hour and a half when you knew there was a dead woman in your bed?" This is the first time he's called me "son" instead of "sir." Mildly offensive since I'm thirty-one and this Brady guy can't be more than six or seven years older than me.

"Oh, come on. I was hung over, maybe still a little drunk. And this kind of hassle, I was totally not expecting. So I made some coffee. Then I took a shower. And then I got kind of distracted on Instagram. It might only have been an hour. Like I said, not sure. Anyway, what's the diff? Eventually, I poked her a few more times and figured she was a goner. And that's when I called nine-one-one. So you've got the lot of it. Now, unless you need something else, I'd really love to step out and grab a bite to eat while you guys get this whole thing cleaned up."

Feeling things to be adequately wrapped, I rise and make my way towards the door.

"Please take a seat, son. We're not going to be done here for quite some time."

I'm his son again. I drop my shoulders, pull an exasperated mug for Officer Brady. He shakes his head slowly and walks back to join Officer Kundy.

By my watch, maybe only an hour left to grab a good table at The Oxford Exchange. And a bad table at the Oxford Exchange really isn't any kind of brunch at all.

PENNY

"Aren't you a little young to be tramping around?" An old guy remarks from a two-top just outside the Starbucks "wait for your drinks here" area.

"I graduated university last year." You always say university instead of college. That's how they know you're not from the states. Catelyn *never* traveled as a U.S. citizen. I try to remember Catelyn's insulted look, put that expression on my face.

"Really? Sorry, I…" The old man, stammering, like a bartender who's just been handed a legit I.D. by someone who looks as young as, well, me.

"It's okay." I flash him a no-worries grin. "Happens all the time. I suppose looking so young will be a real gift when I'm older."

"How old are you?"

"Nineteen, graduated a bit early." Fifteen, actually. But it's not like I'm asking for booze or cigarettes, so why would this guy think I'm lying? I let the awkwardness settle, wait for him to redirect the conversation.

"How long have you been in the states?" He eyes my backpack.

"Three weeks."

"Where are you from originally?"

Here I smile, nod backwards at the maple leaf on my red-and-white backpack.

"Je peux voir que vous venez du Canada. Je veux dire, d'ou venez-vous au Canada?" the old man chuckles.

Here I take a deep meditative breath, try to control my frustration. Of course, I know what he's asking. But only from context. Because I don't speak French. Because I'm not really Canadian. That's the trouble with old people. You're more than likely to run into some know-it-all who does, actually, speak French. And just can't wait to show it off.

Why I decided to be a Canadian backpacker is, Catelyn always considered Canada to be a kind of short bus version of the United States. And I don't think she meant it in a bad way. It's just that Canadians have this super friendly, sorta goofy vibe about them. An aura of heartbreaking innocence, like the way you feel watching those close-up, wide-angle lens videos of puppies on YouTube. And an innocent vibe is helpful when you're pretending to be something that you're not. Especially if you're a fifteen-year-old runaway trying to pass for a legit backpacker.

Also, Canadians speak an almost normal version of English. You just have to stick a wonky accent on a few words, like, say "a-boat" instead of "about." According to Catelyn, no one ever gets called out for having a fake Canadian accent.

And the best thing about Canadian backpackers is that they wear their country like a badge of honor – all reds and whites, maple leaf patches plastered everywhere on their stuff – just to make totally sure that nobody mistakes them for citizens of the cruel superpower neighbor to their south. The Canada ornamentation is a distraction. And when people are distracted, you're more in control. If you ever want to hide in plain sight, you could do worse than dressing up as a Canadian backpacker.

"J'ai dit, d'ou viens-tu au Canada?" the old man says again, smiling expectantly.

The one landmine when you're pretending to be a Canadian backpacker is that almost everyone in Canada speaks at least a little bit of French. Catelyn said that most of the world just ignores this whole 'French charade' thing that Canadians do, because it's essentially harmless. Like how you'd ignore some guy on a bus who's talking to his imaginary friend about comic books. As long as he's not talking to his imaginary friend about blowing up the bus, you just roll with it. No harm, no foul – just like Canadians and the whole French thing. But it can be a real pain in the ass when you're pretending to be a Canadian backpacker.

"Est-ce que tout va bien, mademoiselle?"

I don't understand what the old guy is saying now but can clearly hear suspicion creeping into his voice. A Canadian who doesn't speak French? What kind of sinister ruse is this? Old guy's obviously read too many spy novels. Though how he could possibly consider this a "see something, say something" moment, I have no idea.

"I'm sorry, sir." I'm the picture of innocence. "I was thinking about asking you for a ride, but I got kind of a rape-y vibe when you started speaking French."

If you ever want to halt a conversation with any guy over the age of thirteen, just mention that he's giving off a rape vibe. Never fails to shut them up.

Old guy exchanges his suspicious expression for a look of semi-guilty bewilderment.

I give him a wink, walk away.

Don't bother to hit up a couple of senior ladies at the next table, the awkward glitch with old guy killing any hope of a ride from this particular Starbucks. Consider walking back towards Union Station. But as helpful as my Canadian flag backpack might be when it comes to getting rides from strangers, it's also a giant bullseye for some of the sketchier types who hang around train stations.

So I lug my backpack towards downtown with no idea how to find my way to the West side of South Tampa. No real idea of what I'm going to do when I get there, even though I have a destination.

I have a few days, a week on the outside, before someone notices that I'm gone and starts looking. I picture my face on a milk carton, a copy of my school portrait hanging at the foot of the stairs in the house where I used to live, right up until yesterday. The picture's almost two years old, but it's the one Dad would pick. It's the only one he's got. But who'd believe that smiling thirteen-year-old girl—who looks like everything's right with the world—would ever run away from home? Who could guess that eighteen months after that picture was taken, my world would collapse. For a second time. And there aren't any pictures of me since then. I think it's the last happy picture of me that will ever hang on any wall anywhere.

Oh, God. What am I doing here?

Catelyn's number one life rule: Don't Panic.

No matter how bleak things look – you never, ever, ever panic.

Instead, you remember that the universe rewards people who don't panic, and you trust it with your whole self. Panic is what happens when you let yourself think about how bad things could possibly get. Real travelers, Catelyn says, live their lives day-to-day. Sometimes minute-to-minute, always open to – always trusting that – an opportunity will come up to turn bad situations into good ones. When you panic, you can't see those opportunities. Panic is for suckers, Catelyn used to say. And Penny Sullivan is no sucker.

So I step from the sidewalk into the shade of an enormous oak tree, pull off my Canada pack and stand with my back against the thick grey trunk. I shut my eyes and breathe, the way that Catelyn taught me, the way she says that Navy Seals breathe when things aren't going great.

In, two-three. I let the image of Catelyn come into my mind.

Hold, two-three. I let in the thoughts about how Catelyn had the same blood type and DNA as I've got, and she's the closest thing to a real hero that I've ever met.

Exhale, three-four-five-six. There was nothing Catelyn couldn't do. And I'm made of all the same stuff as she was.

In, two-three. Every great adventure starts with what suckers see as a hopeless situation. But Penny Sullivan is not a sucker. The universe is kind to people who don't panic.

Suddenly I feel, more than hear, an explosive crack just a few feet behind me. Oddly, my mind remains calm while my body reacts with a jerk forward that sends me stumbling over the Canada backpack at my feet.

On hands and knees, I lift my head into a black cloud of exhaust smoke. I'm looking at a parking spot on the opposite side of the tree I'd been leaning on. A motorcycle that could be a prop for the TV Land sitcom *Hogan's Heroes* is sputter-blasting dark smoke and backfire. Skinny guy, trying to coax the bike to life. Pink Floyd tank top, cutoff sweatpants, doesn't notice me until he glances into the side mirror. At which point he startles, nearly drops the bike sideways onto his leg.

"Whoa, Jesus! Are you okay?! I didn't even see you!"

Skinny guy releases the hand accelerator, bike stalls. He's looking over his shoulder at me on the ground. I'm getting the weird impression that he thinks he might have hit me with his motorcycle, despite the fact that the bike is parked and doesn't even seem likely to start.

"Yeah, I'm fine." I pull myself up. "You just scared me is all."

"You came right out of nowhere. Sure you're okay?" He shakes his head.

Part of me wants to mention that the bike hasn't moved an inch since I've been here, but I feel like that conversation could get strange.

"Totally fine." I pull the pack onto my shoulder.

"Whoa. Oh, *Can-a-da*!" He's checking out my backpack. "Right?"

"Sure." I slip my other arm through the strap of my pack.

"Take off, you hoser! Beauty, eh?"

"You bet." I turn back to the sidewalk.

"You know…those guys! The Canada guys. Bill and Ted. Take off, eh!"

"Bob and Doug." Coincidentally, not forty-eight hours ago I was watching YouTube videos of *Great White North* to hone my Canadian accent. Another tip from Catelyn.

"Say again?"

"You're thinking Bob and Doug McKenzie, the *Great White North* guys. Bill and Ted were the guys who had, you know, an excellent adventure." I punctuate this statement with a brief air guitar, then stop because it feels stupid.

"Right on. A classic. You get that up in Canada?"

"Yes. We get all the movies up in Canada." I'm about to mention that Keanu Reeves, AKA Ted, is actually from Canada, when I realize that it doesn't matter.

"So, hey. Where you headed? You need a lift somewhere?"

"You want to give me a ride?" I look at him, then the bike. "On that?"

"Hey, I almost killed you. The least I could do is give you a lift, right?"

"I don't have a helmet."

"Neither do I. You don't need one in Florida."

Of course…because the only reason to wear a motorcycle helmet would be state law.

"My aunt has a place in Beach Park." This, in fact, is true. "You wouldn't be headed in that direction?"

I'm not sure what I want his answer to be.

"No way! I'm headed to a gig in Beach Park right now."

The universe has a dark sense of humor.

"A gig? Are you, what, an artist?"

"I like to think so."

"Musician?" Because what else could he be?

"Painter."

"Oh. Murals?"

"Houses. Interior and exterior." Yeah, that makes sense.

He kicks the starter hard. After a couple of coughs the engine catches a regular rhythm, almost as if it had been waiting for me before starting properly. Penny Sullivan is a traveler. But she's not necessarily the type of traveler who'd climb on the back of a definitely unstable motorcycle with a probably unstable stranger. This is what I'm thinking as I climb onto the back of the bike, shout my aunt's address into his ear.

"Rufus!" he replies. I'm not sure if this is some kind of hipster slang, so I shout the address again.

"Right! Got it. Rufus!" He shouts again, bobbing his thumb at his face until it finally dawns on me that Rufus is his name. And he's waiting, eyes expectant, for me to reply before driving off, probably to kill us both. This is so not me.

"Catelyn!" I shout, bobbing a thumb at my face. It just comes out.

"My friends call me Roofie!" he shouts, accelerating into traffic.

He continues to shout conversation at me for the next ten minutes, but I can't make out a word over the wind and engine noise. So I just enjoy the ride – a fifteen-year-old runaway girl, pretending to be a Canadian backpacker, wearing no helmet on the back of a deathtrap motorbike driven by a thirty-something stranger nicknamed after a popular date-rape drug.

It's the best I've felt since hopping the overnight train to Tampa from Penn Station about thirty hours ago.

SAMMY

"I already told Officer Brady everything that happened." Older guy, grey hair, grey mustache, brown suit. Looks kind of like this old television character, Barney Miller, from…I can't remember the name of the show.

"I'm going to have to be a little more thorough, *Mister…?*" he lets the sentence hang.

"Okay, I understand, *sir*." Figure I should address him formally as well.

"It's Detective."

"Yeah, you told me that."

"No, I mean, you address me as *Detective* O'Hare. Not sir."

"Okay, *Detective*. I understand."

"Mister…?" He repeats. Why do I feel like we're playing some kind of parlor game?

"Detective…?"

"Jesus! What's your name, son?"

"Oh, sorry. It's Sammy. Uh, Sam."

"Full name, please."

"Samuel."

"Samuel…" He rolls his hand in front of my face, signaling for more.

This guy knows my full name. I already gave it to Officer Brady. He just wants to hear me say it. Fine, if that's what it takes for these cops to stop pestering me, remove the body and clean up the mess so I can get to brunch...

"It's Samuel Davis Junior."

"Your name is Sammy Davis Junior." O'Hare smirks.

"You think I'd make that up? My family is in the entertainment business."

"Your surname is Davis, then?"

"My surname is Junior. My middle name is Davis. My first name is Samuel. Same as my father."

"So, your name is actually Sammy Davis Junior, Jr."

"Sure is."

Okay, long story short. My grandfather, Bud Junior, owned a television station back in the 1960's which produced its own content. Sammy Davis Jr. was featured in one of his productions on the night my grandmother gave birth. And because our surname is Junior, my grandfather thought it would be just hysterical to name his son Sammy Davis. My grandfather had a sense of humor. My father does not. Dad passed me the name as a kind of misplaced revenge, I think. We don't discuss it. He and I don't discuss anything, actually. Which suits me just fine.

"Okay." Detective O'Hare sighs, like he's done digging into my unique familial naming conventions. "Why don't you just tell me what happened here?"

"I woke up and she was dead."

"According to Officer Brady, you first noticed that the victim, one Janice Pirelli..."

"Pirelli?"

"Yes, Janice Pirelli."

"Are you sure it's Pirelli?" I wouldn't have pegged her as being of Italian descent. She has red hair, for Christsakes. Had red hair. Though she still has it, even though she's dead now.

"That's what it says on her driver's license. You didn't know her last name?"

Maybe she dyed her hair red. But it's not, like, exotic or emo. Not scarlet or purplish. It's normal, redhead red. Doesn't make any sense…meh, no point losing sleep over it.

"I went through all this with Officer Brady."

"So, you noticed Miss Pirelli had defecated in your bed. And then you poked her with a broom…"

"The sweep-end of the broom, I didn't poke her with the handle."

"Right, I've got that. And then you made some coffee, took a shower and kind of hung around for a while before calling nine-one-one."

"Wouldn't say I just hung around. I checked my e-mail and got caught up on Instagram, like I do at the start of every day. It's a kind of morning routine for me."

"But it's not routine for you to wake up next to a dead body."

"No, that's true."

"Do you have a problem with your eyes, Mister Davis Junior?"

"Just, Junior. And no, my eyes are fine. Why, do you have a problem with my eyes?" People say that my eyes are my best feature. They're a vivid green, which is unusual, and makes them stunning.

"Officer Brady found eighteen empty bottles of Visine in the drawer of your bathroom."

"Yeah, keep meaning to throw those out."

"Why would you have eighteen empty bottles of Visine, Mr. Junior?"

"I just, you know, when the bottle runs out and I've got the stuff in my eyes, it's easier to drop the empty in the drawer than it is to walk over to the garbage can. So, I'm kind of a slob. What are you, my mother?"

"But why so much Visine, Mr. Junior? Most people take six months or a year to go through a single bottle of the stuff."

"Yeah, well, most people don't have bright green peepers like mine. I like to keep the whites white, okay. Shows them off. I feel like this conversation is getting a little too personal."

"Did you know that Visine is a toxic substance, Mr. Junior?"

"No, I...wait, really? But it's okay to put in your eyes, right? I mean, that's what it's for, isn't it?"

"When digested in sufficient amounts, the Tetrahydrozoline in Visine can cause nausea and diarrhea. Excessive amounts can be fatal."

"Yeah, sure, but it's okay to put in your eyes, isn't it? How could they sell it all over the place if it wasn't okay to put in your eyes?"

"Yes, it's fine to put in your eyes." Detective O'Hare squeezes the bridge of his nose with thumb and forefinger, like he's got a brain freeze.

"Good. Because I use a lot of that stuff."

"You're missing my point, Mr. Junior." Detective O'Hare, suddenly all serious and authoritative-like.

"No, I am not," I snap back. "Wait. What's your point?"

"We were able to do a preliminary blood test on the victim." Detective O'Hare calmly looks at a single sheet of paper given to him by one of the medical examiners. "Are you aware that Ms. Pirelli was pregnant?"

"Ms. Pirelli? Like, Janice's mom?"

"What? No, Mister Junior, *your* Janice Pirelli. Was pregnant. Why would a blood report have anything to do with her mother...?"

I don't hear the last part because the room is spinning. This can't be right. This can't be right. We were careful. We were pretty careful. We tried to be careful, at least. Probably. We were pretty drunk, though. No! Oh, man. I can't be a father. My life isn't together enough to have a baby.

"I...that can't be right. Can you have them check again?"

"Are you okay, Mr. Junior?"

"No. No, I'm definitely not okay. Are you sure it's mine?" Girl would show up at the bar a couple of nights a week, go home with me, disappear in the morning. I can't be the only guy with whom she had this type of relationship. Still...suddenly, blind screaming panic. "What?!"

"What, what?" Detective O'Hare, reveling in calmness while my world explodes.

"Why are you looking at me like that?!"

"You do realize that the pregnancy was terminated when Ms. Pirelli died." Like he's talking to a little kid. Like how Officer O'Hare talked to me earlier. But at this point, I couldn't care less.

"Oh. Thank God." I collapse in my chair, exhale, unaware that I'd been holding most of my breath. "Wow. Of course. Sure. She wouldn't be pregnant anymore. Man, looks like I dodged a bullet there, huh?"

"You seem relieved."

"Yeah, for sure. I mean, it's sad and all – not just about the baby but about Janice, too. Very sad, all of it." My mind inadvertently shifts to Belgian Waffles. "But, man, this thing I had with Janice, it was super, super casual. And I am in no way ready to be a father, you know? You have kids?"

"Two."

"Yeah, well, no offence. Me? I don't want kids, don't really see the point of them. But I'm only thirty-one, so maybe that will change someday."

"Let's hope not."

"From your lips to God's ears. Anyway, are we almost done? I know a place across town that does a whole day brunch on Saturday, so if I bolt now I can probably catch the tail end. I'm a big brunch guy, look forward to it all week. Hey, by the way, you guys are going to clean up the sheets and everything when you take away the body, right?"

"You seem awfully casual about this whole situation, Mr. Junior. I find that a little strange. Most people would be more upset waking up next to a dead girlfriend."

"Yeah. Well, like I said, this thing with Janice was way casual. I definitely wouldn't call her my girlfriend, per se. I mean, frankly, we never even talked about what was going on with us. I assumed we were just hanging out, right? Don't know how she felt about me, but that's how I felt about her. Was actually trying to figure out how to end it without getting wrapped up in a whole mess of awkwardness, given how little we ever talked. And if she really was pregnant, that would have made it a hundred times worse. So, all-in-all…"

"So, all-in-all, her being dead is kind of convenient for you, then."

"I suppose you could look at it that way. Silver linings, right? I mean, I do feel bad for Janice and the unborn baby and all, but I guess things could be a lot worse. Why?"

"So, let me try to sum up." Detective O'Hare turns his eyes toward the ceiling, brings them back in a hard stare. Cool, how he did that. Dramatic. "There's a dead girl in the bedroom, with whom you 'wanted to end things.' And you were out with her last night. Turns out she was pregnant…of which you wanted no part. And in your bathroom, you have eighteen empty bottles of a substance that is highly toxic when ingested in sufficient quantities. Does that all sound about right?"

"Yeah, I guess so. Kind of rando, but…"

"Means, motive and opportunity, Mr. Junior."

"I'm not following you."

"Jesus!" Detective O'Hare shouts, suddenly all out of sorts. "You cannot possibly be this stupid!"

"Whoa, hey. That's uncalled for. This thing has totally screwed up my whole Saturday too, but you don't hear me calling you names. Pull it together, man." My genuine offense at O'Hare's unprofessionalism seems to take him aback for a second. I find that entirely appropriate. His Saturday was maybe ruined because of this dead-Janice thing, but that's no excuse to be rude.

"My apologies, Mr. Junior." O'Hare, all demure again.

"No problem. I think we're all pretty shaken up by this whole scene." I love it when I get the chance to be magnanimous. "So, I can go now?"

"I'm sorry, Mr. Junior. But the only place you'll be going this afternoon is down to the station with me."

And just like that, any remaining hopes I have for a Saturday brunch are shattered. My favorite meal of the week.

PENNY

"The white one on the corner!" I shout in the direction of Rufus's ear. He slows the motorcycle, stops at the curb.

"Righteous digs," Rufus shouts over the idling bike. "Bet you don't have houses like that up there in Canada."

"Of course we do." I defend my phony homeland in what I believe would be true Canadian fashion. "What, you think we all live in huts?"

"I pictured it more like log cabins."

"In your mind, everyone in Canada lives in log cabins?"

Rufus tilts his head in thought, obviously figuring his own version of Canada. Answers in the affirmative. I stare at him in wonder, imagining the storybook world in which he must live. A Mexico speckled with nothing but adobe pueblos. An Alaska made up only of igloo colonies. The grass-roofed jungle camps of Africa and the Amazon. It must be nice.

"Well, thanks for the ride." I climb off the bike. "Hope it wasn't too far out of your way."

"Believe it or not, Canada, the house we're working on is right over there." Rufus points to a giant plantation-style manor a few doors down from my aunt's house, opposite side of the street.

When we were visiting my aunt a few years back, Catelyn told me that a lot of the really beautiful houses in South Tampa are empty during the summer. Snowbirds, she called the owners. People who winter in Florida and summer at some other home. Just like my Aunt Sally. Which is exactly why my runaway self is in Tampa on this fine June morning.

"Nice house."

"Yup. Pretty much all we paint are nice houses."

"Do you guys always work on Saturdays?"

"Nope. Get the weekends to ourselves, unless it's some kind of a rush job."

"So, this is a rush job."

"No."

"Then why are you working on Saturday?"

"Ha," Rufus snorts. Then he looks at me funny. His face drops. "No way."

"No way, what?"

"What time is it?" There's a weird urgency in his voice. Not dangerous, but weird.

"I don't know, my cell phone broke." I'm lying. I have a working cell phone. But no way am I turning it on because that would be the easiest way to track me. I'm off the grid.

"Roughly?" Rufus turns off the motorcycle.

"I think my train got in at about twelve-thirty. So it's probably around two?"

"And it's Saturday."

"Last I checked."

"The goddamned bastards," Rufus growls, handing me his phone.

"What's going on right now?" I'm not worried, but definitely confused.

"Look at it."

"Okay. It's an iPhone."

He reaches over, points to the home screen. I notice his phone display reads that it's seven-forty-eight a.m. And, oh yes, the phone also says that today is Friday. Weird. I wonder for a second if I'm the one who's confused. Maybe train-lag...if there is such a thing. But the sun is way too high in the sky for it to be around eight a.m. "That's strange."

"No, it's cruel."

"Okay." I quietly wonder what kind of meds he forgot to take this morning. After a few tense seconds, Rufus sighs. Chuckles and shakes his head.

"Well, at least I got to meet you, right?" Rufus kicks the starter, the bike backfires and begins to hum.

"At least that," I nod, confused.

"Take it easy, Canada."

As he's leaving, I realize how good it felt not to be alone. Even for just twenty minutes or so. Over the roar of the engine I want to say something to keep him around a little longer, but what is there to say? Instead I just wave, shout thanks again for the ride.

Rufus gives me a thumbs-up, pulls away from the curb, heads back the way we came. I shoulder my pack and make my way round the back of the house, controlling anxiety with slow breaths.

I spot my aunt's single lawn gnome, backed against the bamboo hedge that lines the yard. If I were the praying sort, I'd be saying a prayer right now. But I'm more the confidence-in-the-universe sort, so instead of praying I focus on being open to whatever I find. And what I find, when I lift up the lawn gnome, is a single key. Yes! Yes! Yes!

I grab the key, thinking about a hot shower, a soft bed, whatever non-perishable foods Aunt Sally might have left in the house. I make my way to the back door. I do my best to focus on being open to whatever I find, knowing the universe has a plan.

This isn't always easy. Because what I find, when I reach the back door, is a keypad with a little blinking green light. Beside the keypad is a window decal that says "A-1-A Security Systems" in blocky letters.

The last time we visited, Aunt Sally definitely did not have an alarm system installed at her house. No. No, no, no, no, no. The image of Green Bunny, balled up in my backpack, pops into my head. What am I doing here?

No matter how bleak things look – you never, ever, ever panic.

In, two-three.

Hold, two-three.

Exhale, three-four-five-six.

There was nothing Catelyn couldn't do. And I'm made of all the same stuff as she was.

In, two-three.

Hold, two-three.

Exhale, three-four-five-six.

... Maybe eight hours later, I'm counting my blessings. Literally.

It's something that Catelyn says real travelers do every night before going to sleep. You count the ways that the universe has provided opportunities that day, so you can recognize and be grateful for each one. And you don't count the bad stuff that happened because there is no bad stuff that happens. Everything that happens leads, some way or another, to the good stuff. It's important to remember that part.

For example, I'm grateful that I knew about the Panera Bread shop on Westshore, walking distance from my aunt's house. It reminded me of the Panera Bread shop back home because they're all exactly the same. A comfort.

I'm grateful to have made it to Tampa without being abducted and sold into a human trafficking ring. Or found out by the police and sent back home.

I'm grateful for meeting Rufus and getting a ride to my aunt's house. Although, in retrospect, I acknowledge that if anything were likely to get me abducted and sold into a human trafficking ring it would be hopping onto a motorcycle being driven by a stranger nicknamed Roofie. But I could tell there was something nice about Rufus, even if he was kind of an idiot. And I realize that I'm going to have to trust my instincts – well, Catelyn's instincts, if I'm being honest – if this whole fiasco is going to end up being a real adventure, instead of a complete tragedy.

I'm grateful for Swann Circle Park and all of the huge, twisty oak trees draped with Spanish moss. I'm especially grateful for this specific oak tree, right at the northeast corner of the park, which I'd climbed with Catelyn the last time we visited. Grateful for a place to sleep that isn't on the ground with all the bugs. About four years ago, Catelyn and I sat in this same nook, a pocket of three forking branches thick as trunks and cushioned with Spanish moss. That was when Catelyn told me about the time when she and a friend were "nighted" at Yosemite.

It's a word play on "knighted," she told me. They were rock climbing a section of El Capitan when it got too dark to continue and they ended up having to spend the whole night on the cliff face. A rite of passage for rock climbers, she told me. Which was funny, since it was the first I'd ever heard Catelyn talk about rock climbing at all. But they were harnessed in tight, so it wasn't really dangerous, she told me. It was just a long, long, long night. I hug Green Bunny, squished into the crook of my neck, feeling like Catelyn's up here next to me right now so it's okay to just be Penny for a while.

I'm hoping tonight doesn't last as long as Catelyn's night on El Capitan. I know it's not the same thing. I'm only maybe twenty feet above the ground. And I'm nestled into a safe, mossy nook that hides me from any evening walkers but is close enough to turn the houses across the street into nightlights. Sleeping here tonight would be a breeze for Catelyn. And I'm made of the same stuff as she was. Even though she had a friend with her on El Capitan. Which can make things a lot less scary, I think. I shake my head to stop thinking about scary, press my chin harder into Green Bunny, and do my best to make no noise even though I'm crying pretty hard.

No matter how bleak things look – you never, ever, ever panic.

Sob, in two-three.

Sob, hold two-three.

Sob, exhale three-four-five-six.

SAMMY

"So tell me about your week."

"Why don't you tell me why a court-appointed therapist is even working on a Sunday morning?"

"Because I make my own hours and I like to get your session out of the way before the start of what I consider to be my *productive* work week."

"Clever. I don't want to be here, either. In fact, we both know that I shouldn't be here."

"Are we doing this again?"

"Yeah."

"Every single session," Dr. Cater exhales. "Okay, let's talk about why you're here, then."

"Gross misunderstanding."

"Those auto-dealerships didn't think it was a misunderstanding. To them it was a pretty clear-cut case of grand-theft larceny and criminal mischief."

"Yeah, but I didn't actually steal anything, did I? I just moved it. Within eyesight, no less. And the criminal mischief charge, that's too ridiculous to even talk about."

"You removed a thirty-six-foot branded inflatable from the Douglas Honda Auto-Dealership on Kennedy Boulevard. The balloon cost over seventeen thousand dollars. In Florida, that's a third-degree felony. You then installed said balloon three blocks away…"

"At Johnson Toyota. I know, I was there."

"…at the Johnson Toyota Auto-Dealership, thereby defacing that company's property. In Florida, that's a second-degree misdemeanor."

"How is moving a giant balloon onto an auto-lot considered defacing property? It's not permanent, like graffiti."

"Grey area. I think they took into consideration that the balloon was announcing a June-Only, Blow-Out Sale for which the Johnson dealership was unprepared."

"It was branded Douglas Honda; people would have figured it out. Hell, they're only three blocks away."

"I think both companies would have been more understanding if there weren't multiple assault charges related to the incident."

"Hey. I had no part in that, Cynthia."

"Dr. Carter. Exactly what did you think was going to happen when the employees of Douglas Honda showed-up in the morning to find their expensive promotional balloon stolen? And then look three blocks down the street, to see that same balloon flying over a competitor's establishment? Or, conversely, when the people at Johnson Toyota show up for work and find a thirty-six-foot balloon lofting over their own lot, promoting a big sale at *their* competitor's place? Do you even know what kind of people sell cars?"

"I didn't think they'd go all Jets and Sharks on each other."

For real, the way the dealership staff went at it so totally exceeded my expectations.

"You incited a riot."

"Come on. Riot? It was a minor street brawl."

"Eleven people had to go to the hospital. Three of them were over sixty years old."

"Probably a lot of built-up tension between those dealerships, what with being so close. It obviously needed a release. But saying I'm responsible for what happened is like saying World War One all started solely because that Archduke guy was shot."

"How you got off with just two-months of court mandated therapy is beyond me."

"Rich father, expensive lawyers."

"Fine. But I just have to ask again. Why?"

"Why did Monet paint *Starry Night*?"

"Van Gogh painted *Starry Night*."

I just love messing with her.

"People are my canvas, Cynthia. Look, you're a clinician, I'm not expecting you to wrap your head around my specific form of art. But you could at least respect the fact that I'm an artist, and disrupting everyday reality is the way my soul breathes. Go ahead and think of it like performance art, if that helps. But I've never heard of any flash mobs or buskers being sentenced to two months of therapy. I mean, nothing was even damaged or stolen."

"First, please call me Dr. Carter. Second, eleven people went to the hospital."

"That is totally coincidental."

"Tell it to the court. I'm just that lucky municipal counselor they appointed to you. For at least four more sessions. If you're fortunate enough to get my sign off. Can we move on now?"

"We can move on now."

"So how was your week?"

"It was good. It was okay. I mean, I woke up next to a dead girl yesterday morning and that kinda threw a wrench in my weekend, but otherwise things were…"

"Say again?"

"What part?"

"The part about you waking up next to a dead girl."

"Why? You just said it."

"You want to unpack that for me?"

"Uh, not much to it, really. I went home with this girl on Friday night and she was dead on Saturday morning. So now I'm technically the prime suspect in a murder investigation, but…wait, are you seriously reaching for the panic button?"

"Just making sure it's still there."

"Come on, Cynthia…"

"Dr. Carter."

"Fine, Doctor Carter. You know me. We're friends."

"We have a doctor-patient relationship. That's not the same thing as a friendship."

"Whatevs. You at least know me well enough not to get all paranoid when I tell you that I woke up next to a dead girl."

"And you're the prime suspect in a murder investigation."

"Oh, come on. I'm harmless. Wouldn't hurt a fly."

"That's what Norman Bates said at the end of *Psycho*."

"Seriously?"

"How about you just tell me about the dead woman."

"Why so interested? Hey…am I detecting a hint of jealousy?"

"Yeah, I'm jealous of a dead woman that was hooking up with you."

I shrug, give her a dazzling smile. But it falls completely flat. Doctor Carter happens to not be one of those women who fall hopelessly in love on first meeting me. I know, sounds weird, but it's a thing.

It's only a very small percent of the female population, these women who imprint on me at first sight. One in two hundred, maybe? Never figured out why it happens, never been able to define in advance the type of woman it's likely to happen to. Sometimes it's old women, like great-grandmother, lived-through-two-world-wars, old. Sometimes it's young women, like, baby-teeth young. I've learned to maintain a wide berth when it comes to those little love bugs so as to avoid misunderstandings that might legally restrict my being within two-hundred yards of grade schools. Sometimes it's totally age-appropriate women. Like Janice, before she was dead.

American, Jamaican, British, Canadian, Chinese, Continental European, Eastern European, South American, African – it's happened to women of almost every nationality and ethnic diversity…with the odd exception of women from Japan, who seem to dislike me universally. The overwhelming majority of women—those who do not fall hopelessly in love with me—don't understand the attraction any more than I do. I've talked to Doctor Carter about this phenomenon, and she thinks it's all delusional. Ha. If you don't feel it, you just don't get it, I suppose.

"I don't know what's sadder, the fact that this woman is dead, or the fact that she was hooking up with you," Doctor Carter says.

"Don't you just love our playful banter?"

"Tell me about the dead woman. We still have," Doctor Carter glances at her watch, sighs, "Jesus, forty-five minutes."

"I literally talked about the dead girl all day yesterday. Let's talk about something else. You know how people used to paint their jeans and denim jackets back in the sixties? Like with rainbows and unicorns and stuff. Why do you think no one does that anymore?"

"I'm not sure whether it's funny or sad listening to someone who was born in ninety-one reminisce about the sixties. Why would you even bring that up?"

"I watched a documentary about Haight Ashbury. It's weird how I can hate hippies so much but still appreciate the finer details of their apparel. Did you ever own a lava lamp?"

"How'd she die?"

"I honestly have no idea. The police think I poisoned her."

"The police think you poisoned her. I see."

"With Visine."

"That's pretty specific. Why do the police think you poisoned her with Visine?"

"They found a bunch of empty Visine bottles in my bathroom. Did you know that stuff can kill you if you drink it? It's okay to put in your eyes, though."

"No, I mean, why do they think you poisoned her at all?"

"Circumstance, I guess. Dead girl, empty bottles of Visine. Wrong place, wrong time. Oh, and it didn't help that she was pregnant."

"She was pregnant? You were having a one-night stand with a pregnant lady?"

"Settle down, Doc. First of all, it wasn't a one-night stand. I'd been hooking up with her, on and off, for weeks. And it's not like she was eight months big or anything. I didn't even know she was pregnant until they did a blood test on the body."

"You were hooking up for a few weeks. So, does that mean the baby was yours?"

"That...has not yet been determined. But I'm thinking, no."

"I really don't want to ask, but by what deductive reasoning are you led to believe that it wasn't your baby, if you'd been having on-and-off sex with this woman for weeks?"

"God, this is like being back at the police station."

"You are back at the police station."

"I mean in the interrogation room, not in the luxurious office of a court-appointed therapist."

"Manners."

"Why don't we just meet at Starbucks? Everyone else does."

"There's no panic button at Starbucks, no officers right outside ready to wrestle you to the ground if you get violent."

"Does it make you happy, treating me like I'm a criminal?"

"Maybe you are a criminal."

"Right. They should lock me up. Because I moved a big balloon three blocks."

"No, because you're explaining to me what sounds like an open-and-shut case of you poisoning a casual hook-up that you happened to impregnate. Seriously, how are you not in jail right now?"

"Same father, same lawyers. I'm not allowed to leave Tampa, though. Would you please stop giving me that look? I just told you, there's a better than even chance that the baby wasn't even mine."

"And you were going to tell me why you think that."

"Sure, just like I told the nice officers all day yesterday. So, this chick would just show up at the bar when I was drinking with my crew..."

"Your crew. What are you, a white rapper?"

"I mean my literal crew. I'm a contractor. The people I employ to paint with me, in the business we call them a crew. Now, do you want to take a moment and feel bad about your snarky comment, or should I continue?"

"Fair point, my apologies. Please continue."

"So this chick would just…"

"Could you please?"

"What?"

"Just pretend to be more respectful. I mean, the woman was pregnant and died in your bed."

"Fine. This young lady…"

"Better."

"This young lady would just show up, out of the blue. One, maybe two nights a week."

"Always the same bar?"

"No, which is also weird. So, anyway, this chick…sorry, this young lady would sidle up, do a whole mess of shots – and I'm not talking about top shelf tequila or sipping rum. She was like an eighth grader raiding her parent's liquor cabinet, slumber-party style. She'd shoot straight bourbon, then follow it up with Jägermeister and then something like a sweet vermouth. Hell, I once saw her down successive shots of crème de menthe and peach schnapps after shot-gunning a PBR. Honestly, I couldn't figure out how the bartenders, in good conscience, would continue serving her – they should have cut her off on general principle. Totally out of control, she was."

"I get it. She liked to drink."

"You don't get it. It didn't seem like she liked it at all. She certainly didn't know how to do it. By the end of the night, her stomach definitely contained a wider spectrum of alcohol than any bar rag in the place…"

"Hey!"

"What?"

"I thought you were going to reign-in that derogatory crap."

"What'd I say?"

"Did you not just refer to a woman as a, quote, bar rag, unquote."

"No, I did not just refer to a woman as a quote-unquote bar rag. I referred to a bar rag as quote-unquote bar rag."

"Oh. What's a bar rag?"

"It's a rag that you use to wipe down a bar. You don't get out much, do you?"

"My mistake."

"That's twice now that you've slapped me for your own dropped ball. One more and you're knocking a session off my sentence."

"I'm not going to drop one of your remaining sessions just because I misinterpreted something you said…that would be illegal on my part. But you have my apologies."

"That and a quarter might buy me a gumball."

"Go on."

"Where was I? Right, so this…young lady, the way she drank, I almost threw up just watching her. And like I was saying, it wasn't the quantity so much as the horribly irresponsible variety."

"And you thought it was a good idea to take this woman home and have sex with her."

"No. That's offensive. And again, you're wrong. The girl would literally drag me out of the bar. I didn't even know how she could still stand, but she had those wiry, like, yoga muscles I guess, and she was relentless. I'd take her back to my apartment just to get her off the street, for her own safety."

"But then you'd have sex with her."

"Sure, you could say that. But it would be more accurate to say that she had sex with me. The girl would get back to my apartment and, like, devour me. Believe me, she was driving, all the way. Hell, I was too afraid to do anything proactive at all. I figured she'd grab onto any momentum I brought to the table and reverse it on me, like a judo move."

"It just astonishes me how any woman could possibly find you that attractive."

"I know, I don't get it either. Luckily, it's just a weird little minority of the female population."

"At least there's that. Still doesn't make any sense, her being so crazy into you."

"Thanks. Kind of you to say."

"So what's your point? How does any of this make you believe that the unborn baby wasn't yours?"

"Getting to that. I'm just trying to explain that this woman was a force of nature, right? With the drinking, with the sex, like, the girl was on a mission from God."

"Uh-huh. So?"

"So there's no way I was the only one. She had to be doing the same thing with five or six other guys, at least."

"Are you slut-shaming her, now?" Dr. Carter rolls her eyes.

"No, I'm just saying that it would be absurd to think that she would focus her hurricane energy only on me. I mean, I know I told you how some women imprint on me. But come on, look at me. There's nothing special here. Certainly nothing that would arouse that kind of wild energy."

"As stated too often, I've got to agree with you there."

"Again, thanks, you're very kind. So what I'm saying is, it was her, not me. And if it was her, not me, then she would be doing this same thing regardless of whether I was there or not. Ergo, other guys. Ergo, high probability that the baby wasn't mine. Ergo, Friday was just a bad luck night when her engines flamed out and everything will be cleared up once the toxicology report comes back, which should be no later than next Saturday. Ta da!"

"That's not exactly stellar logic."

"Really, how so?"

"As ridiculous as it sounds, isn't it just as likely that this girl had it so bad that she'd stay home on the other nights of the week, recovering and recouping her energy for the one or two nights of drinking and sex with you?"

"You are kind of a wet blanket, Doc. Has anyone ever told you that?"

"Oh, look." Doctor Carter glances at her watch with a birthday party smile. "Our time is up."

PENNY

"Are you hiding?"

My eyes flip open, stare into the face of a little boy hanging maybe six inches from my own. Green Bunny scrunched beneath my chin; I clamp my jaw to keep from screaming.

"Are you hiding?" the kid whispers again.

Quick mental inventory. I'm sleeping in the nook of a giant oak tree, at least twenty-feet high. Catelyn was here, I think. When? And what's with this kid in my face? I nod, buy a few seconds, then stick my head up for quick reconnaissance.

The tree is lousy with children. My ears tune into the background noise of laughter and shouting below me, noise that was there while I slept. It's Sunday morning in Swann Circle Park. Family time.

Wide awake, I stick a finger in front of my lips. With a knowing wink, I breathe him a slow shush. The kid nods. He doesn't move, but also doesn't call me out.

"Don't give me away," I whisper. Slight dramatic glances left and right, before I duck my head back into the nook.

"I'll pretend I didn't see you," the kid smiles sharp. "Me and my sister, can we play next round?"

"Sure."

Part of me feels bad. The kid is going to think I ditched him and his sister. Rotten trick in exchange for not calling out my hiding spot.

Another part of me is coming to grips with what little privacy is available to homeless people, something I'd never really thought about before. But the biggest part of me is grappling with how the hell I'm going to get out of this tree without parents on the ground realizing it was my bedroom for the night. I imagine that would be frowned upon in this part of South Tampa.

I tuck Green Bunny into my shirt, glance down and assess the parent situation at the base of the tree. It looks like there are two couples and a solo dad. All watching their kids creep the branches, hands poised to catch.

Catelyn talked about people's "sneak radar" – that the surest way to get yourself noticed is by trying to act inconspicuous. The trick is to go against your instincts, like steering into a skid, and be exceptionally conspicuous. I'd never driven a car when Catelyn explained this to me, but I understood it from context. Reversal was a big part of Catelyn's personal philosophy.

And right now my instinct is to try and slip down quietly. So instead I sit up, scooch over, lock my knees around a sitting branch, drop backwards and hang upside-down. At twenty feet up, this move draws attention like Cirque du Soleil.

"Holy shit!" shouts the male-half of one couple.

"Larry! Potty Mouth!"

"Sorry," he asides. "Jesus Christ, kid!"

"Don't worry about me!" I shout down. Then I flip myself right-ways and swing down the branches like a spider monkey, thinking, nine years of gymnastics and finally a payoff. I nail my landing with a smile.

"It's not you I'm worried about!" the potty-mouth's partner spits at me. Shoves her finger right in my face. "Look around! These are little kids! An example like that and you're just asking for broken necks! What in the name of God are you thinking, missy?!"

Whoa. With everything else on my mind, I am so not expecting to get bawled out. It throws me. I start to cry. Apparently, I've had some stuff bottled up since I started this adventure.

"God, Susan, you are such a bitch!" the potty-mouth says to his other half. Loud, like maybe he's got some stuff bottled up, too. "Look at her! Does that feel good? Making a teenager cry?"

"Larry, I didn't…"

"I'm done with this charade, anyway," potty-mouth Larry growls, dropping her hand. "And next time you swipe right, you might want to mention you've got a four-year-old straight off, instead of waiting for the third date. Waste of my time."

I assume said four-year-old is the sobbing pigtailed girl who has witnessed this scene from a low branch behind me.

"Larry, wait, I…" Bitch Susan turns towards me. "Don't cry, honey. It's okay."

"I'm fine," I say, pulling myself together.

"I wasn't talking to you," she sneers, reaching past me to grab pigtails from her branch while potty-mouth walks away without even a glance backwards. Solid exit.

Geeze. Catelyn would be proud of this scene I just made. Mission totally accomplished; all attention diverted from the fact that I slept in the oak tree last night. I start walking in the direction of Aunt Sally's house, where my pack is still backyard stashed.

But I don't get twenty feet before I pat the front of my shirt and my stomach drops. Green Bunny! And just like that, I'm frozen. The tears and sobs are back. Even though I know Green Bunny has to be somewhere under the tree, I feel like I'll never find her again. It's like my heart has stopped beating.

Breathe! Catelyn shouts in my head like a drill sergeant. *Breathe first, then figure it out!* And I follow her instructions, letting my shoulders drop. I inhale, two-three. After a minute or so, I'm calm enough to go back and find Green Bunny. But when I turn around, I see Green Bunny walking towards me.

Pigtails, cradling Green Bunny like she's hers. Hugging my Green Bunny! My lizard-brain, telling me to run up and snatch it – mine, not yours! – but then I realize, she's bringing her back to me.

"Thank you," I say, all tears and nose-run.

"My mom said I have to ask you," the tiny girl says, "can I keep it?"

"What? God, no!" Then, because what fifteen-year-old wants to look like she's crying about a lost stuffed animal, even in front of a tiny girl, I say, "It's my little sister's favorite."

"Your little sister. Yeah, sure." She actually snarks at me. What is she, four?

"Mean moms make mean girls." I snatch Green Bunny from her arms. The hell is wrong with kids these days? I turn heel and make my way towards Aunt Sally's place.

When I get there, I look around, make sure there are no neighbors watching, then casually stroll into her back yard. My Canada backpack doesn't look much like a home, but it's the only one I've got right now. So I make the best of it. I pull out a bottle of water, drink most of it and use what's left to brush my teeth. Take a hobo shower with Aunt Sally's garden hose, wishing I'd had the forethought to pack soap. I dry my hair with a sweatshirt, pull it back into a ponytail. Then I take two twenty-dollar bills from the side pocket of my pack.

Money isn't a problem – I've squirreled away a little over twelve-hundred-dollars in birthday and babysitting money, all cash. But the problem is, what hotel or hostel takes cash from a too-young looking backpacker with no identification? I was counting on Aunt Sally's house for a home base. And that tree in Swann Circle Park isn't gonna cut it for another night. I have no plan. And I'm all alone. Once again, my brain takes a hard swing back to freak-out town.

You are a traveler. Catelyn's voice inside my head. *Remember the rules.*

So I breathe. I put my toothbrush and toothpaste back in a side pocket of my pack.

And I don't panic. I stash my pack in the bamboo hedges.

I remember that when day-to-day doesn't work, I can live minute-to-minute.

I can be open to the next opportunity because I am made of all the same stuff as Catelyn, and Catelyn could handle anything. So I can handle anything.

I walk towards the front of Aunt Sally's house. Now I have to step up and be the traveler that Catelyn was, because I'm the only thing left that's made of the same stuff as she was.

Because Catelyn's dead.

And it's my fault.

SAMMY

Jeff double-takes when I walk in the door. Flashes me a quick gunslinger stare, then plasters an ingratiating smile across his lousy face. "Where you been, Sammy? Hell, we were about to start calling hospitals."

"You the only one here, Jeff?" I sigh.

Here is The Blind Goat, one of the better local hangs on the lower east side of northwest South Tampa. Why it makes me sad right now is, I don't want to be alone with Jeff.

"Just me and you so far, buddy. Come on, where'd you disappear to this weekend?"

"Long story, Jeff. And I don't feel like telling it to you."

"We're not even on the job, man." Jeff shakes his head deliberately, like a slow clap.

"We're always on the job, Jeff." I sigh again. The Goat is our Sunday afternoon spot, great for a mellow goodbye to the weekend and soft hello to the coming week. But it won't be mellow or soft for me if I have to spend more than ten minutes alone with Jeff.

Here's the thing about Jeff. We're hazing him. He hates it, and right now I hate it too, because it just takes so much damn energy. And energy is something I really don't have much of at the moment.

Why we're hazing Jeff is that he joined our crew about three weeks ago. Beer and Mealy and I—Beer and Mealy are my partners—we all went to high school with Jeff. We were friends with him, too. Kind of. I mean, he was part of the group. Nothing special, just part of that group of friends you have in high school. We'd see him around when we were home from college, too. Thanksgiving, Christmas break, summer vacations. Like my grandfather used to say, he was fine in his own way, he just didn't weigh very much. Homonym humor, my grandfather loved that stuff.

So Jeff graduates from college, starts a company that develops some social app or something, raises a ton of venture money and becomes a pretty big deal for a while. Then it all goes to his head and he proceeds to fail spectacularly, which often happens to children who "get too big for their breeches," as my grandfather also used to say.

Mismanagement, narcissistic investments, unchecked expense accounts, all the bad stuff. Almost overnight, the Jeff brand stopped trending. He became a pariah that no venture firm would touch with a barge pole. But none of that is why we're hazing Jeff. Well, it is kinda, but in a roundabout way.

So here's the bigger back story. Beer, Mealy and I, we started this house painting company back when we were in high school. Long story, not interesting, except the money was good and jobs kept popping up, so we kept it going during summers when we were home from college.

Then we graduated college and we all decided to do some painting while we took the time to figure out something really special to do with our lives. It's a tough question, what to do with your life. Not something you want to rush. Then, about a year and a half ago, we all turned thirty.

But why we're hazing Jeff, it has nothing to do with our perpetually stalled lives.

So Beer, Mealy and I, we were the guys who graduated college and didn't go on to become doctors or lawyers or corporate c-suite executives. We were the guys who stayed home, doing the exact same job we did in high school. What our old classmates thought of us, I can't even imagine. Like three idiot kids standing at an airport fence, watching as our old classmates would soar to incredible heights and do amazing things. Jeff included.

Some of those ex-classmates, they'd launch and soar away forever. Great jobs, great spouses, great kids, all around great lives. But as happens, some of those ex-classmates would launch, stay aloft for a while, and then come crashing back to the tarmac in a giant ball of flame, engine gutted by a whole flock of seagulls.

And Beer, Mealy and I, like three idiot kids standing at an airport fence, we'd watch these bleeding catastrophes, too. Then we'd go and paint stuff.

Jeff wasn't the first. Over the past ten years or so, we've hired seven ex-classmates, all males. Life's burn victims, we called them, returning home to live with their failure and their parents. And where do you think these poor bastards turned up looking for short-term work?

Do a brother a solid, wouldja? Just something to bridge the gap while I decide what's next, they would say. I want to take my time and really figure out how to make something meaningful out of my life, they would say. Oh, we know all about that, we would think, but not say. Just look at how great it turned out for us.

So we'd hire our old friends. Sure, we'd love to work with you – welcome to the Island of Lost Toys and all that. And did they appreciate it? You bet they did. For, like, a day. Sometimes two.

See, here's the thing about these Gary Coleman types, these darlings of the world one minute who go completely pear-shaped the next. It does a job on their egos. And I'm not throwing shade here, that kind of thing is not easy on a person. But you know what's not easy on a contracting company? Hiring one of these fallen superstars to do long, repetitive hours of menial labor on the low-end of society's totem pole, that's what.

At first, we were patient, we were accommodating, we tried to be nice.

Hey, buddy, did I mention we start work at eight?

No, bro, we don't take our lunches at restaurants.

Yes, muchacho, I understand you had an interview, but you can't just skip work when something better comes up.

No, pal, we've decided it's not a good idea to drink on the job.

We'd listen to hours of friendly, unsolicited strategic advice: how to expand the company, efficiencies, cost-cutting, employee morale. Brand awareness for Christsakes. And through it all, these brilliant MBAs would not be painting *a single goddamned thing.*

We tried to reason with these people, but there was no reasoning with these people. We got mad and they got mad. Ultimately, we had to fire their asses. Working for a house painting company can sometimes feel like you've finally hit rock bottom – but getting fired by that painting company is like the universe saying uh-uh and handing you a hydraulic drill.

It made us feel bad.

So, after the fourth time we had to fire a former friend and classmate, Beer, Mealy and I, we all agreed. If we were ever stupid or compassionate enough to again hire a flamed-out ex-classmate, we'd have to make some changes. Our Island of Lost Toys needed a caste system. We had to break these people down before we could build them back up – like marines in a wartime boot camp…only more so. Because war might be hell, but at least it has its interesting moments.

Painting, on the other hand, is like a conscious lobotomy. It is the endless repetition of endless repetition. Beer once said a painter's brain is like a normal person's appendix – it serves no practical purpose, and when it does turn on, nothing good can possibly come of it. A brilliant summary of my life's work.

We decided on hazing because a plebe system was really the only system any of us knew about for this kind of thing. But we were humane. Well in advance of hiring, we'd explain to the desperate job hunter exactly what we were doing and why we were doing it. We were very clear on the fact that he'd be pond scum for a minimum of eight weeks, maybe more. The lowest of the low, that part of the totem pole buried six feet deep and visible to nobody. Nothing but grunt work. Repetitive grunt work.

And also, he'd be the equivalent of a leper in our small social system. And finally, he would be recognized as a human being *only when we decided* that there was no chance of him backsliding into the airbag narcissist we knew was hiding somewhere deep in his soul.

Nate Cunningham, former quarterback on our high school team who'd lost everything in the commodities market, he was the first one to agree to these terms. He quit on the fourth day. A week later, we heard that he'd died of a heroin overdose. Dude didn't even smoke pot in high school.

Rufus, we call him Roofie, he was the next to agree to these terms and is still working with us today. But Roofie was never really a flame-out like the others. He just bummed around for a few years after community college and then came back home to live in his parent's basement. By the time we finally recognized him as a human being, he'd forgotten all about the hazing thing and just figured we were always a bunch of inconsiderate dicks. Roofie's one of the good ones.

Jeff is our latest gesture of tough love. It's been three weeks, which is longer than any of us expected him to last, but the jury's still out on whether he'll be a long-term player. I expect, no. So, long story short, that's why we're hazing Jeff.

By the way, Jeff's real name is Dillon. But we decided that he's not remotely cool enough to pull off a name like Dillon, so we all call him Jeff. He does his best to hide it, but this drives him absolutely batshit crazy, so we try to address him directly as often as we possibly can.

The bartender at the Goat is new and she pauses a beat to look at my eyes when she hands over my beer. Asks, "Are you wearing color contacts?"

"Am I what?"

"Color contact lenses. Your eyes, they're like electric green." Wow, how rude.

"I'll tell if you'll tell." I stare openly at her breasts. "Are those things real?"

"Excuse me?"

"No, no. Excuse me. I thought we were pointing out each other's attractive features and then asking if they're fake." The bartender stares, expressionless. "Hey, weird question, are you crushing on me right now? You can be honest."

"Uh, that would be a hard no."

"Cool. Just checking. I got a tab, name's Sammy Junior." I raise my glass to the bartender in a no-hard-feelings gesture. The fact that I come here regularly enough to have a tab ought to keep her from totally ghosting us for the rest of the afternoon.

"You make friends everywhere you go, huh?" Jeff laughs. He's trying so hard.

In lieu of response, I take a pull from my beer and give him the finger.

"Hey now!" Beer shouts from the door. "There's our little lost boy! I was looking for your picture on milk cartons this morning."

"Ha!"

"Shut up, Jeff." I meet Beer halfway, we bro-hug, he walks past me to get a drink.

"You okay?" Mealy's slipped unnoticed into the bar behind Beer. I swear, the dude walks in shadows. You could be painting in the same room with Mealy for, like, six hours before you even knew he was there.

"It's been a weekend, bud."

"Talk about it?"

"Nah, save it for the job tomorrow. Where's Roofie?" Mealy's not a tall guy and I glance over his head at the door. "Oh. Hey, Roofie."

"You're a tool." Roofie tries, and fails, to look angry at me.

"No, Jeff's a tool. What's your problem with me?"

"Messing with a man's phone is not in bounds."

Oh, right. "Wow, man, I completely forgot about that."

"That just makes it all the worse."

"Tell me."

"Yeah, you pulled it off. I woke up at seven-fifteen on Friday morning, drove to the house, and eventually discovered that it was actually two p.m. on Saturday."

"That's messed up, dude."

"Shut up, Jeff."

"No, he's right. It's messed up. What happened to 'frogs don't kill frogs,' huh? You guys randomly decide to haze me again or something? What am I, Jeff, now?"

"I'm right here, you know."

"Shut up, Jeff. And no, Roofie, we're not hazing you again. We would have done the same thing to Beer. You spent, like, an hour spouting off about how zazen your life has become since you set up your phone to handle 'all the small stuff'…like time management. You can't soapbox something like *that* and not expect people like *us* to mess with your phone. Jesus, how long have we known each other?"

"That's a fair point, I guess."

"Anyway, it was worth it, right?"

"How do you mean?"

"What do you mean, how do I mean?"

"I mean I don't understand what you're saying. Worth it?"

"He didn't go in the house," Mealy surmises, wide-eyed.

"You didn't go in the house?"

"No. I gave someone a ride and figured out your clever ruse before I got there."

"Dammit, Roofie!" I shout, even though it's not his fault. "Okay, let's go. Jeff, grab Beer and close out the tab. We need to get to the house, pronto."

"Why do we have to go back to the house?" Roofie looks longingly at the bar. "We're gonna be there tomorrow morning, anyway."

"The first reason is because that brilliant stunt we pulled with your phone had a payoff at the house, and you missed it. The second reason is because that payoff we set up might be a bit of a fire hazard." Kind of

46 SEMI-GLOSS

feel bad that Mealy had to light all those candles on his own when I didn't show up yesterday, but he's being a sport by not mentioning it. Or maybe he's trying to minimize his complicity in the impending disaster of a gag that was entirely of my making.

"Goddammit, Sammy. You guys burn down another house and I swear I'm gonna quit and start my own company.

"It was a frickin' tool shed, Beer. When are you gonna let that go?"

"How about this? I'll let it go if we get to our current job site and don't find a big, smoldering pile of ash instead of a house."

"Deal. Let's move."

"You burned down a tool shed?"

"Shut up, Jeff."

PENNY

I spend the whole day alternating between Starbucks and Panera, always open to opportunities that never show up. I end up walking back towards Aunt Sally's place feeling lonelier than ever. And I'm thinking, the jig is up. Nothing wears on optimism like hours of waiting for something, anything, to happen. Catelyn would have found an opportunity, a slip-edge into some kind of adventure, new places, new friends. But I'm not Catelyn, even though I'm made of the same stuff as she was. I pull out my iPhone, my fingers on but not pressing the side buttons that will bring it back to life.

Dad's not going to care. I mean, he'll probably get semi-animated and go through all the motions – disappointment, outrage – but his heart won't be in it. Dad's heart is just a burned-out fuse. It took three years for mom's cancer to grind him to dust. And in a hot second, Catelyn's death just blew that dust away. Now he's only a corpse waiting to happen. Shame about the living daughter, though.

We should think about boarding school, Dad said a few weeks back.
Sure, Dad, I said.
There's a good one in Buffalo, he said.
Whatever, I said.
I'll have my secretary set it up, he said.
You do that, I said.

Why I left for boarding school in June? Wouldn't hurt to get a head start with summer sessions, Dad decided. And neither my dad nor I was interested in me hanging around home until September. And then I was on the train to Penn Station, with a connection to Buffalo. And then I was off the train at Penn Station, and on my way to Tampa.

Some adventure. I got a ride on a motorcycle and slept in a tree. Catelyn would be so disappointed. And soon I'll be back on a train to Penn Station, with a connection to Buffalo. My fingers put pressure on the side buttons of my iPhone, just a click and it's all over. One click and I'm back on the grid.

Real travelers, sometimes they have to live life minute to minute, Catelyn's voice in my head. *Just get through this minute, is all.* But I can't do it. I can't do it because I'm not a real traveler. I'm trying to be, but I'm not. Sob. I just want my sister back.

The distant coughing of an old motorcycle shakes me out of my miserable trance. There are tears in my eyes as I look up to see that I'm right in front of the house Rufus pointed out yesterday. I quickly wipe my face and, for reasons I can't even fathom, dart towards the side of the house.

I'm crouched behind one of the trees lining the driveway, totally obvious to anyone looking from the opposite direction, when Rufus pulls into the driveway. I see him sprint to the front door and pull what looks like a house key from beneath the doormat. Then a pickup truck pulls into the driveway behind Rufus's bike. I duck into a crouch to observe.

"I forgot the alarm code!" Rufus shouts at the truck.

"Nine! One! One! Nine!" the truck shouts back.

"Nine, one, one, nine. Got it!" A few seconds later, Rufus shouts. "It's not working!"

Crouching behind a bush at the side of the driveway, I look totally suspicious from the back. So I make a dart to the side of the house. More cover. Lean my back onto the side of the house, slide into a seat on the grass where I can hear the guys talking.

What am I expecting to happen? Am I just going to pop out and say, "Hi"? These guys are like, twice my age. And if they're anything like Rufus, probably a little bit sketchy. What would Catelyn do? And I smile, because I could so picture Catelyn hiding at the side of a strange house, spying on some weird guys. Life, minute by minute.

I stare at the sky, then at the backyard. Maybe a backyard oak tree would make a better bed than one in a public park? And right there, I decide that no matter what happens, I'm not sleeping in a tree again tonight. I've already been nighted, and if once was enough for Catelyn, it's enough for me.

What are they even doing in there? Do painters have, like, Sunday strategy meetings to plan the week? Doubtful. What does it even matter? I yawn, drop my chin to my chest, and decide to close my eyes. It feels really good to close my eyes.

SAMMY

"No smoke, so that's positive." Mealy is wedged between me and Beer in the front seat of the truck as we make a turn off of Swann Circle. Roofie is ahead of us on his bike, Jeff on back.

"It's been almost thirty hours. No smoke wouldn't be a cause for relief at this point," I reply. "Anyway, I don't think we're looking at a burn down scenario for the entire house, here. It was just those little tea light candles."

"How many?" Beer grunts.

"A lot."

"How many exactly?"

"Roughly two-hundred-eight."

"That's an oddly specific rough estimate."

"I bought four bags of fifty-two candles, I'm assuming Mealy lit them all up."

"Yeah, I did."

"You guys really went all out," Beer says.

"I never do anything half-way. Shame, though, all that effort. I really wish Roofie could have seen it. It must have looked spectacular. Did you take any video, Mealy?"

"No. Should have."

"You guys do know there are battery-powered tea lights, right?" Beer says.

"Wouldn't have had the same effect. Roofie was supposed to enter the house around two p.m. With all that daylight, you'd hardly even be able to see battery-powered candles."

"So you decided to risk burning the whole place down, just to make it look prettier."

"That was my decision, yes."

"Looks okay from the front," Mealy says as we pull into the driveway. Roofie's already struggling at the front door.

"I forgot the alarm code!" Roofie shouts back to the truck. So he would have had trouble getting into the house yesterday, even if he hadn't figured out that I'd messed with his phone. Sigh. Best laid plans.

"Seriously? We've been working here for two weeks." Beer exhales, sticks his head out the truck window. "Nine! One! One! Nine!"

"Nine, one, one, nine." Roofie repeats, "Got it!"

"Maybe we should put a Post-It note by the keypad," Mealy says.

"No need," I reply. "After that furtive exchange, if we ever forget the code again we can just ask any neighbor within shouting range."

"These rich people probably all know each other's codes anyway," Beer says.

"It's not working!" Roofie shouts.

We walk to the door. Beer shoulders past Roofie, presses the pound on the keypad and the beeping stops.

"Oh. So, nine, one, one, nine, pound – got it."

"Let him go in first." I grab Beer's arm.

Beer steps aside, lets Roofie pass. From the doorway, we see him approach a path of, thank God, burned-out tea candles. He proceeds along this path up the stairs. We follow a few yards behind him, through the reasonably sized master bedroom and into the obscenely giant master bath. In Florida, rich people really seem to love their master bathrooms.

A few dozen burned-out globs, once tea candles, surround a giant, stand-alone soaker tub that sits elegantly beneath a bay window. The tub is filled with slick, grey-green water evidencing the stale remains of bath salts, bombs and bubbles. On a small reading table next to the tub, a Sports Illustrated Swimsuit Issue, circa two-thousand-three. Also a few Victoria's Secret print catalogs. Roofie walks slowly to the table, picks up one of the magazines, flips through it.

"Poor-man's porn," Roofie says wistfully. Then he dips his fingers in the tub, lifts them, sniffs. "Lavender."

"I really wish you could have seen it yesterday, man. When the tub was fresh and all the candles were lit up…"

"Shush," Roofie turns and gently places two lavender-scented fingers on my lips. "This might be the nicest thing anyone has ever done for me."

"Please stop touching my lips now," I say through his fingers, restraining the urge to swat his hand away and thereby ruin the moment. Roofie drops his hand slowly.

"How do you know me so well?"

"Dude, at least twice a week, you talk fantasy about how nice it would be to have a really romantic evening of self-love. I just figured I'd give you the gift that you never give yourself. And I know you'd didn't actually get to experience it…"

"The thought itself is enough."

"Right. So, we're cool vis-à-vis me messing with your phone?"

"Sammy, you can mess with my phone anytime you want."

"Yeah, thanks. It was really just a one-time thing."

"Okay!" Beer belts, thankfully shattering what has become a long and awkward pause. "It looks like no damage done, except for a bunch of melted wax that Jeff can scrape tomorrow."

"Dude." Jeff slumps his shoulders.

"Consider yourself lucky that you don't have to clean this mess up tonight, Jeff. Let's get back to the Goat."

PENNY

I hear the front door of the house open again, guys talking. How long have I been asleep? Fifteen minutes? Half an hour? The guys walk back down the driveway, their voices becoming clear.

"Roofie," one voice says. "Don't forget the alarm."

"Sure thing – uh, just give me that code one more time…"

Nine. One. One. Nine. Pound. I say to myself, lip-syncing the voice from the driveway.

I don't know. What I'm thinking…it might be a step too far, even as desperate as I am.

Bolting from Penn Station to Tampa, I knew that crossed a line. But this, what I'm thinking now, this is like a one-way, no return ticket to crazy town. Straight-up felony. Maybe misdemeanor, I don't really know law. Why does it have to seem so easy? *Minute to minute,* Catelyn in my head, *one minute at a time.*

When the truck and bike are out of eyeshot, I make my way to the front door. Casual, like I totally belong where I am. Cool, like I'm Tyler Durden. Like I'm Catelyn. I reach under the mat, grab the key. Stick the key in the door, press the buttons on the alarm pad, open the door and walk right in. I am inside. I am inside of a really nice house. A really nice house that is going to be empty until around eight a.m. tomorrow morning. How about that!

I am so taking a bath, first thing! I'm no grubbier than I was a few hours ago, overnight train trip, overnight in a tree, but right now I can't even stand the smell of myself. It's like having to pee – you can wait and wait and wait, but it only becomes pants-wettingly urgent when the bathroom is actually in sight.

I run up the stairs, only peripherally noticing a pathway of burned-out tea candles at my feet. At the top, I notice the pathway continues down the hall, so I follow it. Why not? It leads me through what has to be the master bedroom. And into the huge master bath!

Oh, my God.

What the hell kind of bizzaro sex games have these guys been getting up to here? Burned out candles, tub filled with a stew of melted bath bombs and salts. Actual physical copies of an old Sports Illustrated Swimsuit issue, Victoria's Secret catalogs. It's like grandpa's bathroom back in New Jersey. Big time cringe.

Okay. None of my business, I don't judge. But that doesn't make it any less creepy. I end up settling for a shower in a Jack-and-Jill shared bathroom that connects two bedrooms at the front of the house.

After my shower I find a small laundry room on the second floor, run a wash for the clothes I've been wearing since Friday. Then I wrap myself in a bath towel and set out to explore the house.

The plastic tarp-covered furniture, paint cans and gear in most rooms make the place seem more like a construction site than a luxury South Tampa mansion. Downstairs is open floor plan, so I focus on finding a place to hole up on the second floor. The enormous master bedroom and bath suite takes up almost half of the upstairs area and it looks like they haven't even started painting it yet. Too much exposure, too much potential for leave-behind evidence when the workers come in. That, combined with the creep show in the master bath, no way I'm sleeping in here.

Two bedrooms facing the front yard, the shared bathroom where I took a shower between them. These are only partially painted and I'm nervous about any light slipping out the street facing windows, so no dice. And then I notice a closed door at the far end of the hall.

I push the door open. It's obviously a guest room. Longer than it is wide, windows facing tall bamboo hedges. A walk-in closet, a small in-suite bathroom at the back. And best news, the walls are still damp with drying paint. This feels *just right*.

After celebrating my Goldilocks moment, I pull a plastic tarp from the queen-sized bed that's been moved to the center of the room. The bed is fully made up, sheets and a comforter. Aside from the plastic tarps covering the bed, a chair, and wall-mounted flat-screen, there aren't any paint cans or other gear in the room. Is it just sheer luck that the perfect room for me was painted before the others?

No! The universe always takes care of real travelers who are brave enough to keep moving forward, even when it seems like all hope is lost.

I remember my fingers, pressure on the buttons of my iPhone, split seconds away from turning it on and ending this whole fiasco. Was that really just an hour or so ago? And here I am, in a self-contained guest suite, in a South Tampa mansion!

Real travelers can live minute to minute when they have to. And if you can keep hope alive, the universe always takes care.

Big smile. Big, like Catelyn's smile. A memory flash of the last time I saw Catelyn's big smile, but I shut that down quick, avoid turning the moment sad.

The past isn't real, the future isn't real, the only thing that's really real is right now.

This smile on my face right now, that's what's really real.

When my clothes are dry, I dress and head downstairs to check out the kitchen. Lift the tarps covering cabinets, nothing but a few packages of dry pasta, canned veggies, condiments. Open the fridge. Hey now. Two six packs of Miller Genuine Draft, bottles!

What the hell, it's been a day. I pluck one out of the cardboard sleeve, twist off the cap and down half of it. Take a breath, down the rest of it. I'm not much for beer, usually. Could never understand how people like the taste. But that MGD I just downed, that was, like, maybe the best thing I ever drank.

I treat myself to another bottle and it's not until I'm almost finished that a thought hits me. A chilling thought. Stupid, stupid, stupid! Somehow, I'd just assumed that the beer belonged to the people who own the mansion. But the type of people who live in a house like this, the beer they'd drink would probably be expensive microbrews or something. Rich people beer. Miller Genuine Draft is what kids used to drink at my old school. It isn't rich people beer, it's…oh, man. It's the type of beer that contractors would drink. And I've just had two of them. I look at the cardboard six pack sleeves, two glaring gaps, like missing teeth.

Maybe they won't notice?

Of course they're gonna notice.

Maybe they'll think the house is haunted?

Yeah, put money on that.

I consider running down to the gas station on the corner of Kennedy and Westshore, see if I can convince someone to buy me a couple bottles of Miller Genuine Draft, because I have zero chance of buying beer myself. But that gas station is already kind of sketchy even in the daytime, can't even imagine what it's like after sundown. Bad idea, got to stay away from situations lending themselves to human trafficking.

I rummage the cabinets, looking for any kind of golden food coloring or powder that might pass for beer if mixed with water. The beer bottles are clear but the tops are twist-offs, so if I can fill them up again it would at least buy me some time. But I'm finding nothing. And I'm panicking.

And the two beers I drank are going right through me so now I have to…hmm?

No! Don't even think about it. I'm not the type of person who would even consider doing something like that.

Still, desperate times?

No! No way.

I mean, though, it would buy me some time. If I put them in the last two slots of the cardboard sleeve at the very back, I could find a way to replace them by tomorrow night. Go to Panera when it opens, blend some lemonade with a hint of iced tea. That might work. And as long as nobody drinks them before I slip back in here...hell, it's all I've got.

Sigh.

I grab a drinking glass from one of the cabinets I'd rummaged earlier. I'm not a guy, not going to roll the dice and try to pee directly into the bottles. I take the glass into the bathroom, already feeling ashamed of myself. Conscience has to count for something, I think.

It takes over an hour because I need to pee three times before I have enough to fill the bottles. I carefully pour the pee into the bottles, twist the tops back on and feel utterly disgusted. The term "cruel and unusual" comes to mind. The bottles are warm when I replace them in the cardboard sleeve, reshuffling to make sure they are at the very back. It looks okay. I mean, it might not hold up to detailed inspection, but I don't think anyone would notice at first glance.

Okay. I need some air.

I slip out the back door, making sure the alarm is still off and reminding myself to reset it before I go to bed. Run quietly through the shadows towards Aunt Sally's house, retrieve my pack. And I'm back at the mansion about ten minutes later, no incident. The walk has helped me to feel a little less gross about what I just did with the beer. I'm sure I'll be able to figure out replacements before anyone drinks them. No harm, no foul...right?

I take another shower, just because it feels good to shower. I wash my clothes again, even though I only wore them for a few hours. I can't turn on my phone, so I have no idea what time it is. Any clocks that were in the house have been taken down for the paint job, but I noticed an old digital alarm clock on a shelf in the walk-in closet earlier. I retrieve it, turn on the television to get a sense of the time, set the clock to nine. Then I set the alarm for five, so I'll have more than enough time to get lost before Rufus and the other guys show up for work.

I pull on some sleep sweats, stow my backpack behind some hanging clothes in the walk-in closet, climb into the bed at the center of the room. I close my eyes. Then I open my eyes, get out of bed, go to the walk-in closet and dig through my backpack until I find Green Bunny.

Back in bed, Green Bunny crammed under my chin, I start to count my blessings. There are a lot of blessings to count for today, I think, eyelids heavy. Maybe too many…maybe it would be okay to count them all tomorrow…

SAMMY

"You know, I was a tough boss. But I never treated my employees like you guys treat me."

"Is that a complaint, Jeff?" Beer asks.

"It's not a complaint, just a fact. I never treated my employees like this."

"And how'd that work out for you, Jeff?" I chime in, take a slug of my beer.

"My company going under had nothing to do with the way I treated my employees."

"We're not having this conversation, Jeff." Beer cuts him off. "You know the rules. You agreed to the rules. We don't want to hear anything about what you did before you started painting with us."

"Fine, whatever. I'd rather hear what happened to Sammy yesterday, anyhow."

"That's not something I'm comfortable talking about in front of the help, Jeff."

Jeff clenches his jaw, says nothing.

"What did happen to you yesterday, anyway?" Beer strips a chicken wing with his teeth.

"Tired of talking about it. What with the police all Saturday and my court-appointed therapist this morning, the whole story's getting a little stale."

"So the police were involved." Beer casually sucks meat from another chicken wing.

"Anyone hurt?" Mealy, so considerate.

"No, everyone's fine. Oh, right, but you know that girl Janice I was kind of involved with? She's dead."

Three jaws drop. Mealy, Roofie and Jeff gape at me in variations ranging from shock to horror. Beer strips another chicken wing with his teeth, takes a lazy pull from his beer.

"Wait, Janice is *dead*?" Jeff's eyes fill up, the big baby.

"Oh, God. Don't go making this about you, Jeff. You didn't even know her."

"I did too know her. I talked to her probably a dozen times on those nights when she was, like, stalking you or whatever."

"Really?"

"Yeah, she was sweet and smart and way too good for someone like you."

"Huh, maybe, I wouldn't really know. So this might sound like a weird ask, but was English her first language?"

"She was born in Ohio. Of course English was her first language."

"That's tough, man," Roofie says, hand on my shoulder. "How'd you find out?"

"Unpleasantly." I feel no need to explain that Janice defecating in my bed was my first real clue. Respect for the dead and all.

"Was it a car crash or something? Drunk driver? Hit and run?" Mealy asks.

"No, nothing like that."

"Then what? I mean, how'd it happen?"

"Not sure, really. She just didn't wake up."

"Wait, she was in your bed? She died in your bed?" Roofie stutters. Jeff has turned a lovely shade of green by this point, the child.

"Yes," I sigh, "that would be where she passed away."

"And the cops think you did it," Beer says, flatly.

"What makes you say that?"

"You just said you were with the police all Saturday."

"Yeah, but I could have been there as an insider, like, helping them crack the case."

"Were you?"

"No, they think I did it."

"Why, exactly?" Mealy asks.

"A few reasons, actually. I had a bunch of empty Visine bottles in my bathroom, and…"

"Wait, you lost me," Roofie says.

"Visine is poisonous when ingested in sufficient quantities," Jeff explains.

"How the hell would you know that?" Beer asks.

"Because the app my start-up built was for the pharmaceutical industry. Duh. I was in the business."

"Oh, really? I didn't know you had a start-up, Jeff. And you say you built an app?" I'm obviously just pissing him off here.

"Screw you, Sammy. At least I didn't poison my girlfriend."

"She wasn't really my girlfriend."

"Tell her that."

"Can't, she's dead."

"So get back to why the police think you had something to do with it. Just because of the Visine bottles?" Mealy asks, apparently the only one genuinely interested in my well-being.

"Yeah, that. And it also turns out she was pregnant."

All three of the guys, their jaws are on the table again.

"Yours?" Beer sucks another chicken wing.

"Unconfirmed. Probably not."

"Whose else could it be?" Jeff barks.

"I have some thoughts on that, Jeff." But for some reason, my thoughts turn to what Dr. Carter suggested earlier today. I start to wonder if Janice really was seeing five or six other guys on the nights she wasn't ravaging me. Or if, instead, she spent those nights recharging. Like a vampire or a spent smart phone, just gathering her energies and thinking about me.

What if Janice was that one percent of one percent who imprinted on me so hard that it consumed her, possibly even killed her? What if, in a round-about way, I really *was* the one who killed Janice? These thoughts don't seem to evoke any remorse or sympathetic emotional response in me, just a kind of intense curiosity about whether there might be more women like Janice out there. How it might be a good idea to avoid them going forward. Because what I'm dealing with right now, it's a colossal hassle.

"What thoughts?" Jeff spits.

"You know, you're getting way uppity here, Jeff. Remember the rules."

"Screw your rules, a girl's dead! A *pregnant* girl's dead!"

"I think we've established that, Jeff. And while a part of me would like to know why you care about this so much more than I do, another part of me just doesn't seem to care. Now, get out of my way, I've got to do something."

Here I climb up and stand on my bar stool, grab my and Mealy's pint glasses from the bar, clink them together like I'm calling for a wedding toast.

"What are you doing?" Mealy asks.

"Public service announcement."

"Here we go." Beer smears a final chicken wing in plate sauce. "He's lost it."

"I haven't lost anything," I say, looking down on Beer, both literally and figuratively. "I'm being responsible, here."

"Of course you are," Beer, smearing chicken wing on plate. "Please continue."

There are about forty people in the place, a mix of young hipsters and middle-aged locals, and I have their attention.

"Hey, everyone! This will only take a minute, okay? And it's really a question for the ladies. Though, actually, if you're a dude and it resonates, I should probably know that as well. So be honest, because this is important. Does anyone here feel an *unnatural attraction* to me, right now?"

"That question's kind of redundant, isn't it?" a female voice calls from a group in the back.

"Right. Ha, ha. Very clever." I nod at the smart alack. "But seriously, show of hands. Does anyone feel this overwhelming need to love me?"

"Dude, if you want to hook-up, get down and put in the work like the rest of us!" hipster guy shouts from across the bar. I wave him off with a sarcastic thumbs up.

"Okay, last chance. Anyone? Show of hands? Tell me now, because if you are weirdly attracted to me, your life might be in danger! Anyone? No? Okay, great. Enjoy your evening!" I climb down from my barstool and hand Mealy back his pint.

"That last part was priceless," Beer says. "You're going to have to beat the chicks away with a stick."

"You think that was a play?"

"Originally, I did, yes. But when you mentioned how anyone attracted to you might be putting their lives at risk, I had some doubts. Lucky you're not in a chat room, you'd be on forty government watch lists with that stunt."

"Yeah, you might want to rein it in a bit. At least until you're no longer the prime suspect in the investigation of your pregnant girlfriend's murder," Mealy says, seriously.

"How many times? She was not my girlfriend." I turn my head. "Jeff, you have something to say?"

"Nope. I'm good."

We all stop talking to watch Roofie climb up on his own barstool.

"See what you started?" Beer rolls his eyes.

Roofie proceeds to tell the crowd that he would also be interested to know if anyone at The Goat is attracted to him. And that, unlike with his friend Sammy, any interest would be received with zero intent to harm. He gets a few "Woos!" from the girls in the back, but otherwise no takers.

"You mock what you don't understand," I say to Roofie when he's sitting again.

"No, dude, seriously. I mock nothing. What you did there was super-efficient. You really cut through all this hunter-gatherer crap and got straight to the point. Totally impressive. Except the part about how liking you might put a girl's life in danger, I mean. That part you might want to re-think."

"Okay, so whatever that was aside," Mealy sighs, "you wake up next to a dead pregnant girl and the police think you poisoned her. I don't get it."

"Don't get what?"

"Why you're drinking beer with us," Beer says, "instead of being gang-raped in a prison shower right now."

"Oh, that. Yeah, Senior sent lawyers."

Jeff's jaw clenches, like it does whenever I mention my father. It drives him bananas, the fact that I could easily take over my dad's crummy production company, but instead just continue to paint houses. I should really find a way to bring Dad into casual conversation with Jeff more often. "I'm stuck in town until they clear this mess up, though."

"Like you were going to leave anyway." Beer finishes his beer and waves the bartender for another.

"Nice to be a trust fund kid when the chips are down, huh?"

"Nonsense, Jeff. It's nice to be a trust fund kid all the time."

PENNY

An electric shock blasts through my leg and for the first time in my life I feel like I'm going to die. Like I'm really going to die. Right here, this clear cool water, rainbow fish in herds, not shy, swim right up to my face. Like in a dream. Like I'm dying in a dream.

I open my eyes, upright, tangled in sweat-damp sheets. No idea where I am. A bed in the middle of an empty room, the sun coming through windows with no blinds. I'm not screaming, not crying, because I'm not breathing. I gasp, first breath, hours or days since I've taken a breath.

Breathe, like the Navy Seals breathe when things aren't going great.
I don't count off the inhale, hold, exhale. But I breathe.

I know the dream better than I know my surroundings right now. I've had the dream so many times. But where…oh my God, what time is it? I hear noises through the floorboards, realize I'm not where I'm supposed to be. Glance at the door. Closed. Good. Good. Take a breath.

What happened to my alarm? The digital clock at the corner of the bed, I grab it. Seven-forty-two. I press the alarm button. Five! What the…oh. I see a red dot beside an etched-white P.M. in the plastic. I set the alarm right, but I set the clock wrong. I make a mental note to feel stupid about this when I have time. Right now, need to make sure I don't spend the whole day hiding in a walk-in closet.

I put the tarp back over the unmade bed. Quietly, quietly. No time to put on street clothes, today I'm ultra-casual in sleep sweats. I slip on shoes, grab twenties from the wad in my pack. Brush teeth? No. Wash face? No. Brush hair? Loose ponytail. And I'm out the door. The guestroom door, that is. How I'm going to get out of the house without being seen? Come on, universe! Serve something up for me!

The voices seem to come from the kitchen. A wave of shame washing over me for the whole pee-in-the-beer-bottle fiasco. I slink down the stairs, feet close to the wall so no creaks. Once down, I slip behind the staircase so that my view is blocked from the kitchen. This would be much easier if the floor plan wasn't so open.

Now, decision time. Do I make a break for the front door and risk running into someone coming in? Or do I wait here and hope that the guys in the kitchen come out together, so I can slip around opposite to the back door?

I decide to sit tight.

"Next item on the agenda, how are we feeling about Jeff?"

I'm not one for eavesdropping, but the voices in the kitchen, it's like we're in the same room.

SAMMY

"Next item on the agenda, how are we feeling about Jeff?" I ask.

Beer, Mealy and I usually get together for a check-in meeting at the start of most workdays. Not that we typically have anything to say that we can't say in front of the crew, but having partner meetings is a subtle way to reinforce our collective leadership position.

"It's only been three weeks. Too soon to discuss," Beer says.

"I think he's holding up pretty well." Mealy.

"Yeah, see, I'm not so sure. There's a weird, quiet boil about him that makes me uneasy. Anyone else picking up a school shooter vibe?"

"No more than I'd expect. I mean, we are treating him like a farm animal. If anything, we should maybe stop calling him Jeff. I think he's developing a twitch." Mealy.

"Lighten up, guys. Jeff's fine. Next item, we've got about six point nine million spindles on the main staircase and upstairs hall railings. Day workers?" Beer.

"Hell yeah." I say, no question at all.

In case you don't paint houses for a living, spindles are the awful ornate legs that connect a stairway banister to the floor below. Right, you've never even thought about them. But for painters, spindles are Satan's teeth. Painful, body contorting work. And they rate a perfect ten, tortuous repetition category, on the suicide probability scale.

68 SEMI-GLOSS

Because there are never just a handful of spindles. They always come in millions.

"Fine," Mealy votes, not happy about it.

"What? You want to paint those spindles yourself?" Beer.

"No, it's the right call. I just...it's fine."

"I'll tell Roofie to collect the truck and gather up two or three guys from the Wal-Mart parking lot on Kennedy." Beer pulls out his iPhone and makes the call.

"Dude. It's been, like, fifteen years. You've got to get over this day worker thing."

"They throw off my game is all."

"Mealy, man. You're a Jedi painter. No need for performance anxiety."

"You know it's not the painting, it's brain-jobs. Outsiders don't get it. Messes up my chi."

"Dude, most of them don't speak English."

"Doesn't matter. It's like...remember playing with Star Wars figures when you were a kid?"

"Sure."

"It's like Star Wars figures in your living room, yeah? You've got this whole universe going on – the coffee table's an imperial fortress, ashtray's a tar pit, Cheerio under the couch is some kind of rebel quest artifact. And you're really in it with, like, Han and Chewy...and then your dad walks in, kicks his feet up on the coffee table, turns on the football game and poof! All the magic vanishes. Now you're just the weird son playing plastic dolls instead of doing something respectable, like football or baseball."

"You don't *do* football or baseball," Beer says, ending his call. "You *play* football or baseball. God, you're such a girl."

"And yet you have no problem hanging around with Beer. Interesting." I used to wear a dress, have stuffed animal tea parties in my dad's office lobby, just to embarrass the hell out of him. Real man's man, my dad. You never really think about anyone else's childhood being so different from your own.

"It's fine. I usually forget about it after the first hour or so."

"You know what a psychologist would say about all of this?" Beer doesn't wait for an answer. "A psychologist would say, get a grip, Mealy. You paint houses for a living. Nothing you do matters. And I mean that in the best way possible."

"He's right, man. Freedom's just another word for nothing left to lose. Baby, you were born to run. You don't have to live like a refugee."

"Speaking of which, today's brain job is what?" Beer asks.

"Oh, I have a good one!" Mealy's the best at brain-jobs.

"Let's have it."

"Okay, so last week I got a call from this Human Resources lady. Jeff listed me as a reference," Mealy continues.

"Jeff's still looking for a job?" I interrupt.

"And he listed *you* as a reference?" Beer.

"Yes, and yes. First, who else is he gonna use as a reference? Everyone in his old world hates him. Second, I am technically an owner of the business where he works. Third, he sure as hell wasn't going to list one of you guys."

"Fair point."

"I wonder what he said he does?" I muse. "Probably something like Strategic Consultant for a large-scale real estate improvement firm."

"Doesn't matter. So, this lady calls me last week, right? And I'm trying to be all professional as she works through this list of totally insipid questions that could only have been thought up by some collective, brain dead, bureaucratic HR department."

"Or, just, HR department."

"Right. And the hardest part for me is that she keeps calling him Dillon, so I have to keep remembering who she's talking about."

"Get to the brain-job," Beer sighs.

"Getting there. So, I'm all positive and complimentary and bored-to-death until she comes to the last question, which just blew me away." Mealy pauses dramatically.

"And it was?" I ask, just to round-off his drama.

"Quote, 'As a current employer, what would you say is the potential candidate's biggest weakness?' End quote."

This cracks us up, for obvious reasons. As if anyone who's agreed to be a job reference would answer that question honestly. Human Resources departments, they've got to be the stupidest people in the world. And that means something, coming from a guy who paints houses for a living.

"So, what'd you say?"

"Oh, I played the game. Not the right context for messing with Jeff. Told her maybe Jeff was too dedicated. She asked, who's Jeff? Told her I meant Dillon. Said he sometimes took the job too seriously, didn't think enough about himself, blah, blah, blah. I'll tell you, though, nothing makes me feel better about painting houses than talking to some nitwit trapped in a perfunctory corporate environment. Never gonna happen to me, don't care how much they pay."

"All great. When do we get to today's brain-job?" Beer, antsy.

To comprehend what is a brain-job, first you need a basic understanding of the house painting business. Basically, painting stuff sucks. Mind-numbing repetition that makes you bend and stretch in ways that are no good for your body, for hours and days and months and years. Dante's inferno would have been more accurate if he'd described dead souls painting the endless circles of hell straight into eternity. It's the kind of work that gives you a warm, fuzzy feeling about suicide as a back pocket exit strategy.

In most jobs, the smartest excel. In painting, it's the opposite. Mental softness and occasional befuddlement are the qualities we're looking for. I might have mentioned before, it helps to think of a painter's brain the way you would a normal person's appendix – it serves no practical purpose, and when it does wake up, no good can come of it.

Brain-jobs, they're our secret weapon. Our competitive differentiation. What helps us paint longer, more accurately, and with far less dependence on drugs and alcohol than other contractors in the greater Tampa Bay area.

We came up with the idea the summer of our senior year in high school. We'd marathoned all three *Lord of the Rings* movies one night before a job. And we started the next day with an impassioned discussion about the socio-political climate of Middle Earth. It's actually a pretty pregnant topic, what with elves, dwarfs, trolls, goblins, orcs and humans. And after three straight Peter Jackson movies not six hours prior, we had the wherewithal to take it seriously.

We remained fully engaged in that single pointless discussion until the sun began to set. And then we realized how much painting we'd gotten done, without even noticing it. With our brains fully engaged in the meaningless, our bodies just clicked into autopilot and we painted the whole goddamned house. It was honestly the first time we'd ever finished a workday and not had a desperate urge to drive into oncoming traffic on the way home.

Mealy was the one who put two-and-two together, realizing what we'd discovered. The secret to success in the paint game. A single fertile and pointless topic to fully engage our appendix-brains while allowing our bodies to go through the motions of painting.

So Mealy put some effort into it. Potential outcomes of Marvel vs. DC comic characters, absent their primary superpowers, in battles to the death. How long after a hot celebrity dies would you still have sex with her corpse, itemized by name and number of days. Exactly how commercialism destroyed every *Star Wars* film released after *Empire*. You get the idea.

We painted like the wind.

"Today's brain-job is…what's the most awesome answer you could give to the job reference question 'AS A FORMER EMPLOYER, WHAT WOULD YOU SAY IS THE POTENTIAL CANDIDATE'S BIGGEST WEAKNESS?'"

Beer and I contemplate this for a moment. Nod and smile. Mealy really does have a gift.

"That'll do, pig," Beer says warmly. We hear the truck pull into the driveway and head out to brief the day workers.

PENNY

"That'll do, pig."

And with that, the guy ends what was probably the strangest conversation I'd ever eavesdropped in my life. Brain-job? Whatever. For some reason the absurdity of it brings my heart rate down to something approaching normal. As the guys walk out of the kitchen, I sneak around the staircase and quietly slip out the back door.

I jog from the backyard to the grass strip that separates the driveways of this house and the neighbor's, walk super casual toward the street, head down, eyes on my feet. No reason anyone would think I'm not walking out of the neighbor's house. Playing it cool, just straddling both driveways, totally inconspicuous.

And then some dude jumps from the bed of a pickup truck and lands almost on top of me. Of course, I scream. A high-pitched thing that would probably shatter crystal. And I was so close to pulling off a perfect exit.

"Jesus, what the hell, man!" I shout, falling backwards. Then actually feel a little bad for the guy, who hadn't expected to land inches from my face, and is clearly freaked-out by my earsplitting scream.

"Ay, dios mio! Lo siento, estas bien?" The man grabs my shoulders to steady me.

"No hablo espanol," The only Spanish I know. "It's fine."

"You are...okay?" he asks, English broken. Hands still holding my shoulders, but not in a creepy way. He's more startled than I am.

"Okay! Bring it in!" shouts a tall, scraggly looking guy – thinning hair, gut and a beard – from the front door. Didn't get a look inside but think he's one of the guys who were talking in the kitchen.

My guy nods, gives my shoulders a kind of "sorry" squeeze and we exchange weak smiles. He walks toward the tall guy while I try to control my flight instinct. *Real travelers walk into ticklish situations, not away from them.* Sigh. I flash a glance at the tall guy, who pulls a mug like, are you waiting for an engraved invitation or something? Okay. In for a penny, right? I know who I am and what I'm made of. Put on my biggest Catelyn smile and jog towards the front door, calling, "Sorry a-boat that!"

"Right, listen up." Tall guy, inspecting us like a drill instructor. Me, the guy who nearly jumped on me, and some other guy, all lined-up in the foyer. "I'm Beer. That's Sammy. That's Mealy. Bosses, okay? Capire?"

"Capire es Italiano, somos de Cuba," replies the guy to my left.

"He says 'capire' is Italian. They speak Spanish," the little boss guy. Mealy?

"Tell them I don't speak either." This guy Beer, playing bad cop for whatever reason.

"Is fine. We speak some English, no problem. I am Carlos and that is Juan."

"And I'm Catelyn," I say proudly, to nobody who seems to care.

"You all paint before?" Beer asks.

"Si," Carlos and Juan nod.

"Sure," I say. How hard can it be? And as intimidating as this guy Beer is, he smells oddly good. He smells clean. Weird.

"Good. It's fifteen an hour, cash obviously. We work till four. Buckets, paint and brushes over there. You're all on these spindles." Beer turns, points at the base of the wide stairway, moves his arms upwards to the hall banisters. "Carl, you start on the west-side hallway. John..."

"Juan," Juan corrects.

"Whatever. You start on the East hallway. Girl…"

"Me?" Did he seriously just call me 'girl'?

"Right. You start at the bottom."

I look up the staircase. Banister spindles, something you'd never notice unless you have a reason to notice. You ever see a single ant on the sidewalk? And then slow-follow it with your eyes, until you realize it is one of six thousand ants swarming a melting Snickers Bar on a hot summer day? That's how I feel, looking at these banister spindles right now.

"I want it done fast, but accurate. No drippies." The hell is a drippy? "You get paint on the baseboards you wipe it pronto. No nets. You tank, you're out. We cool?"

Carlos and Juan shrug, nod. I shrug and nod, too. Then follow them to the living room, where – oh how lovely, half a bare male butt – bent and rocking a plastic pail. Cut-off jean shorts slung so low that my instinct is…intentional. Pervert. Like, maybe time to bail, Penny.

Then the butt stands up and I recognize Rufus. Okay, maybe it's not a predatory work environment, maybe Rufus is just clueless.

"Okay, guys…whoa! Hey, Canada!"

"Hi, Rufus."

"Roofie!"

"I don't think I want to call you that."

"Okay." Rufus shrugs. "I didn't know you were on the job!"

"Just earning a few bucks. That's Carlos. That's Juan."

"I know. I hired them. But I didn't know you were working today." He says it like I've been painting with him my whole life, but never on Mondays.

"Last minute decision."

"Right on!" he says, as the three boss guys walk into the living room.

"Let's get moving," the Beer guy says.

"Hey, how do you guys know Canada?" Rufus asks. And I'm thinking, the jig is up.

"How do we know Canada? Timmy Wilkinson's bachelor party? Montreal? You were there, Roofie," Beer says.

"No, I mean, Canada," Rufus replies, pointing at me.

"Your name is Canada?"

"I'm from Canada."

"And your parents were, like, super patriotic?"

"No, I mean, Rufus just calls me that. My name is actually…"

"Doesn't matter, Canada." Beer interrupts before I can even say my dead sister's name. "Like I said, fellas, no nets, keep a rag on you at all times and don't let any drippies set. Fast but careful, right?"

Juan, Carlos and I, we all nod.

Roofie hands each of us an empty quart-sized bucket. Flashes his bottom as he pulls the plastic lid from the big pail of paint.

Carlos and Juan step forward. I step back, watch what they do. Carlos squats, Rufus tips the big pail of paint to fill his bucket. Carlos stands, grabs a paint brush from the windowsill, heads toward the stairs. Juan does the same thing. So I do the same thing. But that's where follow-the-leader comes to an end, because we're all starting at different ends of the staircase. So I sit on the bottom step. And I start to paint. It's not so bad…

"Oh Jesus Christ, Canada!" little boss Mealy whisper-shouts not thirty seconds later, glancing left and right like he stole something.

"What?" I ask, feeling shame with no apparent cause.

He quietly pulls the paintbrush from my hand, gapes like it's a dead baby, darts into the living room. Did I pick the wrong brush or something? A second later he's back with another paintbrush. He scooches me aside, quickly brushing the spindle I'd just been painting.

"You've never painted before," he says, not like a question.

"Not true." Technically, I did do some watercolors in middle school art class.

"Come on," Mealy continues to repaint my spindle.

"What gave me away?" I sigh.

"Look at my brush." He holds the brush vertically in front of my face.

"Okay." The brush is as clean as his hands, only a little edge of paint hanging in a solid line along the tip. My hand, paint is sploshed all over, just like my old brush. A realization starts to dawn.

"The only part of the brush that touches paint is the tip. This half-inch, here. The rest of the bristles, the ferrule, the handle – all day, should be as clean as your hands. Well, not *your* hands." He looks at my sploshed paws. "Clean hands."

"So, am I, like, fired?" I might cry.

"No, relax. Painting's not hard. I can show you how. See this?" He points at a part of the spindle he hasn't repainted, little rivulets of paint rolling towards the floor. "You've got drippies everywhere. Only use the last half-inch of the brush, make broad strokes, don't bend your wrist. Like this." He strokes the brush, the rivulets disappear, leaving a smooth layer of paint. "See? No more drippies."

"I can do that. Thank you," I say sincerely.

"I'm Mealy."

"I guess I'm Canada." I want to tell him my name, my real name, this guy who's being so nice to me for no reason. "Mealy. Is that your last name?"

"I've known my partners since high school. You ever read *David Copperfield*?"

"Charles Dickens? No, never read that one."

"We read it sophomore year. There's this character called Mealy Potatoes because of his complexion." Mealy points at his own pale face. "Kind of stuck."

"Want me to call you something else?"

"No, I own it. Painters don't posture."

"Cool," I say, meaning it.

"How old are you anyway?" he asks, but not like a boss would ask.

"I graduated university last year. Figured I'd backpack around the states for a while before heading back to Vancouver and getting a real job." My standard non-answer redirect. When you're east of the Mississippi, you say you're from Vancouver. West of the Mississippi, it's Toronto. You never say you're from Montreal – not just because of the French thing, but also so people don't think you're a dick. "My aunt has a house down here, so I'm crashing with her for a few weeks."

"Cool," Mealy replies, unconcerned with my elaborate back story. "How about you start on the other side of the staircase?"

"Oh, yeah. Sure." I scooch across and lightly dip my brush so that paint only covers a half-inch strip along the edge of the bristles. Make a long vertical stroke on the first spindle.

"Good." Mealy's watching. "Start with the trim work at the top, careful when you cut the banister. Then sweep any extra paint down towards the meat of the spindle."

"Like this?"

"Yeah, try to keep your wrist straight."

SAMMY

"Oh, hell no."

I walk into the front bedroom, where I'm going to spend most of the day cutting ceiling trim, to find Jeff. On one knee, painting the floor trim. What kind of bad-karma universe sticks me in a room with Jeff for the better part of eight hours?

"There's a limit to the amount of abuse I can take, Sammy," Jeff says coolly, not looking up. "I'm playing your game like a good soldier, but there is a limit."

"BASIC OBJECT PERMANENCE!" Beer shouts from the adjoining bathroom. "Who's secretary?"

"Roofie," I shout back.

"You got that, Roofie?" Beer shouts.

"Got it, yeah," Roofie shouts from the downstairs hallway. There's always lots of shouting on the site of a paint job.

"What's that all about?"

"Basic object permanence is knowing that the things around you continue to exist, even when you can't see or hear them."

"I know what object permanence is."

"It's today's brain-job, Jeff. Something you'd know if you got here on time."

"I was on time."

"Ten minutes early is on time, Jeff."

"So?"

I refuse to respond, and he continues. "Tell me the brain-job."

"Roofie's secretary, Jeff. You can ask him."

"Is it really necessary, you being such a dick to me?"

"Yes, Jeff, it is. Hey, how about you and me have our own private game today?"

"And what would that be?"

"The quiet game."

"You've got problems, man."

"Jeff, I'm thirty-one years old and paint houses for a living. Tell me something I don't know."

"I'm glad you bought that up."

"Here we go."

"Seriously. What are you even doing with your life? Your dad still wants you to take over Junior-Senior, doesn't he?" He says it like he knows something I don't know.

Stuck in a room with Jeff, discussing Junior-Senior. This is my hell.

"HE HASN'T ACCEPTED JESUS CHRIST AS HIS PERSONAL LORD AND SAVIOR... HAVE YOU?" Mealy shouts from the bottom of the stairs.

"I just can't understand why you would flat-out refuse to take over a successful multinational business?" Jeff, continuing a conversation I do not want to have.

"Only you and my dad would ever refer to Junior-Senior as a successful multinational business, Jeff."

"It produces programs that play on every continent."

"*The Goop Group* plays on every continent, Jeff. Other than that, Junior-Senior mostly produces advertisements for ambulance-chaser law firms and used car dealerships local to the greater Tampa area."

The Goop Group is Junior-Senior's cash cow program. You know the show. Five gelatinous blobs representing a full spectrum of racial and gender diversity, goop-goop-gooping to each other in the harsh sunlight of Candyland Park. Little babies and really old people, they love it. Everyone between the ages of five and ninety-five, they hate the show with a passion typically reserved for child predators.

"Dude, Junior-Senior is literally a powder keg waiting to be ignited. With the right vision…"

"Jeff, let me stop you right there. If Junior-Senior were literally a powder keg, we would have to call the bomb squad. You know what's more annoying than the incorrect usage of literal and figural, Jeff?"

"Whatever."

"I literally cannot come up with anything more annoying. It's got me figuratively over a barrel."

Jeff identifies as one of those tunnel-vision business types with a command of the English language that would make a fourth grader cringe.

"So you're just going to waste your life being grammatically correct and putting paint on wood. Seriously, dude. All Junior-Senior needs is some forward-thinking management to bring it into the twenty-first century."

"The correct usage of literal and figurative isn't grammatical, it's a matter of word definition. Oh, and I don't suppose you know any forward-thinking managers who are available to help bring Junior-Senior into the twenty-first century, do you, Jeff?"

"I literally raised millions of dollars in venture capital before I even graduated college. That is the definition of visionary management."

"That's actually right, Jeff."

"How do you mean?" Jeff, dubious.

"I mean that was the correct use of 'literally' in the sentence you just said."

"SHE HAS REALLY BAD LACTOSE INTOLERANCE AND IS ALWAYS EATING CHEESE!"

"Man, Beer's on fire today. And I mean that figuratively, Jeff."

PENNY

"We call him Beer because he started drinking beer in the third grade," Mealy drones, not breaking meditative focus on, like, his twelfth spindle. I've only painted seven so far.

"That's a little on the nose, isn't it?"

"I don't think any of us were trying to be clever with the nickname. I mean, we came up with it in the third grade."

"That's fair. So, I get Rufus is 'Roofie' though it's maybe the worst nickname ever…"

"…and yet Roofie has no problem with it whatsoever," Mealy, trancelike.

"…so what about that guy, Jeff? Why doesn't he have a nickname?"

"He does."

"What is it?"

"Jeff."

"His nickname is Jeff."

"Kind of. See, Jeff's real name is Dillon. But we don't think he can pull off something that cool, so we decided to call him Jeff instead."

"Why 'Jeff'?"

"Hold a minute…" Mealy stops painting, takes a beat, then shouts towards the top of the stairs, "I GUESS I'D HAVE TO SAY PERSONAL HYGIENE?!"

I see Carlos and Juan exchange a glance across the upstairs hallway, then go back to painting their spindles.

"Where was I? Right, we think 'Jeff' is a better fit for his personality. It's making him a little crazy, though. Another month or so, we'll probably tone it down. Don't think we'll ever go back to Dillon. Maybe 'D' or something. That has a double meaning, but I think he'd like it better than 'Jeff.'"

"Hang on a second," I pause my brush. "Explain what you just said."

"Okay, Jeff's real name is Dillon..."

"No, no, no. I didn't follow that part at all, but it's not what I'm asking. What's with that personal hygiene thing you just yelled?"

"Oh, that. Just something we do to keep our minds healthy."

"You shout random stuff."

"Not random. Pointless. There's a difference."

"Are you messing with me right now?"

"Not at all. Look, you've been painting spindles now for, what…three hours?"

"Three hours? It doesn't seem that long at all."

"Right. Actually, that's probably counter-productive to the point I'm about to make, but I'll try to explain it anyway." Mealy, his meditative painting drone, so focused on the spindle in front of him. "Why the past three hours flew by, it's not because painting spindles is entertaining. You understand that?"

"I don't know, it's not so bad."

"No, what's not so bad is having a mindless conversation like we've been doing. Painting spindles, in and of itself, plain sucks."

"If you say so. I wouldn't necessarily call this a mindless conversation, but whatever."

"Don't get me wrong. It's been fun talking to you. But it's not, like, this conversation really mattered to either of us. We weren't mentally or emotionally invested, is what I mean. We weren't talking about depressing stuff like politics or global warming or what to do with the rest of life. We were engaged, but with no real impact or direction. You agree?"

"Sure."

"And that's what kept your mind off the fact that you've painted, like, six spindles…"

"Seven."

"Whatever. So, picture a thousand more spindles to paint, each one exactly the same as the last, no variation or novelty whatsoever. Depressing?"

"Not really," I say.

"Imagine it as if you were alone in the house. Or if we'd already talked each other out and had nothing more to say. Or worse, imagine if we didn't like each other and didn't want to talk."

"You like me?" Suddenly, my nose tingling, my eyes filling up.

Am I crushing on this little ginger guy? I mean, he's kind of cute. We're probably on a peer level, like, emotionally and mentally, despite the fact that he's more than twice my age. But I don't think it's a crush, really. After the past few days, the past eighteen months even, I just think it's really, really nice to hear someone tell me he likes me.

"Sure, I like you a lot," Mealy drones. "But imagine I didn't. And we'd have to sit here painting next to each other, not liking each other, for hours and hours. That can happen on a job. Look at Sammy and Jeff, upstairs. So, can you picture it?"

"I think so." I try to remember my worst times over the past two days. How I felt then. But it's no use. I'm so happy just having a conversation with someone who likes me right now, I feel like I could paint spindles for the rest of my life. "Yeah, I think I got it."

"Now look at all the spindles we still have to paint."

"I could vomit." I sigh, looking at the endless banisters. I'm not being honest, but at least I'm saying what Mealy wants to hear.

"Exactly. Sit with that a second. Are you starting to feel like ending your own life might not be the worst way to wrap up the day?"

"Uh, no."

"Fine. Too soon. The vomit thing makes my point."

"Are you going somewhere with this, Mealy?"

"Yeah. What I'm saying is, the key to painting isn't technique. Hell, your technique is fine and it's only been a few hours. No, the key to painting is finding a way to replicate that perfect balance of entertaining, meditative distraction that keeps your appendix-brain from turning on itself…"

"My appendix-brain?"

"Analogy, I'll explain some other time. I'm riding a train of thought here, don't interrupt."

"Okay."

"What was I saying? Right…finding a way to replicate that perfect balance of entertaining meditative distraction that keeps your, quote-unquote, brain from recognizing a rock-bottom reality and starting to drill."

"Strange, but I think I'm actually following you, here."

"Yeah, that's because it makes sense," Mealy hums. "My partners and I have known each other since kindergarten, we can't bank on talking about new stuff to carry our days. And our future prospects are pretty much limited to painting with each other until we die. So faced with these obstacles, we had to come up with artificial ways of achieving that perfect balance of entertaining, meditative distraction."

"Like our conversation this morning."

"Exactly. And the solution is brain-jobs. That's our secret weapon."

"Brain-jobs."

"Think of it like a hand-job, but for the brain."

"Gross," I say, offended but intrigued. "Give me an example."

"Right. So today, we are trying to come up with the most awesome responses to an HR person who's making a reference call for a potential job candidate. And the question we're answering is, 'WHAT WOULD YOU SAY IS THE POTENTIAL CANDIDATE'S BIGGEST WEAKNESS?'"

"I don't get it. Do people really ask that on job reference calls?"

"Yes, totally. It's a stupid question, but it's real. And if you do have to give a reference for an employee or former employee, you're gonna say something rote so you don't screw up their chance of getting the job. But in brain-job context, we're not trying to come up with the best answer for the candidate. We're trying to come up with the most perfect response to that absurd question set-up. Then the secretary records the answers in a Notes document on his phone, and we vote for the top answer at the end of the day."

"So it's like a game."

"Yeah. Something you can spend the whole day thinking about that doesn't weigh on your brain, but it keeps it pleasantly occupied. End of the day, it means nothing at all. It's the journey, not the destination. Get it?"

"I get the concept. Not really into the whole 'hand-job for the brain' analogy."

"Well, don't think about it like a hand-job from someone you're, like, in a relationship with. It's more the five-dollar hand-job you'd get around midnight down at the bus station."

"That certainly warms me up to the metaphor."

"Simile. And it's just an analogy for a pleasant, meaningless brain-massage."

"And you didn't consider calling it a 'brain-massage'?"

"We don't work with a lot of women."

"SOMETIMES YOU NEED TO SMACK HER AROUND SOME TO MAKE HER PAY ATTENTION, BUT SHE MAKES ONE HELL OF A SANDWICH!" the other boss, Sammy, shouts, making his way down the stairs.

Sammy stops when he gets to me, stares. He's got these sparkly eyes, a bright shade of green that's right on the edge of artificial. Mealy gave me some back story on him. As I wonder whether he's wearing color contacts, it occurs that we've been staring at each other for a beat too long.

"Can I help you?" I give him my biggest, most confident Catelyn smile.

"What are you, like, twelve?"

"I graduated university last year." Jesus, print me a t-shirt.

SAMMY

"Can I help you?" she beams a smile at me. Maybe this thing with dead-Janice has me a little thrown off, but that type of long-stare-smile feels like trouble. I need to put some ice on it.

"What are you, like, twelve?"

"I graduated university last year."

"Same academic track as Doogie Howser?"

"Sammy, this is Canada. Canada, Sammy." Mealy doesn't look up from his brushstroke. "She does good spindle work."

"Yeah, we met earlier. Mealy, you know I don't have a problem with hiring illegal immigrants, but I think we're crossing a line when we dip into the child labor market."

"She's a friend of Roofie's," Mealy says.

"Oh, so no chance of any weirdness. That's good."

"I'm right here, you know," she says.

"Of course I know, we were just discussing you. Maybe you'd be more comfortable painting that spindle with your fingers instead of a brush?"

"So I look young for my age. What about it?" she's smiling no more, so that's good.

"HE DOESN'T PRIORITIZE SOCIAL SHOPPING ON MOBILE APPS!" Jeff shouts from upstairs.

"You're embarrassing yourself, Jeff!"

"What? That's a good answer!"

"So Peanut, I'm gonna need to borrow your babysitter for a few," I say to this girl, Canada.

"Really, dude?" Canada stops painting long enough to glare.

"He's not going to stop if he knows it bothers you," Mealy drones, laser-focused on the spindle in front of him.

"Let her figure that stuff out on her own. Meet me in the kitchen when you finish up that spindle." I step over them, head to the kitchen.

"That trim in the master goes on for miles." Beer pulls a can of flavored seltzer water from the fridge, which he stocked with soft stuff this morning. He pops the top and takes a sip. "Jesus, it's been like three hours and these things are still warm."

"Why aren't you sticking one in the freezer every time you get a new can?" I ask.

"Because that's what I do with beer."

"You understand that it's a transferrable process, right?"

"Mixing beer and soft stuff rituals puts me too close to the edge."

"You think putting a can of seltzer in the freezer puts you one step closer to drinking on the job?"

"I do, yeah."

"Fair enough." I'm not interested in learning more about the Jenga! stack mechanics that balance Beer's on-the-job emotional and mental health. Lifers in the paint game are complicated beasts, we all deal with the demons in our own ways.

"What's up?" Mealy walks into the kitchen.

"I'm worried about that girl, Canada," I say.

"Seriously?" Mealy replies. "What do we care how old she is?"

"It's not her age, though I don't buy for a second that she's old enough to buy cigarettes."

"If we've got to re-do those spindles she's been working on all morning I'm going to fire her and Roofie, as a matter of principle." Beer is so easily riled.

"From what I've seen, she paints fine," I sigh.

"I'll vouch. So, what's the problem, then?"

"I think she might have imprinted on me."

"Oh, Jesus Christ." Beer knocks back his seltzer like he's chugging lager. "You think every girl you meet imprints on you."

"That's not even remotely true. I think every girl I meet *might* imprint on me. And the overwhelming majority don't. But Mealy, you saw how she was staring at me earlier."

"No, I didn't."

"Well she was. And she's a minor, no matter what she says about graduating from whatever the Canadian equivalent of a normal American university is."

"That would be just a university. No dif," Mealy sighs.

"I've just got to make sure it's not a problem. In case we're thinking about taking her on for the rest of the job. You know, precautions."

"Come on. She's nice. You're gonna weird her out."

"Look, this Janice thing, it's got me spooked, okay? I'm not going to let another girl get so hung up on me that she ends up dead. I have more than enough hassles to deal with right now."

Beer grabs another seltzer, says, "I imagine a direct approach would work best in this situation."

"Seriously, Beer. Don't encourage him."

"I know how to handle it. Just wanted to give you a heads-up in case things go sideways."

"Just don't freak her out in front of Carl and Mike."

"Carlos and Juan," Mealy corrects.

"Right. We've got too many spindles to lose those guys. Really, Sammy, why don't you just have Mealy ask Canada if she thinks you're hot or whatever?"

"Sure, because that wouldn't be weird at all," Mealy says.

"I'll be subtle," I say.

I walk back to the stairs. Canada is cutting the top of a spindle, eight steps up, the type of concentration usually reserved for little girls and coloring books. "Hey, Great White North."

"Hey, Mr. Show Business." She doesn't look up from paintbrush on spindle. Even if she actually were a young-looking twenty-something, which I'm sure she isn't, it would still disconcert me to hear her throw out Sammy Davis Jr.'s nickname from the nineteen-seventies.

"A little young to be an SDJ fan, no?"

"I'm not a fan. Sammy Davis Junior sexually assaulted my great grandmother. He's a prominent figure in my family history."

"Seriously."

"No. Not seriously."

"Jesus, what's wrong with you? Put down the brush for a second, okay?"

"I'm working."

"Yeah, well, we need to do a job interview type of thing."

"A job interview," she doesn't break concentration on the spindle. "Isn't that something that usually happens before you hire someone?"

"You think telling me how to do my job is a good way to start this interview?"

"Fine." She pauses her brushstroke, turns to face me.

"So, I know this is just a dinky house-painting company, but it's important to me and my partners that we run a professional organization."

"SHE NEVER REMEMBERS TO PUT THE SEAT DOWN AFTER SHE PEES!" Roofie shouts from somewhere in the house.

"So what do you want to ask me?" Canada's eyes crinkle as they look into mine.

"I can't help but notice you noticing my eyes."

"Are those color contacts?"

"Why does nobody think it's offensive to ask me that? No. These babies are all natural. So, would you say you find my eyes attractive?"

"Excuse me?"

"Alluring. Seductive. Beguiling. Answer the question."

"Okay, fine. I mean, I wouldn't say they're *unattractive*. They're definitely striking. Noticeable, I mean. But I'm more of a brown-eyed girl, myself."

"Your eyes are blue."

"I mean I like guys with brown eyes." She's saying this so as not to hurt my feelings. Positive sign.

"Well, that's just stupid."

"Not that your eyes aren't nice and all," she backpedals. A sad awkwardness, sure sign that she has definitely not imprinted on me. Probably finds me just as unattractive as the super-majority of females in this world. Good. That's good. "Maybe we can just get on with the interview?"

"Got what I needed," I say. "Get back to your spindles."

"That's it? That's your whole job interview thing?"

"Yeah."

"You just wanted to know if I think your eyes are pretty?"

"It runs a tad deeper than that. But no worries, we're square."

"How're things in crazy town?" Mealy asks, walking towards the stairs.

"She's clear."

"Phew, that's a relief."

"Sarcasm doesn't become you." I give Canada a nod, continue my way up the stairs to the front bedrooms.

"The hell was that all about?" Canada asks Mealy.

He'll tell her the whole story. That's okay, it's a good story. And I'm happy to expose some of the idiosyncratic details of my personal life if it will distract the two of them from spindle work. It's called taking one for the team. It's what painters do.

PENNY

"I don't get it."

"Join the club. But I've seen it happen. Like a cat to catnip. Stranger things…"

"What can these girls possibly find so attractive about him?"

"That is a mystery for greater minds than our own," Mealy monotones.

"And this happens a lot."

"Not at all. Very small percentage of women affected. Frequency's probably comparable to, like, identical twins. Not something you see every day, but you know they're out there."

"How does he even come into contact with these women? It's not like house painting is a socially geared career or anything."

"It's less about him being a house painter, more about him being a functional alcoholic. Sammy spends a lot of time in bars. But this particular brand of lightning can strike anywhere. Supermarket. Gas station. Grade school."

"Grade school?"

"Seen it happen. We were doing a window frame job at a Catholic school not far from here. One of the little girls, maybe second or third grade, clamped onto Sammy like a pit bull. Every recess, she'd find him wherever he was painting, just sit there with googly eyes. Bring him crayon drawings of the two of them kissing, prince and princess wedding scenes, the house where they were going to live, that kind of thing. Got so bad after a few days that the priest who ran the place had to ask Sammy to leave the job, not come back. No blame or anything, just that he was a disruptive influence at the school. Sammy was pissed."

"But he left."

"Yeah, Sammy wasn't going to die on that particular hill, given its proximity to that town called pedophilia. Even with a priest, that's the type of tangle that should be avoided, no matter how right you are. But Beer was able to negotiate a premium on the job due to loss of manpower, based on site-factors beyond the company's control. So it all worked out fine. For us at least. The little girl though, couple days after Sammy left, she showed up at school with her father's hunting rifle, shot the place to high hell."

"No! What?!"

"Sorry, just messing with you." Mealy's voice doesn't rise or fall a single octave. "That was a joke. I'm sure the little girl was fine. Think the weirdness wears off pretty quick, once Sammy's out of sight and mind. Point is, thing doesn't seem to age discriminate. We had this librarian in high school, she must've been about a hundred-forty years old..."

"That's okay, point made. So the ones that are, like, age appropriate. Does he date these girls?"

"I wouldn't call it dating, per se. But yeah, that's the romantic pond he fishes in, metaphorically speaking."

"So he just, like, has sex with them." I've never even come close to having sex.

"Exactly how much graphic detail do you want to get into, here?" Mealy's voice like a brushstroke.

"Seriously, none. I just mean, has he ever had, like, an actual relationship with any of them?"

"Not to my knowledge, but I've only known him for about twenty-five years. Maybe some girl hurt him real bad in preschool, I don't know."

"So how does it usually end?" Surprised I'm not more offended by this conversation on behalf of my entire gender. But it somehow feels more like we're talking about lab rats than actual women.

"The last one didn't end well, but most of them..." Mealy breaks his paint trance, looks at me. "My guess? These girls hang around long enough to pick up on Sammy's near-sociopathic apathy towards anything even approaching intimacy, at which point some kind of self-respect hormone kicks in and overwhelms whatever weird magnetism attracted them to him in the first place. So they slink off, full of self-loathing, and hopefully a little wiser. But that's just a theory I have."

I nod at Mealy; he nods back. This is nice.

"SHE DOESN'T PUT OUT! OTHERWISE, SHE WOULDN'T BE LOOKING FOR A JOB, AM I RIGHT?!" Beer, from the front room.

"What's his deal?" I ask Mealy.

"Who, Beer? How do you mean?"

"I don't know, he walks around like a big, grumpy boss. You and Sammy aren't like that."

"Beer's old school. Thinks every crew needs a jerky boss-type to keep motivations in line, and he's a natural fit."

"Why?"

"Because he's a boss and he's a jerk."

"Can he paint?"

"Look at you." Mealy breaks his trance again, turns, smiles at me. "Six hours on the job and you're ready for a stare down."

"I've done thirteen...no, fourteen spindles. Check 'em out, they're perfect."

"I'm digging the attitude, Canada. And you do good work, faster with every spindle." He's back to the monotone.

"So, can Beer paint or is he just good at bossing people around? He doesn't look very fit."

"It's a shame that the muscles conditioned for painting have no cosmetic value. If they did, Beer would be Mr. Universe. Yeah, he can paint. There's a scene in *Clone Wars* where Yoda fights with a light saber, you see it?"

"No."

"Too bad. That's what Beer's like with a paintbrush."

"Okay."

Mealy doesn't explain further.

"And he does some of his best work without ever even picking up a brush."

"You mean he's good with one of those roller things, too?"

"No. Well, yeah, Beer can roll like the wind. But I'm talking about his mouth," Mealy drones.

"His mouth."

"Yup, his mouth. Tell me, who do you think decides when a house needs painting?"

"Is it God?"

"Seriously."

"I imagine it would be the people who own the house."

"Wives, that own the house. Rich or poor, most guys wouldn't even notice if the walls were painted at all. But these big mansions, nine out of ten jobs, rich wives make the decision. That's where Beer's mouth comes in."

"This conversation is getting weird."

"It would be less weird if your mind wasn't in the gutter. The way Beer talks to rich wives, it's like how Obi Wan talks to storm troopers."

"You use a lot of Star Wars analogies. So, you're saying Beer's your sales guy?"

"Prosaically put, but yeah."

"Well, that makes sense. I mean, yeah, he's just dripping with charm and charisma."

"Rich wives aren't stupid, Canada. Charming, charismatic people have real jobs in the real world. One shows up to discuss house-painting and you better check the silver cabinet when he leaves. I'm not talking about interior design here. Beer sells paint on wood and drywall. What's the first thing that comes to your mind if I ask you to describe Beer? Don't think, just say it."

"He's a skinny, fat guy, weathered, like an old young man."

"Can you picture him in a suit and tie? Work-casual khakis and a golf shirt?"

"Ha."

"Exactly. But does he smell? Body odor, bad breath?"

"Oh my God! I actually noticed how clean he smelled when he was staring me down this morning."

"I bet you did. It's disarming. Beer looks like a guy who would waste his life on brainless grunt work. He's disgusting, but only on the surface. Rich wives don't know it, but he's an archetypal model of who they can trust to paint their houses. That's half the battle, right there."

"What does that have to do with his mouth?"

"Once his body establishes an unspoken trust, Beer's mouth is what makes the kill. It's like how a snake stares into the eyes of a feed-mouse, what Beer does to these rich wives. Except with Beer, it's not the eyes that hypnotize, it's his mouth."

"I have no idea what you're talking about."

Mealy pauses his brush, closes his eyes, like he's mid-stride of a decision.

"Come on, man. At least give me one practical example, instead of just feeding me these *Star Wars* Zen koans." This seems to push Mealy over the edge, and he carefully lays his brush across the top of his paint bucket.

"Okay, come up here a minute," he sighs, no longer speaking in his monotone trance voice. I scamper up three stairs, crouch over his shoulder. "Take a look at this spindle up here, the one I haven't painted yet. Look at how the texture is off balance, here, and here, and here." He points. "You can tell by the way the light diffracts, how the brush strokes used to paint this spindle were inconsistent, sloppy. Not uniform. Now look at the spindle I just painted, compare the two. Can you see how my spindle reflects the light evenly, like ice on a pond?"

"Yeah." I nod. "Sure, I can see it."

"No, actually you can't. Because I just made all that stuff up. The old spindle is perfectly fine. Honestly, I don't even think these things need another coat of paint at all."

"Whoa." I am seriously impressed.

"That was nothing. Give Beer a ten-minute walk through and he will mortify your typical rich wife at the thought of ever having invited anyone into her cheap, shoddy-painted mansion. Beer could sell Evian to people who live in Fiji."

"Give me another example."

"No. Once you understand a magician's tricks…"

"One more. Come on."

"Fine."

He stands, so I stand. We walk to the kitchen. He points at the wall. "Look."

"Okay." I'm actually excited right now.

"So, top left, you see how it looks dingy."

"That's a shadow."

"Beyond the shadow, I mean. Where the light hits it."

"Okay, sure."

"Now, I'm not doing this any justice, but Beer would explain how the previous contractors probably used a flat latex paint, which is alright in one sense because you don't want your walls reflecting light like mirrors. But flat paint like that, it absorbs moisture in the air. And that makes dust and dirt stick to it, like, on a microscopic scale. So what you get is not mold, per se, but it's in the same ballpark. And that's what makes the wall look so musty, right?"

"Uh-huh."

"Beer would recommend a light acrylic latex semi-gloss paint, which wouldn't noticeably reflect light, but it'd be easier to clean and would provide a moisture barrier, so it wouldn't attract the dust and dirt, and ergo you wouldn't have that microscopic bacterial musty problem."

"Great. Got it. So how much of that is true?"

"None of it, actually. I mean, the previous contractors probably used a satin or semi-gloss paint just like we're going to use. It looks a little dank because houses are dusty. You could probably wipe it down and it'd look as good as if we'd repainted it. But rich wives don't know that. Most rich wives don't even know what a semi-gloss paint is. But when Beer subtly talks like it's a trade secret or something, well…"

"So it's a scam. You just, like, lie to people."

"Whoa. Hold up. You're getting a whole wrong impression here." Mealy might actually be offended and it's got me a little worried. "I mean, of course it's kind of a scam. But I don't lie to people."

"Sorry, I didn't…" I backpedal.

"Beer lies to people. Because he's better at it than me or Sammy."

"Ah."

"And Beer's a master up-charger. I mean, he'll quote a job and then, throughout any work visits, mansplain areas that could be better served by an optional up-charge, until he's almost doubled the original quote. And the rich wife still recommends us to her friends. Guy's a true Jedi."

"How do you price a job in the first place?" We walk back to the stairs, take our places at the spindles.

"That's complicated."

"Like we don't have enough time for you to go through it," I say, looking up at the endless rows of spindles.

Here Mealy launches into a solid five-minute explanation of the complex methodology used to price a residential paint job. For the first time all day, I'm having trouble suppressing my yawns.

"…so finally, you take all the estimated man-hours for woodwork, multiply it by one-point-eight and add it to all the estimated man-hours for surfaces, multiplied by one-point-six, then take the sum and add forty percent for set-up, break-down and spot cleanup. And that gives us the base price."

"The base price?"

"Yeah, it usually comes out on the low side. So we'll, like, triple it. Then sometimes we claw back a few hundred, it's really all about the cosmetics at that point."

"I see. So it really is kind of a scam."

"It's business, so, I guess. Show me a business that isn't. Anyway, it's standard free-market practice. No one is forcing these rich wives to accept the price."

"Did Beer just come up with this whole thing on his own?"

"Nope. Learned almost all of it from his uncle. He was one of the greats."

"One of the greats?"

"Most successful house painting contractor in the greater Bay area, in his prime. Taught Beer everything he knows."

"So, what? He retired?"

"In a manner."

"Meaning?"

"Meaning he's no longer among the living."

"Oh. Sorry. I mean, my mom died of cancer a year and a half ago. How did Beer's uncle die?"

"Yeah, he drove his pickup off a causeway in St. Pete, about a sixty-foot drop, straight into one of those luxury yachts you see out that way."

"Oh my God."

"It's okay, really. Apparently, that was how he always wanted to go out. Beer said he talked about it all the time, back when they were painting together."

"Was anyone else hurt?"

"Just Beer's uncle. Oh, and everyone on the yacht. Both gas tanks exploded, at least that's what I read in the newspaper clip. Beer says his uncle had a few resentment issues, vis-à-vis the ultra-wealthy set, which he hadn't quite been able to work out through more traditional means."

"Like therapy."

"Like self-medication, actually. Big time boozer, did a lot of coke, that kind of thing."

"Sorry that didn't work out for him."

"Beer says he ultimately got the catharsis he needed, so I guess it's all good."

"Can we talk about something else now?"

"Sure. Hey, it's almost time to break-down anyway."

SAMMY

"Alright, let's break it down!" Beer shouts, descending the stairs. "Empty your buckets into the main tub, wash your brushes – and wash them entirely – in the slop sink by the back door!"

"Hey, Canada." I make eye contact, first time since our earlier talk. "AS A FORMER EMPLOYER, WHAT WOULD YOU SAY IS THE CANDIDATE'S BIGGEST WEAKNESS?"

"THAT'S TOUGH… AND I CAN ONLY PICK ONE?" she shouts past my head. Impressive, I think.

"Weak," I say. But the effort makes me smile.

"Blow me." She's smiling. No lingering awkwardness. This one might be a keeper.

"Roofie, shortlist! Jeff, beer!" Beer, shouting, though we're all well within his indoor-voice range.

Suddenly, Canada's spooks. Eyes round as saucers, like a kid who just got felt-up on Santa's lap. She puts her brush and bucket on the stair, darts to the kitchen.

"You can't just leave those there, Canada!" I call after her. Everyone on our crew cleans their own brush, empties their own bucket. This is why we don't hire teenage girls. I walk up to Beer, who's reading from Roofie's phone. Mealy joins us.

"You want to take a look?"

"No, Roofie's always pretty good with the short list. Long as you're okay with it, I'm square."

"Mealy?" Beer asks.

"Anything contestable?"

"Not that I can see."

"Miller Genuine Draft, big spenders." Jeff walks into the dining room. Puts two six packs, minus one bottle, on the table.

"You don't have to drink it, Jeff." I look at Canada, who is literally pouring an entire bottle of beer down her open gullet. Tears in her scrunched-up eyes, body quivering with involuntary jerks. This little chick really likes her beer.

"Alright, everybody votes!" Beer says in his outdoor voice. Canada has finished her beer, takes a stagger, retches like she's going to puke, slams the empty bottle on the table. Then takes a kind of breath that looks like she's trying to keep her body from exploding, moans, and grabs another bottle from the sleeve. Twists the cap, sobs, and proceeds to dump that entire bottle into her gaping mouth and glugging throat.

Beer pauses his speech and joins the rest of us, staring openly at Canada's erratic behavior. When she's finished dumping the last of another beer down her throat, she slams the empty on the table and does the same gurgling retch dance, bent in half, body twitching. Aside from Canada's heaves, the room is completely silent. And then, if you can believe it, she grabs a third beer and twists the cap.

"Okay, Betty Ford, let's dial it back a bit, huh? We only have a twelve pack and there are eight of us," I admonish.

"I! Need! It!" Canada's voice, desperate hiccups, like Meryl Streep after making Sophie's choice. Now that was a good movie. Kevin Klein? The guy's genius.

"Uh, go ahead. It's yours," Mealy says gently. Canada takes a gulp, but it's more human-sized this time around.

"Dios mio," Juan or Carlos says, crossing himself.

"I'm not a psychologist or anything..." Beer mutters.

"Do we even know her well enough to stage an intervention?" I ask the group at large.

Canada, face pale, eyes tear-wet, appears to be pulling herself together. She's swishing beer around her mouth but not swallowing.

"Drink a little slower and you might be able to taste it without all that swishing," Roofie says gently.

"You do realize how selfish that was," I say. "Way too comfortable, much?"

"I'm sorry, okay? I, I'm just…" Canada, some tears, pauses. "I got nothing. I'm just sorry, okay?"

"I think we're all better off pretending that never happened." Beer raises Roofie's phone, returning things to relative normal. Carlos and Juan, don't know which is which, look as if they're steeling themselves for more impromptu weirdness, like maybe an Amway recruit meeting or something.

Beer shouts the shortlist and we raise hands to cast a vote. Despite the fact that there are eight of us, the tally is twelve votes because Juan and Carlos don't understand the rules and raise their hands on every vote. It breaks down like this:

AS A FORMER EMPLOYER, WHAT WOULD YOU SAY IS THE CANDIDATE'S BIGGEST WEAKNESS?"
- BASIC OBJECT PERMANANCE. (Beer, four votes)
- HE HASN'T ACCEPTED JESUS CHRIST AS HIS PERSONAL LORD AND SAVIOR, HAVE YOU? (Mealy, two votes)
- SHE ALWAYS FORGETS TO PUT THE SEAT DOWN AFTER SHE PEES. (Roofie, three votes)
- HE USED TO WORK FOR JEFF. (Sammy, two votes)

CONSOLATION PRIZES:
- NO ENTIENDO QUE QUIERES QUE DIGA. (Juan, Best Effort)
- HE SOMETIMES USES BRICK-AND-MORTAR TACTICS TO ADDRESS DIGITAL MARKETSPACE OBSTACLES. (Jeff, Most Embarrassing)

PENNY

"THAT'S TOUGH…AND I CAN ONLY PICK ONE?" I shout right through Sammy's head. Not great, but at least it shows I can play the game.

"Weak," he replies after a few seconds. But he's smiling.

"Blow me." I smile, too.

"Roofie, shortlist! Jeff, beer!" Beer shouts.

A beer actually sounds pretty good right…

Wait…Oh my God! The beer.

There's a devil on my shoulder, telling me it's like a game of Russian Roulette – to just take my spin with the rest of them. These guys are clowns. There's no way they're going to peg me for this fiasco. Hell, it could have happened at whatever shady place they probably got the beer. And it's not gonna kill anyone. I remember, there was a boxer who used to drink his own urine for, like, the nutrients or whatever. I'm healthy. I'm clean. It's totally no big deal. Play it cool, ride it out. Do not be an idiot.

But Catelyn's on my other shoulder. *Sometimes the universe needs a sacrifice, especially when you've had a very good day.* Shut up, Catelyn! Goddammit, are you freaking kidding me?

But this is the best day I've had since my sister was with me, these guys treated me so right. Like a human being. Like one of their own. And the last thing they deserve is some, disgusting…whatever I set up here. They'll think it was a sick prank, probably end up blaming each other. I so hate knowing what I have to do right now. I put down my brush and bucket, bolt past Sammy.

"You can't just leave those there, Canada!"

That guy Jeff is reaching into the fridge when I get to the kitchen.

"Let me get those!" I try to shoulder my reach past him, but he's already got hold of the two six packs. I crouch as he pulls them out, scan the bottles.

"Relax, little lady. I got this." Patronizing dick. "You're Canada, right?"

"Yeah." My eyes on the bottles…are the two on that end a little paler? God, my pee was a great match.

"I'm Jeff."

"Yeah." I just got to pull the trigger; this waiting around isn't getting me anywhere.

"Looks like you could use a cold…hey, whoa there." I snatch one of the back bottles from the cardboard sleeve.

I cannot think about this. I have to make things right. I twist the cap…did it twist off easier than a bottle that hasn't already been opened? I don't look at it. *Come on, traveler, the only way out is through!* My whole body is suddenly gag reflex. Yup, that was the right bottle. It's cold now, but definitely my pee. I push down all my bodily instincts, try to open my throat, pour it straight past my mouth and into my stomach.

Some conscious part of me notices Jeff staring quizzically, like a snapshot, like noticing some side-walker's cool haircut from the window of a car skidding out of control right before it hits a telephone pole. I see him shake his head, then walk out of the kitchen. With the other bottles! I follow, still pouring and gulping my own revolting pee.

There are voices in the dining room, but I don't know what they're saying. I just focus on draining the last of this god-awful bottle.

"Alright, everybody votes!"

I make it to the dining room table somehow, slam the empty bottle down. I can't throw up. Got to hold it together. Everybody's in this stupid room. I've still got work to do. My arms are hugging myself. I take a deep breath, can't control a small moan, grab the sister bottle from the cardboard sleeve, twist the cap. Oh God, here we go.

This is the most disgusting thing I've ever done in my entire life.

It isn't over quickly, but after some ungodly stretch of time, it is over. I don't know what's happening with my body, with these guys in the room right now, but it's over. *That's what we call taking one for the team.* Shut up, Catelyn. I grab another bottle from the sleeve on the dining room table. Actual beer this time. Twist the cap.

"Okay, Betty Ford, let's dial it back a bit, huh? We only have a twelve pack and there are eight of us."

"I! Need! It!" Feral, like it's not my voice. Like the dog in that short story I read at school, locked with its owner in a primal standoff over a fossilized bone.

"Uh, go ahead. It's yours." Mealy, what a sweetheart. I swig, swish the beer to get rid of the pee taste.

"Dios mio," Juan crosses himself.

"I'm not a psychologist or anything…"

"Do we even know her well enough to stage an intervention?" Sammy rants.

I just swish.

"Drink a little slower and you might be able to taste it without all that swishing." Roofie, not exactly helpful, but sincere.

"You do realize how selfish that was. Way too comfortable, much?"

Shut up, Sammy. You have no idea what I just went through to save your asses. None of them know, they're just staring at me. No one but me had to drink pee, at least. But what they just witnessed; it wasn't exactly placid. I need to say something.

"I'm sorry, okay? I, I'm just…" I sob, but just a little. My head is entirely empty explanation-wise. "I got nothing. I'm just sorry, okay?"

"I think we're all better off pretending that never happened." Beer, thankfully ending the debacle and shifting attention to their game, their brain-job.

Throughout it all, I swig and swish the rest of my beer, wondering if every day ends with this type of performance art. It's like I imagine a business meeting might be at any company, if all the meeting participants were tripping wildly on LSD. Oddly formal in its ridiculousness.

Beer ends up winning the day, does what they all call "the happy fella" dance. Hops on one foot, his right hand pantomimes screwing in a lightbulb, his left hand pantomimes strumming a ukulele. I know this because the idiots are shouting with admiration, "He's screwing in the lightbulb!" and "He's strumming the ukulele!"

So it's obvious this dance has been performed many times before.

And I like it. Not just because it makes me feel like less of a relative idiot for my own earlier performance, but it's good to see a hard-ass like Beer not afraid to act the fool in front of his employees – three of whom he met only this morning. This is what people mean when they talk about company culture, I think. Sure, it's an acid trip circus, but it's definitely a culture. What's going through Carlos and Juan's heads though, hard to imagine.

"Okay, that's it!" Beer halts the victory celebrations cold. And just like that, he's a hard ass again. "Day crew!"

Carlos and Juan walk over to Beer, and I follow. Beer pulls a roll of bills, counts out one-hundred-twenty dollars first to Carlos, then to Juan, then to me. It suddenly occurs to me that I'm actually getting paid for today! *They're* paying *me*. I feel like it should be the other way around. Feel like I should give the money back, but that would be too weird.

"Nice work. We're at this place for another week, at least. You're all welcome to stay on."

"Gracias," Carlos and Juan choir.

"Me, too?" I ask, not believing what I'm hearing.

"If you don't get gutter-drunk on that one-twenty and are here at eight, sure."

"I, uh, thank you. I mean, I don't have a drinking problem or anything, really."

"It's been said that the first step is admitting you have a problem. Me? I don't really care long as you're here, sober, at eight a.m." This drinking problem mix up's gonna stick around, I guess. "Roofie will give you guys a ride back to Wal-Mart or wherever you need to go."

"Oh, I'm staying with my aunt and it's right up the…" Beer cocks his head, at once communicating apathy and mild surprise that I'd think he'd care. "I don't need a ride."

"You guys need a pick up tomorrow?" he asks Juan and Carlos. They nod. "Roofie'll get you at seven-thirty, same spot."

"I'll get here on my own."

I wonder if I would consider it a work-from-home type situation, what I've got going on here.

SAMMY

Weird, but that thing Dr. Carter said yesterday, it won't leave my head. What if Janice wasn't wrecking wild abandon on a half-dozen other guys? Does that kind of make me responsible for her waking up dead? Could this be the start of a trend? Jesus, I do not need this kind of hassle in my life. Where's Mealy? That's my problem, I didn't talk to Mealy, like, at all today. That's why my head's so out of whack.

I scan the yard. Mealy's at the end of the driveway with Canada, probably discussing how they didn't spend enough time talking to each other for the whole entire goddamned day.

Beer, Roofie and Jeff walk over.

"Where we headed?" Roofie asks.

"Mad Dogs and Englishmen. Meet us after you drop the guys off."

"And why are we trucking all the way down to MacDill?" Beer, finishing his second MGD, never short-changed when it comes to beer.

"The White Whale. My heart needs curb-stomping."

"Can't go. Meeting up with this chick at six."

"That's awesome, Jeff."

"What? I go out with girls all the time."

"I meant the part about you not coming to Mad Dogs."

"Hey, feed Brutus for me. Looks like this might be a late night," Beer tells Jeff.

"Come on, man. I need to shower."

"You've got time. It's part of the job."

"Seriously? You want me to feed your dog? I didn't sign on for personal errands."

"Yeah, Jeff. You did. You have keys to our apartments for the specific purpose of doing personal errands like feeding my dog. This was discussed."

"Fine, whatever." Jeff sulks off, Eeyore missing his tail.

"Canada's got dinner with her aunt. Where we going?" Mealy, late to the party.

"Mad Dogs."

"Eesch. A White Whale night. You okay?"

"Yeah, I'm okay. It'll be good for me."

The reason we ever go to Mad Dogs and Englishmen is not because it's a cool little gastropub with clean taps and decent music. There's only one reason we ever go to Mad Dogs. And her name is Fiona. The White Whale.

How do I explain this? Fiona, she's like a reverse me. Yin to my Yang. The only person I've ever met who gives me perspective on what that small percentage of women who imprint on me must feel. Cat to catnip, I swear I would just roll around on her in a sensory fit if she'd let me. And naturally, Fiona wants nothing to do with me. Doesn't even register my existence. If you don't believe in some kind of Higher Power or order to the universe, then explain that karma.

It's early enough for us to grab four seats at the inside bar, which is good because it means I'll be able to smell her. Don't judge. She's Irish, doesn't hardly ever use deodorant, and for some reason I find that overpoweringly seductive. And it's not like I've got a body odor fetish or anything, it's just, like, Fiona. Seriously, stop judging.

"Are you sure this is a good idea?" Mealy asks, waiting for the Guinness to settle.

"Where the hell is she? It's Monday night, right?"

"They probably haven't switched shifts yet. Relax, people are starting to stare."

"You don't actually think this is going anywhere, do you?" Beer knocks back a Jameson's while the daytime bartender tops off our Imperial pints, sets them in front of us.

"No, as a matter of fact, I don't. I'm wholly convinced that Fiona is a hopeless situation. What I'm here for is the rejection."

"Why?"

"I'm going celibate, at least for a while."

"Who are you? Mealy?"

"Come on, that was unprovoked." Mealy takes a pull from his Guinness. "This Janice thing, you're finally starting to feel bad about it?"

"I wouldn't say I feel bad. It's just such a pain in the ass, you know? I don't think I could take the hassle if another girl imprinted on me to the point of death. I mean, I totally missed brunch on Saturday."

"You don't actually think she was so into you that her heart stopped beating?" Beer rolls his eyes, shoots another Jameson's.

"I don't know why her heart stopped beating, but she definitely wasn't poisoned."

"You're jumping to conclusions." Beer bangs his shot glass on the bar in punctuation.

"So, what?"

"So, she could have had an aneurism. She could have had a heart condition. There are a million natural causes that make more sense than the idea that she, like, loved you to death."

"Yeah, you're right. And once the lab reports come back from the police it will all be straightened-out and that'll probably get my mind right. But until then, my best course of action is a full stop on any sexual activity."

"Then why are we even here?" Mealy asks.

"Like I said, I'm here for the rejection. I think getting my heart ground to fine dust would be a good way to kick-start this whole no sex thing. Oh, there she is…" Black leather miniskirt. Belly-button ring. Just kill me now.

"Dare are me boys, 'oweya, Mealy?" Of course she remembers his name.

"Hey, Fiona. Just coming on?"

"Aye. Yer gran', Beer?"

"Be better with another Jameson's."

"Comin' roi up! Yer nade anythin', Sandy?"

"Sammy. And no, I'm fine." She always remembers Mealy and Beer, but I'm Sandy. In what universe is that possibly fair?

"What'd I miss?" Roofie saddles up to the bar, takes his saved stool beside my own.

"Nothing worth catching." Beer shoots his third Jameson's.

"Dare yer man is! Oweya', Roofie, what's de craic?!" Here she actually reaches over the bar and gives Roofie a hug.

Roofie. Sweaty, dirty, skinny, ugly, dumb-ass Roofie. And me, I'm Sandy.

"My wild Irish rose." Roofie, sweet enough to make me puke.

"Sure, 'tis been a while since oi've seen yer guys."

"We're working a job on the other side of town," I say. She doesn't even look at me.

"Ye eatin' the-nite?"

"We'll take a look at a menu." She reaches behind her, grabs a menu, puts it in front of me – all without ever meeting my eyes. It's like she's doing this on purpose, but for that to be the case she would have to actually know I exist. God, I love her so desperately.

"I don't get it." Beer pulls the menu from my hands.

"You don't get what?"

"The attraction."

"Of course you don't."

"Oh, come on," Roofie butts in. "She's adorable."

Adorable. Like a bunny. Or a chipmunk. My friends are idiots.

"I don't know, Beer. Maybe it's the heart wants what the heart can't have or something. Anyway, I never asked you to get it. Just step up and be a wingman on this crash-and-burn mission, would you?"

"Sure thing, Maverick."

"Too soon," Roofie sighs. Big *Top Gun* fan, Roofie. Crushed him when Goose died.

"And this is helping you?" Mealy asks.

"I'm getting what I need, yeah."

PENNY

"Sure you don't need a ride?" Mealy, standing with me at the end of the driveway, making sure I'm okay.

"I'm crashing at my aunt's place. She's only a couple houses away."

"We're probably just gonna get pizza or something. You're welcome to join."

"Thanks, maybe tomorrow. I should hang out with my aunt tonight."

"Cool, eight a.m. tomorrow, then." He jogs off to join the other guys.

I walk toward Aunt Sally's place, disoriented at the sudden fact that I'm alone again. I take a lap around Swann Circle, part of me glowing with how great today felt, another part of me sinking fast. Because feeling so good, it just feels so bad when it's gone.

I begin to count my blessings, even though the day isn't over yet.

1. I'm grateful I didn't get busted for squatting in the paint house last night.
2. I'm grateful I overslept. If I hadn't, I wouldn't have been sneaking down the driveway at the precise, perfect moment to run into Carlos.
3. I'm grateful Mealy was the boss who saw that I didn't know how to paint. Pretty sure Beer would have fired me. No idea

what Sammy would have done.
4. I'm grateful that I know how to paint now. That's a valuable skill for a homeless girl.
5. I'm grateful for Mealy, all day long.
6. I'm grateful no one else drank my pee. That was heroic, what I did. Even if nobody knows it. Catelyn would be proud of me.
7. I'm grateful for the extra hundred-twenty bucks in my pocket!
8. I'm grateful the guys are letting me come back, so I have somewhere to be tomorrow.
9. I'm grateful for the paint house, somewhere safe and cozy to sleep tonight.

Catelyn always said there are no coincidences, but you have to believe. If you don't believe, if you don't see how even the bad things happen for the right reasons, then you won't be able to get into the groove where the universe can really take care of you. Even when you're only a second away from disaster, you still have to keep believing.

I take another lap around Swann Circle, then head back to the paint house. I dig through the trash in the kitchen, eat a few pizza crusts and one whole cold slice leftover from lunch. Drink a glass of tap water. The empty house doesn't bother me much, reminds me of being back at home.

Dad hated being in the house when I was there. Any excuse to be gone. I try to remember if it was always like that, even before Mom and then Catelyn, if there was ever a time before Mom died when he loved me like fathers are supposed to love their daughters. But Mom got sick when I was so little, like my whole life was her chemo and remission and recurrence. Wash, rinse, repeat. Maybe that broke Dad. Maybe he would have loved me otherwise. But who could love an unexpected, late-in-life pregnancy that leaves you the sum total of a slowly dying wife, a teenage rebel and a little kid?

I'm never having kids. I'd never want to be responsible for someone having a life that might end up like mine.

After my shower and change of clothes, I set the digital alarm clock, correctly, for approximately seven a.m. Pull the tarp off the unmade bed, slip under the comforter. Think about all the blessings I counted earlier. Let the whole crazy sequence of today's events help me to really trust in the power of believing. Yawn. Painting is exhausting, even though you don't feel it at the time. But it was a good day. A great day. Got to remember. Yawn… Always… Even when you're only a second away from disaster…you got…to keep…believing…

This clear cool water, rainbow fish in herds, not shy, swim right up to my face. That whole life passing before your eyes thing, it's happening. But not my life, not just my own. If I didn't beg Catelyn to come back, Dad wouldn't have taken us to Bermuda, I wouldn't be dying a cool water death with the rainbow fish. Water in my nose, in my mouth. My leg, it burns so much I'm blind. I give up. Sink.

Kayak rent guy with the horrible teeth, his voice in my blackness. Keep yer eyes open for Man 'o War. They come in colonies, so you see one, open yer eyes, cause yer gonna see more.

Jerks and pulls…my armpit, my jaw twisted against a shoulder blade, I feel it hurt like a whisper, drowning in the blare of burn from my leg. My eyes are open. Have they been open the whole time? A pattern of tiny purple sea horses, Catelyn has a bathing suit like that. They're colonial, so you see one…open yer eyes, cause yer gonna see more. Catelyn doesn't see the tentacles, burn strings, so many, so long, little heads. She feels them now, fork in electric socket, jerking on top of me. Now I know she's dying, too. Catelyn, wake up! Wake up!

I open my eyes to familiar disorientation, trying to figure out where I am as the dreams tear out of my head. Light outside the windows, but grey light. I didn't oversleep. I roll onto my back, look at the ceiling. Try to breathe.

You're on an adventure. Right in the middle of it. And on an adventure, the panic butterflies always come when you wake up. They're only shadows.

Catelyn would say thinking about the big picture when you just wake up is like thinking about the big picture when you're way hungover. Nothing good can come of it. I understood what she meant from context. When you wake up on an adventure, just focus on right now. You're safe. You can breathe. That's enough.

In, two-three. I know waking up times can be the hardest.

Hold, two-three. The panic butterflies are only shadows. They're not real.

Exhale, three-four-five-six. I can breathe right now. I am safe right now.

SAMMY

"Jesus, she's here early." Beer pulls into the driveway. Canada, sitting on the front stairs of the house, so fresh as a daisy that I could puke. Totally not what I need right now. *Livin' on a Prayer* comes on the radio.

"*You Give Love a Bad Name*," I croak.

"*Shot Through the Heart*," Beer shouts.

"That was mine," Mealy sighs. "Man, I can never think of Bon Jovi songs."

"I can name ten right now. But you can't use them if I tell." Beer puts the truck into park.

"Just give me a second, okay?" Mealy slides over my lap and gets out the passenger side. Good call on his part, I wasn't planning to move anytime soon. I take deep breaths while Beer turns off the truck radio, turns on the Bose Smart Speaker 500, which is already tuned to the KQID Classic Rock Internet channel. Seems that Tommy's currently got his six string in hock. And Gina's not the only one who's dreaming of running away. I'd like to drive into oncoming traffic right now.

I watch Mealy walk up to a smiling Canada, then he suddenly turns and shouts.

"*She's a Little Runaway!*"

I swear, Canada's knees actually buckle. Eyes like saucers. She looks like she did right before her kooky alcoholic jag yesterday. This chick is way too weird for my hangover.

"Foul. It's just *Runaway*." Beer walks right past Mealy. "Doesn't count."

"Oh, come on, man!" Mealy so rarely gets excited.

"You're not on the clock until eight, just so you know," Beer says as he passes Canada. She actually looks worse than I must look right now, which is totally saying something. I pull myself out the passenger-side door, limp towards the house even though there's nothing ostensibly wrong with my legs.

"The hell's the matter with you?" I ask, passing Canada, her countenance rapidly changing from utter panic to subtle confusion. "You're not gonna get fired for drinking before work if you need it that bad."

"Oh God, you smell awful," Canada says weakly.

"So do you." I'm traumatically hungover. Being mean makes me feel a little better.

"What did he mean, right there?"

"What did who mean, right where?"

"Beer," she asks, voice cracking. "Mealy and Beer."

"I don't know what you're…oh, yeah. Mealy's answer didn't count. It's like on *Jeopardy!* Answers got to be precise. No wrong words or anything. What do you care, anyway?"

"I don't know what you're talking about. Explain. Please."

"You're seriously killing me here, Canada. Twofer Tuesday."

"Yeah, you're gonna have to unpack that a little for me."

"Ahhhgh. Do you realize how much pain I'm in right now? Fine," I take a breath, throw up in my mouth, swallow it and continue. "Every Tuesday, KQID plays two songs in a row by the same artist. What, did you grow up on Mars or something? Anyway, on Twofer Tuesday, when we hear the first song, everyone tries to guess the second song. Make sense? So, we just listened to *Livin' on a Prayer* and Mealy guessed the next Bon Jovi song would be *She's a Little Runaway* but the actual title of the song is just *Runaway*, so his answer doesn't count. Do. You. Get. It. Now?"

"Whoa. Okay, I get it. So that's, like, the brain-job for today?"

"No more questions, Canada. Your boy's hungover in a sick way. I'm sure you can relate."

"All cool. Go drink a lot of water."

"Roger that." There's a blank space, just for a blink. And then I get up and proceed to the house, wondering how much I'd have to pay one of the day workers to kill me. I always drink too much on a Fiona night. *My Life* is coming through the speakers when I walk in the house, but it's Billy Joel. Not Bon Jovi's *It's My Life*, which would have made sense. I'm confused. Maybe the radio station made a mistake.

"Sammy!" Roofie shouts towards my ear, causing me to nearly piss myself. He's already situated, painting left of the door. Did I pass out? Juan and Carlos are painting spindles in their respective East-West sides of the hallway upstairs.

"When did you guys show up?"

"About ten minutes after you did."

I stick my head out the front door and notice our other pickup parked in back of Beer's truck. Guess I missed that.

"You don't remember anything about last night, huh?"

"Nothing more than the heartbreak. Generally, I mean. No specifics. Nothing good happened, like, between me and Fiona, I imagine?"

"Yeah, no. Other than her maybe liking you some less, everything seemed on par."

"Good. Not unexpected. What I was looking for, at least."

"Sup, Sammy! Who had the best sex ever last night, you might ask!" Jeff bursts in from, I don't know where.

I cannot help but vomit on his sneakers and bare legs.

"That...was not intentional...Jeff." I groan. There are limits to hazing.

"You are a goddamned animal! These're the new Jordan's!" Jeff shouts. Roofie's arms keep him from pummeling my defenseless self.

He's totally not taking this hazing thing as well as everybody thinks. Thankfully, *Refugee* wafts through the speakers.

"*Mary Jane's Last Dance*," I gasp.

"*American Girl!*" Jeff shouts, breaking our tension. That's probably the best answer, actually.

"Uhm...*Refugee!*" Roofie shouts.

"That's the song playing now, dude." I aside, painfully.

"Sorry! *Don't Come Around Here No More!*" Roofie shouts.

"*Don't Do Me Like That!*" Beer.

"*Free Fallin'!*" Mealy.

"*Learning to Fly!*" Canada.

Mealy is painting spindles opposite Canada, halfway up the stairs. Somehow, it seems best to approach her for a brief recap of my immediate past. I ask Mealy to give me a minute, take his brush, and continue on the spindle he was painting. The type of guy you'd want in a foxhole with you, that Mealy.

"If you wouldn't mind, the last thing I remember..."

"You face-planted on the lawn," Canada says, kindly. "The guys thought it best to leave you be."

"What time is it?" I don't even remember pulling myself off the front yard.

"Not sure. My phone's broke. Probably a little before eleven?"

"Seriously? I missed three hours of Twofer-Tuesday? Jesus, that's almost as bad as missing Saturday brunch. Is anybody up?"

"No one has answered correctly, if that's what you're asking."

PENNY

So, I'm sitting on the front steps like an A-one perfect employee when the guys pull into the driveway. Trying to wipe the smile off my face so they don't think I'm weird, but I'm just so happy to see them. Mealy, my sweet Mealy, slides out of the truck and walks towards me with a big smile. Then he stops suddenly, turns back towards the car, shouts.

"She's a little runaway!"

Freeze. Knees give, but I'm still standing. All my blood in free-fall from my upper body to my feet. The hell? *Whatever happens, you never, ever panic.* I'm busted? *Breathe.* The jig is up? *Breathe through it.* The hell is going on right now? *Keep breathing, two, three.*

"Foul. It's just 'runaway.' Doesn't count." Beer's voice, he looks at me. "You're not on the clock until eight, just so you know."

I'm still asleep. This is a dream. Another nightmare. I'm going to wake up. I pinch myself and nothing changes. But I think I've pinched myself in dreams before, so that doesn't really help. Beer just continues on into the house. Part of me wonders if he's going to call the police. I look at Mealy, who's distracted, but he gives me a quick smile. Not the kind of smile you'd give to someone you're about to turn-in to law enforcement. This is so a dream right now. Has to be.

"The hell's the matter with you?" Sammy walks up, a reek of alcohol so strong it burns my nose. I'm definitely not asleep right now. "You're not gonna get fired for drinking before work if you need it that bad."

"Oh God, you smell awful." Rude, but knee-jerk honest.

"So do you." Clearly not too hungover to be mean.

"What did he mean, right there?"

"What did who mean, right where?"

"Beer," my voice cracks, not sure I want to know the answer. "Mealy and Beer."

"I don't know what you're…oh, yeah…" And Sammy proceeds to tell me all about Twofer Tuesday, which clears everything up damn quick.

It's weird how the universe is taking such good care of me, and at the same time messing with me, hard. *Everything's a lesson, just depends on how you look at it.* Whatever, Catelyn. If I have another one of these mini strokes, these guys are going to have to put me in a psychiatric ward.

"…Do. You. Get. It. Now?"

I tell Sammy I get it. He tells me question-time is over. I tell him to drink water. He collapses face-first on the lawn in front of me.

I so love my new job.

"Probably best to let him sleep it off." Mealy, head sticking out the front door. "Come on, you're on spindles with me again today."

Yay!

What's more, classic rock was Catelyn's jam! We'd spend hours listening whenever she was home…in her room, in the car. And I spent about a million hours listening to it after she died. Not that a deep knowledge of classic rock gives me any edge in guessing a second song from the same artist, especially when these guys have probably been doing it for over a decade. But at least I'll build some cred with my answers, totally not look like a stupid fifteen-year-old.

"These go in the front bedrooms, hallway and kitchen." Beer hands me two small wireless relays, same to Mealy. "Test 'em for sound quality."

"Upstairs or down?" Mealy asks me.

"I got the bedrooms," I say, scampering up the stairs. These guys obviously have the run of the house, but I still feel nervous about them walking rando into the room where I've been squatting. Mealy heads into the kitchen.

"Sounds good up here!" I shout from a front bedroom.

"Great, Canada! So how 'bout you just shout out if there's a problem?" Beer, such a dick.

Jersey Girl comes on and I let out a quick sob. Every time. Catelyn used to sing it to me because we lived in New Jersey.

"*Thunder Road!*" Mealy shouts. Damn, no time for memories.

"*Born to Run!*" I yell.

"Shit," I hear Beer. "Uh, wait, uh, *Hungry Heart!*"

I totally stole Beer's song!

"*Thunder Road!*" Jeff bursts through the front door.

"Already got it," Mealy's voice.

"Ugh. Okay. Uh, *Dancing in the Dark!*"

"Sure you don't want to take that back? Plenty of time left." Beer, either contemptuous about eighties Springsteen pop, or maybe just about Jeff himself.

"Nope, sticking with it. Oh, yeah, and I think Sammy's dead."

"He's fine, just sleeping it off. Make sure Roofie and the guys don't mess with him when they get here."

I hop down the stairs and walk into the living room. Grab some gear, start negotiating how I'm going to pour paint from the big tub into my little bucket. First step, peel this lid off…

"Whoa! Freeze, Canada," Mealy at the door, scans to make sure Beer hasn't seen anything. "I'm gonna give you some advice here. Never improvise on a job site. We have very specific ways of doing things, so if you don't know exactly what you're doing, stop and wait for someone else to do it. No good's gonna come of broadcasting the fact that you're a total greenhorn."

"Sorry, I mean, I was just taking off the lid…"

"I know. Trust me, okay? I'm on your side, here. The paint in that tub's been sitting all night. So it needs to be mixed, right? Here, watch." Mealy runs his palm along the lip of the lid to make sure it's on tight. Then he flips the big tub upside-down, proceeds to shake and rock it for probably five minutes. "And pouring is always a two-man job. You spill this stuff, it's gonna make a mess. That's a firing offence."

"But it's on the tarp."

"Right, and someone accidentally steps into a puddle of wet paint that shouldn't be on the tarp, then tracks that paint all over the hardwood. Look, I know this isn't brain surgery, but there is a science to what we do, okay? You got to respect it. I don't want to see you gone over something that can be avoided, alright?" And then he tips the tub, fills my little bucket.

"You're right, really sorry. Thank you. Watch and learn, I promise." That was the nicest, most constructive bawl-out I've ever gotten in my life.

"Nothing to be sorry about. You can't know this stuff until someone tells you, right?"

"Right. Thanks. I'll learn and not be stupid." I'm thinking, when I'm, like, twenty-four then Mealy will be, like, thirty-nine or something. That would probably be okay, relationship-wise.

I look at my bucket so he can't see how hard I'm crushing right now.

SAMMY

No one wants to work with me because of the alcohol stink, so I do the right thing and head back to the kitchen, where there's a whole mess of trim work that we haven't touched. I move slow, negotiate standing bed-spins, wonder if I might have a concussion from face-planting earlier. And I think about Senior. I always think about Senior when I'm at my lowest. Think of how my dad would feel, seeing his thirty-one-year-old son in this noxious state. As usual, the thought makes me feel a little better.

"*Have You Ever Seen the Rain*!" I shout, when the supremely recognizable first bars of *Bad Moon Rising* pump through the speakers.

"*Fortunate Son*!" Mealy.

"*Down on the Corner*!" Roofie.

"*Susie Q*!" Beer.

"*My Back Door*!" Jeff.

"Foul! It's *Lookin' Out My Back Door*. Jeff's out this round!" Beer.

"*Lodi*!" Canada. Nice one.

"*Por que gritan todos*?!" Carlos.

I was eleven when my grandfather died. Nineteen-ninety-nine. Right at the end of my sixth-grade school year. Bud Junior, poor bastard almost saw the new millennium. Not a day goes by when I don't wish he'd been my father, instead of just my grandfather.

Senior couldn't stand the old man. Guess that's a generational thing for us Juniors. Grandpa was too rough cloth for dad. Not country club material. Working-class hero. No appreciation for, or interest in, the finer things. Most interesting, because my father never earned a single dollar from the sweat of his own brow in his entire life. Hysterical, because the only reason the polished-up blowfish grew up wealthy in the first place was because of the dollars earned by the sweat of my grandfather's brow.

I never understood it. How can you be embarrassed by the person who gave you everything? Even as a kid, I knew. Knew my dad was just waiting for my grandfather to die, waiting to inherit everything. Like the way a teenage girl waits out the age when she can get rhinoplasty or a boob job, the day everything's going to be better for the rest of her life.

And the twinkle in Senior's eye when he found out that his father had died. I may have known before, but that sealed it for me. There was no coming back. And perversely, that's when the trips started. My father's victory lap, with me in tow, witnessing every moment of his newfound financial independence.

Tower Bridge via the Ritz London. The Louvre ala the Four Seasons Hotel George V. The Acropolis by dint of the Intercontinental Athenaeum. Every summer for the next four years, historical landmarks and luxury hotels. Shanghai. Ayers Rock. The freaking Taj Mahal. The Southern Cross. The Northern Lights. When I was thirteen years old, I'd already set foot on Antarctica by way of Invercargill at the south tip of New Zealand. In addition to hating my father and his inheritance, by the time I was fifteen I'd developed a passionate distaste for geography and all the great historical markers of human civilization.

I know. Poor baby, that's awful, how ever did you survive? Whatevs. It's not like I'm comparing it to military mandated forced labor on the farms of Myanmar or anything, but my childhood still sucked.

See, my grandfather, Bud Junior, he was the best guy I ever knew. All steak, no sizzle. He built a television network and a production company with nothing but brains, bare hands and sheer, bald determination. Conversely, my father has always been a giant bag of air.

JOE BARRETT 127

Think about how that messes with a kid. You know when a fat blowhard in a Ferrari isn't ridiculous to look at? When you're the kid sitting next to him in the passenger seat, that's when.

Hangovers make me melancholy.

Mom figured it out by the time I was two. Twenty years his junior, swept up in the lifestyle like a child. Walked away like an adult. I wouldn't be surprised if Bud Junior bought her airline ticket. She left me with striking emerald eyes and the meal ticket. And I never heard from her again. I picture her as a Reno blackjack dealer, a Phoenix real-estate agent, a New Jersey pharma rep. Wherever she is, she's happier than she would have been if she'd stayed with us.

Bad Moon Rising bleeds into the first beats of *Lookin' Out My Back Door*. And we're not going to hear the end of this one. Jeff's never hit a twofer. Fact that he was disqualified is going to leave a permanent mark.

The summer heading into my junior year in high school, that's when I put the kybosh on Senior's trips. Senior went to the Norwegian fiords anyway, maybe out of spite or maybe nothing better to do. I stuck it out through the brutal Tampa summer, started painting with Beer and Mealy. It was my first independent career move. And I haven't made another since.

PENNY

"What's Sammy's story?" I notice that I'm speaking in the same hypnotic monotone as Mealy when I'm painting.

Mealy proceeds to give me about thirty-minutes of way too much information.

"Wait, so he's already in trouble for the balloon riot thing at the car dealerships…" I've stopped painting, am talking as normal as can be expected given the bizzaro subject matter.

"Technically, they booked him for grand theft three and criminal mischief. It was kind of a grey area, legally speaking. Anyway, he only got a couple months court-appointed therapy." Mealy drones.

"Seems a little light, sentencing wise."

"Yeah, rich father. Lot of expensive lawyers."

"Would he mind you telling me about this?"

"Nah, Sammy's not shy."

"Okay, so now he's the prime suspect in a murder investigation involving his pregnant girlfriend."

"As of Saturday. And he wouldn't necessarily call Janice his girlfriend."

"Right, she's just a rare example of one of those women who, like, imprint on him or something."

"Like I explained yesterday, yeah."

"Which still makes absolutely no sense to me."

"Meh."

"So what is he doing about all this?"

"Apparently, he's off the sex, at least until the murder-thing is cleared up."

"And that's why he went to the Dog place last night."

"Mad Dogs and Englishmen, from a Kipling quote. It's a pub. And yeah, we went there to get Sammy's heart curb-stomped by a bartender he's smitten with who doesn't acknowledge his existence. Thought it would help him, like, kick-off the abstinence thing."

"Hard to imagine Sammy smitten."

"Just this one girl, but he's got it super bad. Why he always gets so drunk at Mad Dogs. Honestly, she's cute and all, but none of us really get why he digs her so much. Karma, I guess."

"I guess. But what's he doing about the murder investigation?"

"Nothing. He's convinced everything will be fine once the toxicology report comes back on Saturday. Apparently, those things take, like, a week."

Love Me Two Times blasts from the speakers. Catelyn loved Jim Morrison, classic poster-in-the-bedroom schoolgirl crush. I never felt the same, but I loved Catelyn so it was easy to love the music.

"*Love Her Madly!*" Mealy.

"*Back Door Man!*" Beer, naturally.

"*Peace Frog!*" Roofie.

"*L.A. Woman!*" Sammy.

"*Today's Tom Sawyer!*" Jeff.

"A rare double fault…you don't see that every day! That's Rush, idiot. And it's just *Tom Sawyer*. You're out this round and the next one." Beer.

"*Alabama Song!*" I shout. Most people know the song, but not the title. Should be obscure enough to gain some points with the crew. Such an awesome way to spend the day.

"Thanks for the great back story and everything, but not really what I was asking. About Sammy, I mean." My drone is back as I focus on cutting the top of a spindle.

"No? What were you asking, then?"

"Well, you're the guy who's good at the brain-jobs, right?"

"Uh-huh."

"And Beer is, like, the boss guy, who's kind of a dick and is good at the business stuff."

"Yup."

"So is Sammy good at anything? Specific, I mean. Or is he just weird, and that's enough."

"Sammy's got talents, sure."

"Such as?"

"Hmm. How to put it? You can think of him as a kind of ambassador. Or maybe envoy's more accurate."

"Oh, sure. That explains everything."

"What I mean is, he's kind of like our own King Moonracer. But instead of flying all over the world looking for misfit toys, Sammy deposits bits of our misfit-toy-lifestyle into everyday reality. Yeah, I think that's a good way to put it."

"I still have no idea what you're talking about."

"Patience, grasshopper. You will."

Break on Through comes out the speakers next, to a choir of groans.

"That should have been a gimme," Mealy drones. We paint in silence through the song, but not, like, an uncomfortable silence. Next up, *Wouldn't It Be Nice*.

"*Good Vibrations!*" Sammy.

"*Help Me Rhonda!*" Beer.

"*Kokomo!*" Jeff. Always the weakest choice.

"Fault. You're already out this round, Jeff. That'll cost you another." Beer.

"*I Get Around!*" Mealy.

"*God Only Knows!*" I shout.

"*Little Saint Nick!*" Roofie.

"In June, Roofie?!" Beer.

"Damn!" Roofie.

SAMMY

"She's a day worker, Jeff. Day workers don't get hazed. They're not in the caste system." How many times does this stuff need to be explained?

"Not fair."

"Maybe not fair, but practical, Jeff."

"How so?"

"We start hazing day workers, once word got out, pretty sure we'd no longer be able to get day workers."

"Yeah, but Canada's not a typical day worker."

"Really, Jeff? She's working illegally in this country and probably under-aged. I'd say that puts her right in the middle of the day worker pack."

"She's a friend of Roofie's. And she speaks English."

"That a Trump t-shirt you've got on under your sweatshirt?"

"I'm not being racist. It's just that English is her first language."

"And?" I hear the opening riffs of *Wouldn't It Be Nice*. Quickdraw, I shout, "*Good Vibrations!*"

The guys shout their answers, Beer slaps Jeff's hand for responding from the penalty box, Roofie guesses a Christmas song in June. All-in-all a pretty normal round.

"And," Jeff continues, "English as a first language means she can play all your stupid reindeer games, just like the rest of us. She's in the middle of the social mix. Not fair that little bitch gets to leapfrog into peer-level social status when I'm still low man on the scrotum pole."

"You know we can hear everything you guys are saying, right?" Canada shouts from the stairs. I wasn't aware that we were being so loud. Not that it matters.

"Seriously, Jeff. Everything was fully explained before we took you on. We created the caste system because ex-schoolmates and townies were leveraging prior relationships to take advantage of us. Canada doesn't fit into that category. You, on the other hand, could be a poster child for why we created the caste system."

"Still doesn't make it fair."

"Or maybe it's that Canada just doesn't suck quite as much as you do, Jeff."

"Thanks, Sammy!" Canada shouts.

"That's it. I'm done. You know what…you didn't deserve a girl like Janice! She's better off dead than with someone like you!" Jeff slams his bucket on the floor, which isn't really a big deal because he's sitting on the floor. But still, I check the hardwood. And where the hell does Janice come into any of this? Dude's gone batty.

"So, what? Are you quitting, then?" That would not be the worst thing, actually.

"No, I'm just done painting with you. I'm gonna work with Roofie in the front room."

"Follow your heart." I resume my brushstroke as he stomps loudly out of the room. Someone needs to school Jeff in proper hangover etiquette. And just when he leaves, the opening bars of *Little Saint Nick* come out of the speakers.

"Unbelievable!" Beer groans.

I climb down the ladder, stick my head around the corner. Roofie is doing the "happy fella dance" on company time. Usually a no-no, but that was such a ridiculous grab I don't think Beer will give him any grief. Screwing in the light bulb, strumming the ukulele, he hops my way for a well-deserved fist bump. Mealy follows Roofie's victory lap at safe distance, walks into the kitchen wearing his we-should-talk face.

"What?"

"Think maybe we're pushing Jeff a little too hard?"

"Not if by quote-unquote, we, you mean quote-unquote, me, no."

"He just walked past me, mentioned he wants you to die."

"Bit harsh."

"Maybe slow your roll a bit?"

"Slow my roll? He's not broke yet and you know it. No way an ego like that moves up the scrotum pole. He reeks of self-importance."

"You're not really in a position to criticize people who reek, right now."

"The three of us agreed. There's not much we can control in this god-awful world, but we can make damn sure not to tolerate narcissists in our workspace. Jesus, painting is bad enough. We either break them or they move on. That rule is in stone."

"What if you're breaking him too much? We don't need another Nate Cunningham situation here." The ex-quarterback I talked about. Died of a heroin overdose a week after he quit. Mealy thinks it was the hazing, I maintain it was coincidence.

"Nate had huge problems before he even came to us."

"Yeah, not like Jeff."

"Come on, man. Bad shit happens to these guys before they even reach our Island of Lost Toys. We can't blame ourselves for what happens when they leave. The only thing we can control is making sure they don't mess our stuff up."

"I'm just saying, be aware, okay?"

"We were harsher with Roofie, practically speaking."

One time, when we were hazing Roofie, we told him that the crew was going on a weekend camping trip. Team-building type of thing. On Friday, he brought a tent, backpack and bunch of other camping gear to the job site. Over lunch we hocked it all at a local pawnshop. My idea.

"Sure, but we left him the pawn tickets and money to buy it all back." Mealy says. This was also my idea.

"Still, that was way harsh compared to anything we've done with Jeff." I insist.

"Roofie's not Jeff. Hell, Roofie was more upset about no camping trip than about us pawning all his stuff. In retrospect, he probably didn't even need breaking. Jeff, on the other hand, is ticking like an emotional time bomb. I mean, we've been calling him Jeff for so long I forget it isn't his real name. That's like Guantanamo-level psychological abuse for someone like Jeff. I'm worried he's gonna crack."

"That's a good thing."

"I said crack, not break. There's a difference."

"Break. Crack. Whatever. He doesn't move up on the scrotum pole until he's a different person. Long run, we're helping him. Who wants to be a douche bag that no one wants in the same room his whole life?"

"You might be too invested in the principle here."

"Aren't we all invested in the principle?"

"Sure. But you're the only one who's driving Jeff so berserk it's got some of us concerned he's going to show up one day and shoot the place up."

"Really. 'Some of us' being…?"

"Me, Beer and Roofie."

My Sharona comes on the radio, accompanied by a chorus of moans throughout the house. Did *The Knack* even record another song? No one even bothers to guess. This happens every once in a while.

"You guys talked about how I'm treating Jeff, then?"

"Yeah."

"Without including me in the discussion." Et tu, Mealy?

"This, right now, is me including you in the discussion."

"Beer's as much of a dick to Jeff as I am."

"That's different. Beer's a dick to everyone. You're only mean to Jeff."

"I got more problems with Jeff than you guys."

"How so?"

"Every day, he finds a way to bug me about Junior-Senior. Every day, a stupid elevator pitch about the massive potential of combining his brains and my birthright. Dude is bananas."

"He's been bugging you about that since high school. Why's it getting under your skin now?"

"It's so much worse after his career collapse. Dude actually has a relationship with my dad, if you can believe it. I think the old man is promising him a position if Jeff can convince me to hop on my family's ship of fools. And for Jeff, it's like a last-ditch effort to get back on the big stage. Which is probably true, but for two simple facts. First, I'll never claim my Junior-Senior birthright. Second, Jeff is a poser, just like my dad. He's only looking to ride someone else's coattails into an unearned power position. And, for sure, that's never gonna be my coattails."

"Jeff reminds you of Senior? Interesting. You never told me that."

"Jeff is what Senior would be without the credit lines my grandfather established through sheer brains and brawn."

"Let me think on that."

"Think all you want. But believe me, breaking Jeff is an act of kindness. For him, and for the world."

PENNY

"Alright, guys! We're breaking down. Roofie takes it!" Beer, top of the stairs.

"Roofie takes what?" I focus on finishing up the base of the day's last spindle.

"The day," Mealy monotones, painting his own spindle. "*Little Saint Nick* in June. That's one for the books."

We finish up our spindles at the same time, mostly because I just tool around with mine until Mealy's done. Roofie's doing that "happy fella dance" in the living room, but there's no ceremony tonight. Maybe because he already celebrated when it happened? We spill and wipe our buckets back into the big tub, take turns washing our brushes in the slop sink.

Beer is paying-out Carlos and Juan, so I step in line behind them and take my hundred-twenty. Tells us we've got work tomorrow if we want it and all three of us nod that we do indeed want it. Carlos and Juan walk out to the truck, wait for Roofie.

"Best crew they ever worked." Sammy smiles as the door closes.

"Still trying to figure us out, I think." Mealy scopes the staircase. "Cutting through these spindles, though. With Canada here, I'd say they're knocked out by next Wednesday. Thursday, latest."

My heart drops, realizing the day-work might dry up so soon. Mealy picks up my expression, smiles, tells me there's stuff I can do when the spindle work's done. Sigh.

"Thanks. I mean, I can really use the cash." And the place to stay. The fun. The friends. The feeling that I belong somewhere. Mealy. I wonder if this painting company could ever legally adopt me?

"So, what's dinner about?" Beer asks the group at large.

"Westshore. I'm way too banged up from last night for anything big. Plus, I spent probably a thousand dollars on booze yesterday so I could use some well-priced beer."

"Fine by me." Beer exits.

"You in?" Mealy asks me. "Westshore Pizza is, like, right down the road."

I wish I could be in. Go out with these guys instead of walking around the neighborhood, sneaking back into this same house. Spending all night alone. But the responsible part of me says it's too risky. I'm a fifteen-year-old runaway pretending to be a Canadian university grad, illegally squatting in the house where somehow, I also illegally work. There are limits. I need to keep a low-profile, wherever I can, at this point. So, no. I'm out.

"Hell, yeah. I'm in," my sister says, with my mouth. Goddammit, Catelyn!

"Cool, ride with us. We'll drop you back at your aunt's place when we're done."

Jeff is driving Roofie's motorcycle, while Roofie drops off Juan and Carlos in the company pickup. I don't ask why Jeff doesn't just drop the guys off so Roofie can ride the bike himself. Political spider webs of the paint trade, I guess.

"Ride with us" turns out to be all four of us – Beer, Sammy, Mealy and me – in the front seat of Beer's pickup. A pickup that has one of those thin back cabs. I offer to sit in back, plenty of room for little me, and Beer asks if I'm a dog. Because, apparently, only dogs sit back there. The smell of the backseat makes his claim seem legit. And anyway, I'm more than happy to be sitting up front with these guys. Like a freshman cruising with a bunch of seniors.

Westshore Pizza is a place I've never been. Strip of outside tables, lined with wide screens facing the parking lot. Kind of feel you'd get in Ocean City, New Jersey. Part Philadelphia, part New York. Which, keeping it real, is all Jersey really is anyway. Feels like a little slice of home on the West Coast of Florida.

We plant ourselves at an empty six-top, on a slightly raised concrete platform off the main patio strip of two and four tops. Mealy and Jeff walk in and place our order, about which none of them have asked for my input. It's one of those places where you order at the counter and they give you a table-flag for semi-wait-service to deliver. I already love it.

"So, Canada. You think I'm being too hard on Jeff?" Sammy asks.

"I, uh, what?"

"Dude, it's…"

"I'm not talking to you, Beer. I'm asking Canada."

"I so totally don't care about how you're being with Jeff. Just be as nice as you can to me."

"Good answer, Canada. Up front. Not like people who've been talking behind my back."

Mealy and Jeff show up with four pitchers of what they tell us is Jai Alai IPA because something called Guayabera is tapped out. Jeff puts a plastic pint cup in front of me. Mealy pours beer into it.

"He's all twisted," Beer says to Mealy.

"Not in front of the help. Can you guys, like, give us a minute here?" Sammy tops off his plastic cup, hands a pitcher to Jeff, looks at me just sitting here. Oh, I didn't think he was serious.

"Sure," I say, getting up. Jeff and I walk through the strip of two and four tops, take a seat at the far end of the patio.

"Just five minutes, max!" Sammy calls after us.

SAMMY

"Just five minutes, max!"

"You're really going to make this a thing," Beer sighs.

"Yes, I am."

"It's no big deal, Sammy. Really." Mealy, uncomfortable.

"It's a big deal to me. When did we start talking behind each other's backs, huh?"

"I mean, we talked about Roofie's manic reliance on automated scheduling just last Thursday, the day before you messed with his phone."

"Okay, fair. But partners, I mean."

"I don't know. We stole Beer's stupid fedora last month. You and I discussed that before we did it," Mealy counters.

"You bastards stole my fedora?"

"For your own good. You're thirty-one, not ninety."

"It looked so good on that guy from *Dexter*. He was around our age," Beer murmurs.

"It just wasn't your look, man. We didn't know how to tell you."

"That's cool, Mealy. I know you were only looking out for me. I don't hold it against you guys." And the Oscar goes to…

"Oh. My. Frickin' God. Did you guys actually rehearse this scene?"

"Told you he'd sniff us out."

"We didn't rehearse anything. It was more like guided improv." Mealy, honest as the day is long. "Look, we're worried you've gone off the rails with this whole Jeff-hazing thing, okay? You're making it too personal. I talked to Beer, then I talked to you. No need to get all bent out of shape about it."

"I'm way hungover, possibly concussed. That's all the justification I need for getting bent out of shape."

"Granted. But maybe you direct your misguided aggression away from Beer and me."

"Sure. I'll point it at Jeff."

"I think we should give Jeff the night off. From hazing, I mean. Think he's earned it."

"Oh, you've got to be kidding me. So, what? We're going to start calling him, uhm…"

"Dillon."

"Right. We're going to start calling him Dillon now?"

"Let's not get crazy, Mealy." Beer refills his plastic pint.

"No, I'm not suggesting we start calling him Dillon for the night. I'm just saying we tone it down, let him take a few breaths without feeling bad about himself."

"You're going soft."

"Not true. Mealy's always been soft." Beer chuckles at his own stupid joke.

"What d'you say?"

"Fine. I'll back off for tonight. See how it goes." I wave Canada and Jeff back to our table.

"Everything copacetic?"

"Shut up, Jeff."

"Dude, really?" Mealy exhales.

"Fine. Sorry, Jeff. I'm hung-over, possibly concussed. Will try to be nicer."

"Whoa." Jeff's eyes widen, then quickly narrow. "Are you messing with me?"

Maybe I have been a little hard on the guy.

PENNY

The room is dusky, I can smell the ocean. A giant ceiling fan makes fat sunset shadows that propeller along the walls. I'm holding my breath for…I don't know how long.

"Where am I?" Catelyn opens her eyes, lifts her head.

"Hotel room. We got stung by those war jellyfish."

"I don't remember." Catelyn looks like she's trying to swallow a deep cough.

"You saved me."

"That's good," Catelyn sighs. Swallows another cough. "Where's Daddy?"

"Still playing golf."

"Didn't anyone tell him what happened?"

"I don't know. Don't think so."

"I feel like garbage." She closes her eyes.

"It's called secondary drowning, and it's very rare in adults." The hotel doctor is talking, not to Catelyn because she's not there anymore. He's talking to me. "It usually only happens to kids when it happens. Your sister compromised her lungs and the damage created fluid that led to her drowning later in the afternoon when she fell asleep. I'm sorry. It's very rare in adults."

"Feels like someone stripped all the skin off the back of my legs," Catelyn croaks, back in the room again. "Hey, don't worry, Penn. I'm fine. Just tired is all. Put those tears away."

"But you're not fine." I sob. "It's called secondary drowning. I didn't know it was even a thing. It's only supposed to happen to kids."

Catelyn coughs. And she coughs again. And she keeps coughing until it's all just one big, long cough. Like a slow, steady buzz.

I open my eyes. The digital clock is buzzing but I can't move my arms to turn it off. I'm not breathing, but that's because I'm crying. But not really crying. It's more like I'm frozen in a kind of soundless wail, like how you feel a split-second before bursting into tears, only that split-second just keeps going on and on.

I'm twisted with guilt, hate myself for being so happy when the guys dropped me off at Aunt Sally's last night. Who do I think I am, feeling happy? Catelyn's not happy. Catelyn's never gonna be happy again.

You're made of the same stuff as me. You've got to be happy for the both of us.

I don't want to be happy for the both of us. I want you to be happy for the both of us. I want me to be dead instead of you. I want to be dead with you.

Then you really would be ending my life. My sister drops the mic.

Sob. Goddamned sob and sob again. Well played, Catelyn. I reach over and turn off the alarm. Remember to breathe like Catelyn taught me. Remember all the other stuff Catelyn taught me, too. I loved her life so much. Everything she did, everywhere she went, such a fearless happiness. Like a little kid who isn't afraid to play with the whole wide world.

And I'm made of the same stuff as she was. And I'm not going to let that die.

Not again.

I get myself dressed to paint. And I don't just put on my clothes. I dress myself in all of Catelyn's fearless happiness, too. I get myself ready to play with the whole wide world.

SAMMY

"What's on the docket for today?"

On Wednesdays, Mealy usually slows things down. Twofer Tuesday is great, but it can be exhausting. Especially when it follows another shout-out joint like we did on Monday. Wednesdays are an introspective time on our job sites.

"I'm thinking, haikus."

"Yes! I am the haiku master."

"Beer, is it even conceivable that you might be the only one who thinks your haikus brilliant?"

"No."

"You've never won haikus. Not ever. What do you make of that evidence?"

"Bad judging. My haikus are so deep and profound, they go right over your heads."

"Parameters, Mealy?"

"Simple. Standard five-seven-five format, obviously. But the last line has to be 'Why won't Mummy die?' verbatim. No shout outs. I'm secretary, people text me their single best effort by end-of-day."

"I can work with that." Beer, nodding pensively.

"Sammy?"

"Good for me. Where's Canada?" Same as Tuesday, we pulled into the driveway this morning to find Canada bright and bushy on the front steps. Smiling like it's her birthday. Who says child labor is a bad thing?

"She's mixing the paint."

"Jesus, Mealy. You're making a twelve-year-old girl mix the paint?"

"She wanted to do it."

"There better not be a single drip on that tarp. You sure the lid was tight?" Beer has an instinctive lack of faith when it comes to other human beings.

"I made sure it's all legit."

"And you're gonna mix it again when she's done, to make sure it's right."

"Of course I am. It's just something to keep her occupied while we're in here."

We hear Roofie and the guys bang their way through the front door. Walk out to meet them, explain today's brain job. Mealy re-mixes the paint in front of a clearly offended Canada. We fill our buckets, grab our brushes and get back to the exact same thing we were doing, every single day we've ever been on every single job.

"Spindles today?" Mealy asks, as I take a seat a few stairs above Canada.

"Giving Jeff the day off, per your advice."

"Day off from painting?" Canada, in distracted, painter-monotone. Girl's already a veteran.

"Day off from me."

"Okay, you keep Canada company for a bit. She's still mad at me for re-mixing the paint."

"Like I said, I'm not mad at you," she says, "but that paint was mixed as good as when you did it yesterday, is all."

"All good, we're still friends. I'm just gonna go cut some trim to break the monotony for a while. I'll be back." Mealy and Canada exchange goofy smiles. I briefly wonder if there's something going on between the two of them, despite the obvious age gap. Then remind myself that I don't really care one way or the other.

"So, Mealy was telling me about your talents," Canada drones, a few minutes or maybe an hour later.

"My talents?"

"Says you're like King Moonracer."

"Oh, yeah. Uh-huh." A few more minutes or hours pass.

"So, do you think you could explain it to me?"

"Thought Mealy already explained it."

"Only gave me that *Rudolph* reference-point. Any further light you might shed would be much welcome."

"You're not gonna understand it."

"I appreciate the confidence."

"It's not a big deal."

"Which is why it's weird that you don't just explain it to me."

"Okay, fine." I sigh, pausing my stroke to look at her. "What's your definition of art, Canada?"

"Is this some kind of *Zen and the Art of Motorcycle Maintenance* thing?"

"No. And I don't think the question could have been any more straightforward."

"What's my definition of art. Like, for real?"

"Yeah."

PENNY

"What's my definition of art. Like, for real?"

"Yeah."

What's my definition of art? I'm briefly overwhelmed by an urge to turn on my phone and Google the definition of art. Truth is, I never really thought about it. Something beautiful? That's too simple. And art doesn't have to be beautiful to be art.

"Something that makes you feel good?" I try.

"A Snicker's bar can make you feel good. Is that art?"

Okay, he's not screwing around. And right now I'm feeling like I could end up looking like a stupid fifteen-year-old here. Not that this question is going to out me, but still.

"How about…something that makes you feel."

"Feel what?"

"I don't know, feel something."

Sammy carefully places his brush on the lid of his bucket, slides down a few steps, and pinches my shoulder. Hard.

"Hey!"

"You felt that. Would you consider it art?"

"Alright, fine. Just give me a minute."

This is, like, harder than a school question. Art. It's so broad. Painting, sculpting, photography. Dance, music, theater. Poems, prose, graffiti, tattoos. Interior freaking design. It can be beautiful, or shocking, or gruesome. There is no simple one-line definition of art, there can't be. But he's not asking for *a* definition, he's asking for *my* definition. For me, I guess, art can be any of that stuff. Anything that makes you feel different about what you think you know...

"Something that changes your perspective!"

"Impressed, Canada. Seriously, I'm impressed."

Thank God he's too focused on that spindle again to notice my full body blush going on right now. I feel like my ears might burn right off my head.

"So, what's an artist, then?"

"I don't know. Someone who gets paid for creating something that can change your perspective?"

"And you were doing so well. You know, van Gogh only sold one painting in his lifetime, and the money he got for it wouldn't buy a pair of shoes today. No one bought Nietzsche's books when he was alive. You don't think they'd qualify as artists?"

Goddammit. Fine, not about money. Simple, then.

"An artist is anyone who can change your perspective."

"So politicians, ad agencies, and car salesmen? These are what you'd call artists?"

"No. I mean, they're trying to change your perspective, but it's really because they want to sell you something. Come on, help me out here."

"Maybe real artists just try to expand your context and are only motivated by the hope that they can get you to think and feel differently about your prior perspective."

"Yeah, that! You're deeper than you act, dude." Seriously, this whole time I'd been thinking Sammy was shallower than a rain puddle.

"I've got a lot of time to ponder life's mysteries. And this is a subject that's actually important to me."

"So what does it have to do with the King Moonracer thing?"

"Getting there. So, by that definition, would you consider Mealy an artist?"

I take a beat. An artist is maybe the last thing that comes to mind when I think of Mealy. No offense intended. I mean, I love the guy. But an artist? I know Sammy's leading me here. By that definition, he said. Expand your context. An artist only wants you to think and feel differently about prior perspectives. Like the brain-jobs. Mealy called brain-jobs their secret weapon. That's because it changes their perspective on sucky paint work.

"Sure. By that definition, Mealy is the very definition of an artist."

"I wouldn't set the bar too high. He's financially motivated."

"You think?"

"I know. Those brain-jobs occupy our appendix-minds, freeing up our bodies to do the horribly repetitive work for which we get paid."

"I actually don't think painting's all that bad."

"Case in point. I think it's purer when art is unmotivated by anything but the art itself."

"Art for art's sake."

"Easy to say, not so easy to find."

"And that's what you do, then? The King Moonracer thing."

"I like to think so."

"Give me an example."

"Better to show you an example. Game?"

"For sure."

"Good. Field trip. You're with Beer and me at lunch."

SAMMY

"Well, this is a breach of protocol."

"What do you mean?" Canada asks, sliding into the front seat next to Beer, who ignores her, continues talking to me.

"How about your whole 'no observation' policy?"

What he's talking about is, I've got this thing where I don't think it's a good idea for artists to observe peoples' reactions to their work. Keeps the ego in check, keeps the art pure.

"Small sacrifice, for the sake of education. Anyway, it's not like we'd get any kind of ego boost here. It's only Canada we're talking about."

"Thanks so much."

"No offense, Canada. Just explaining to our fat friend behind the wheel that we're not seeking your approval or recognition. You're only here because you want to understand."

"Cryptic. So where are we going?"

"Wright's Gourmet House on Dale Mabry. Picking up our lunch order."

"You didn't take my lunch order."

"You're having a turkey salad sandwich and a Sprite."

"Okay."

"What's the name?" Beer asks.

"Fitzgibbons."

"So where to, after we pick up the lunch order?"

"Back to the job."

"I thought this was a field trip."

"It is."

"A field trip to pick up our lunch order?"

"Correct. Look, you're only here to observe, Canada. Bite down on your questions until after, huh? We're here." Beer takes a left on Watrous Avenue, drives a block past Wright's, takes another right and parks halfway down the block on South Sterling.

"Why are we parking here?"

"You're only here to observe, Canada."

"Yes, and what I observed is that there are plenty of parking spots in front of that Wright's place."

"Are you trying to be difficult?" Beer and I climb out of the truck. Canada, still sitting in the middle of the front seat. "Coming?"

"You need me to come help pick up our lunch order?"

"What I need you to do is curb that attitude. Just walk into the deli, kind of step back and look at the sandwich board like you're trying to make up your mind. And don't act like you know us. Can you do that?"

"Are you guys going to, like, rob the place or something?"

"Actually, why don't you stay in the car."

"She's gonna mess it up," Beer says, looking at his iPhone.

"I'm not gonna mess anything up."

Canada slides out the front seat, walks ahead of us into Wright's Gourmet House without another word.

PENNY

This Wright's place is really more like a small restaurant than a typical deli. Maybe thirty tables, most of them already taken by the early lunch crowd. Place is calm, just the low buzz of lunch talk. I walk to the pickup counter and, as instructed, look at the sandwich board like I'm trying to decide.

"Help you?"

"Still looking."

"Take your time. Turkey and pecan salad sandwich is a popular choice."

"Thanks."

Sammy walks into the shop and straight to the pickup counter. He addresses me like a stranger, a hand gesture indicating that I was here first.

"Go ahead, I'm still looking," I deadpan.

"Thanks." Sammy looks at the counter-guy. "Picking up an order for Fitzgibbons."

"Got it right here," counter guy replies, handing over a bag. "Credit card?"

"Cash, if you still take it." Sammy smiles, hands him two twenties.

"We still take it." Counter guy, making change as Beer walks in and heads to the pickup counter. Sammy takes a quick, furtive glance at Beer and then looks the other way.

"Can you hurry it up a bit…actually, just keep the change."

"Got it right here," counter guy holding out a few singles as Sammy walks quickly towards the door.

"Hey, there," Beer's voice, loud enough to raise some diner eyebrows. "Picking up an order for Fitzgibbons."

Counter guy looks at Beer. Then looks at Sammy, who is almost at the door. Looks at Beer again. Nods his chin at Sammy. "That guy just picked up the Fitzgibbons order."

Beer looks to Sammy, pauses a beat, then his eyes go wide with fury.

"You!" Beer shouts, an accusing finger thrust to a point.

Sammy laughs maniacally, darts out the door.

"Who the hell is that guy?!" Beer glares, raging at counter-guy. "Goddammit! Every single time!"

Counter guy, still holding Sammy's change, raises his hands in a wasn't-me gesture.

"Screw it! You lunch places, you're all the same! When is someone gonna take responsibility for that guy?!" Beer sprints out the door, as if he might be able to catch Sammy.

Door closes behind Beer and the deli is pin-drop quiet. I look at counter guy. No expression on his face. Same with the diners. No expression in the whole place. Everyone just looking at each other in silence. Probably a whole minute later, counter guy, loud in the silent dining room, finally asks, "You, uh, make up your mind?"

"Actually, I'm good. Thanks." And I walk out of the shop.

Bizarro.

Sammy and Beer are in the front seat, giggling like a couple of schoolgirls, when I make it back to the truck. I open the passenger door, slide over Sammy's lap to the middle seat.

"What the hell was that supposed to be?"

"That's art, Canada. In its purest form."

JOE BARRETT 153

SAMMY

"What were you expecting?" Mealy's mouth full of turkey and pecan salad sandwich.

"Not that." Canada.

"Well, sure. Be a little weird if that's what you were expecting, no?" I open a micro-bag of potato chips. Seriously, there are maybe five chips in here. The people who make these things should be arrested.

"I just don't know if I'd call it art." Canada, pensive and processing.

"Why not? It altered people's perspectives, didn't it?"

"Told you guys, she's not evolved enough to appreciate it." Beer starts on his second sandwich. He always gets two whole sandwiches, extra mayo, extra cheese. It's like a daily reminder to enjoy the time we have left with him.

"It's just kind of pointless, isn't it?"

"You're kind of pointless." I don't respond well to criticism. "Little piece like that can reframe a person's entire world view."

"Why? Because it makes them think there's some sneaky-weird people out there who hijack sandwich orders? I mean, you paid for it, Sammy. So the guy could have just remade the order for Beer. No harm, no foul."

"No, he couldn't," Beer says. "Because I ran out of the shop chasing Sammy."

"You know what I mean."

"You're missing the point, Canada. Try to unpack what you just saw, like you're on the outside track. How would I even be able to find out every time this one guy places a lunch order? And if I've got that kind of tech, would I really use it to target one poor bastard – not even to steal, but to pay for and then take away his lunch? No matter how you cut it, it's not going to make any sense. Is it just this one guy, or do I have an entire list of targets who I pointlessly frustrate by disrupting their mundane daily tasks? For the people in the deli, that one gesture contained all the unexplained mysteries of the universe."

"Yeah, but why?"

"Why does Banksy paint a picture, put it up for auction and then shred it when it's sold?"

"You're comparing yourself to Banksy."

"I don't like to compare artists. That was just an example."

"You really think anyone in that deli is going to give a damn, one way or another, after Elvis has left the building?"

"No. I'm sure most of them will just shrug it off. Some people drive by rainbows, few stop to really look. But think about the people who do stop and look. When it doesn't add up, which it won't, it might make them question just how well they really know this boring, normal world in which they live. That, Canada, is my definition of art. Much more so than standing in line at the Louvre for three hours to get a glimpse of the stupid Mona Lisa – thing is, like, the size of a postcard."

A few hours later, Canada, Mealy and me, deep in spindle painting.

"So, it's like, performance art," Canada drones.

"Why do you feel the need to categorize everything? It's just art."

"It's like one of those What Would You Do? television shows. But instead of putting people in the context of a socially awkward moral dilemma, you just confuse them with a situation that blatantly makes no sense at all."

"But they still try to make sense of it. Anyway, how's your haiku coming along?"

"I'm gonna take a pass on that. Too busy trying to process your nonsense."

"Third day working with us and you're going to 'take a pass' on the brain-job? You realize your stock is going to drop considerably among the crew."

"Really."

"Yeah, crew doesn't take brain-jobs seriously, our entire foundation starts to crack. I'd at least put in an effort, I was you."

"Fine. I'll table your whole idea of art for now. But it's not resolved."

"Good. That means it's working." Canada pauses her brush, stares at me. Like she's considering my hidden depths or something. "How 'bout you apply that adolescent brain of yours to a haiku, Canada. Trying to figure me out is way, way above your pay grade."

PENNY

She will say I'm bad
But I still won't eat my peas.
Why won't Mummy die?

I re-count the syllables in my head. It's not great, but it should pass for an effort.

"Hey, Mealy."

"Yeah?"

"My iPhone doesn't work. Can I just give you my haiku?"

"Sure…shoot." I recite the poem and he thumbs-it into his phone. "That's not bad, Canada. Not bad at all."

"I can do better, just running out of time."

"Cut yourself some slack. You got through a lot of spindles, even with the field trip."

"Sixteen. How many did you do?"

"I don't know, maybe twenty or twenty-five. But I was here the whole time."

"Alright, let's break it down!" Beer shouts from the upstairs hallway. Asides to Mealy, walking down the stairs, "I can do the short list."

"No offence, but I think all three of us are voting today," Mealy replies.

"How can I not take offense at that…you don't think I'd be impartial?"

"No, I do not. Get Sammy and we'll read them together."

"What's that about?" I ask.

"Beer's got some crazy notions about his haiku capabilities. Need to keep things honest."

We dump what's left in our buckets back into the main tub, carefully brushing out all the paint that can be used another day. Mealy, Sammy and Beer wash their brushes first, then head into the kitchen to do the short list. We hear arguing turn into yelling. Moments later, the three emerge from the kitchen and Mealy takes point.

"Okay, I'm going to read these, in no particular order and without associated names!"

Goddammed shoelaces
Tie these goddammed shoelaces
Why won't Mummy die?

For two years now, I've
Paid insurance premiums
Why won't Mummy die?

Young child, sad, confused.
Time has come to pull the plug.
Why? Won't Mummy die?

Archeologist
Disturbing, cursed profession
Why won't Mummy die?

We all vote, the third haiku wins. Blushing, so cute, Mealy announces himself the winning author. Fist bumps, the "happy fella dance" and Miller Genuine Draft bottles. Another perfect end to another perfect day.

Sammy opens the front door, and why the hell is there a silver Rolls Royce idling behind the trucks in the driveway?

"Oh, you have got to be kidding me." Sammy slouches against the doorframe.

"Is it the people who own the house?" I ask, sounding more panicked than I probably should. But all my stuff is in the guest bedroom walk-in, and with even a cursory going-over I'm sure to be found out.

"What? No. Why would the people who own the house come back when we're in the middle of painting it?"

"So who is it, then?"

"Mr. Junior! How are you, sir?!" Jeff shouts, briefly waves at the car from the open front door, then darts back towards the kitchen.

"That…would be my father," Sammy sighs.

"Huh. Guessing you're not close?"

"Worst human being, ever."

"Yeah. I feel ya." I kindly tilt my head so that it rests on his slouched shoulder, thinking about my own dad. Thinking Sammy and I might have something else to talk about when we're painting spindles tomorrow.

SAMMY

"Senior," I say curtly, approaching the drive-side window.

"Jay-Jay." Short for Junior, Junior. No words for how much I hate that nickname.

"New car."

"Like it?"

"Nope. Don't like to give women the impression that I'm compensating for something."

"I don't think you're in any position to be bringing up your women right now."

"It'll be cleared up once the toxicology reports come back on Saturday morning. And I'm not planning to skip bail. Go ahead and take the retainer fees out of my trust fund, I'm not using it much anyway. This what you're here to discuss?"

"Thought it would be nice to take my son to dinner. Reserved us a private room at Bern's."

"Did you."

"Just said I did."

"How'd you know where I was working?" As if the jogging footsteps at my back were no indication. Jeff straddles up next to me. The bastard is wearing a button-down shirt.

"Good to see you, Mr. Junior."

"Shut up, Jeff."

Unbelievable. I wasn't even nice to him for the past twenty hours, just pedaled back the abuse some for Mealy's sake. How can he possibly think that conspiring with my father to get me out to dinner would in any way extend my armistice? What he did...worse than the attack on Pearl Harbor.

"Please, call me Senior," Dad says, then looks at me. "Who's Jeff?"

This is so gonna suck, tonight.

Why I don't just outright refuse and walk away?

It's complicated.

Sigh. It's not complicated at all, actually. The old bastard is worth nearly nine figures, all earned by my dearly departed grandfather. A straight up conflict might launch me right out of his will. So I let him believe this painting thing is just an extended form of teenage rebellion. That one day I'll come to my senses and take up the family mantle. Like my father, my behavior is passive-aggressive and non-confrontational, two things I hate most in this world (the third is Jeff), but I know no other way to deal with this bag of air.

"I can't go to Bern's like this. There's a dress code."

"I booked a private room. You could strip naked and they wouldn't care."

I consider soiling myself as Jeff climbs into the backseat. It wouldn't get me out of dinner but might make things a little less pleasant for my dad. He explains everything about the new Rolls Royce Ghost to me all the way to the restaurant, and still hasn't finished talking about it when the hostess seats us.

"Why don't you order us some wine, Dillon. I've got to take a trip to the men's room." I hope to God it's prostate cancer that's making him have to pee. Jeff sneaks a glance my way and I get a glimpse of his apprehension regarding the secondary logistics of tonight's meal.

"Actually, I think I'll go with you, sir." Well played, Jeff.

"It's Senior, Dillon. None of this sir, stuff."

"You got it, Senior." They walk out of the private room about thirty seconds before our waiter walks to the door.

"Good evening! Have we all dined at Bern's before...oh!"

Now, this is funny.

The waiter stops short just inside the door, looks me up-down. Appears to be considering whether to call security. Bern's has a pretty strict dress code, and I've just spent the day on a commercial paint job. I'm filthy. I stink. And there's a rip in my t-shirt big enough to expose my left nipple. I lean back in my chair, steeple my fingers beneath my chin, tell the waiter to come in and to shut the door behind him. He opens his mouth to say something, but that never happens. So we just stare at each other for a few more seconds.

"Paulo!" my father's voice booms from the hallway, breaking all of our wonderful tension. The hell? Senior was gone less than a minute. What, did he pee, like, three whole drops? Should have just gone in his pants, that kind of effort. Maybe he really is sick. I try not to get my hopes up. "You've met my son."

"Your son." Paulo, I think, needs to pull himself together.

"Bit of a rebel. We both know what that's like, I guess." Sure. I mean, Paulo looks younger than me and is dressed in a monkey suit, kowtowing to rich old men for a living. He just reeks of rebellion.

"Mr. Junior, I...it's so nice to see you this evening." They actually shake hands. Junior Senior, a real man of the people. Oh, and here's my good friend Jeff. He washed up at the job site, and in that shirt, he doesn't look nearly as hobo as I do. "And your other son?"

"Just a friend of the family," Senior replies, Jeff exhaling a long if-only sigh.

"Dillon," Jeff says, reaching to shake the waiter's hand, just like my father did. This is embarrassing, right here.

"Paulo, very nice to meet you." Pronounces it Pow-loo. What a tool. You're a waiter, dude. Probably from New Jersey.

"Do we need the sommelier, Dillon, or are you good picking the wine?"

"I think I could take a stab at it, Senior." Jeff grins like a cavalier toad. Flips through a wine list the size of an old-school phonebook. "There are three of us, so how about we start with a white? Then we can switch to a red with dinner?"

"I like it," Senior nods.

"So, let's start with the Meursault 2016, A Mon Plaisir, Clos du Haut Tesson, Roulot. Just one bottle, no need to put it on ice if it's already chilled. And with dinner, let's see…oh, the 2003 Clos Du Val Cabernet sounds nice." I don't need to look at the list to know those two bottles alone are well over a thousand dollars of wine. In case anyone was wondering how Jeff bankrupted his start-up.

"Very good, sir. And any appetizers for the table?"

"Let's just do a dozen oysters and the Foie Gras à la Plancha. Anything else, boys?"

"Tell me, Paul…"

"Paulo."

"What I said. So, tell me Paul-oh, what's the chicken finger situation in this joint?"

"That will be all for now, Paulo. Thank you."

"Certainly, Mr. Junior. The wine will arrive momentarily."

"Perhaps you'd be more comfortable in a highchair. I saw some down in the lobby," Senior says when Paulo's left. I just love getting under his skin.

"Have 'em bring one up. You don't think I'd sit in it?" Legit, I would have no problem sitting in a highchair for this entire dinner. Senior purses his lips. The wine arrives.

"Who would like to taste?" some waiter who's not Paulo asks, opening the bottle.

"You go ahead, Dillon."

"Oh no, Senior. Please, you go ahead."

"I'll taste it," I interrupt.

"No!" Senior and Jeff say, simultaneous.

"Jinx! You have to buy each other cokes!" It's not like I won't be drinking wine tonight, they're just worried about the shenanigans I'd get up to with the waiter if I ended up being wine taster. These two are so transparent.

"Excellent," Senior declares after maybe forty-five seconds of wine-tasting pantomime.

JOE BARRETT 163

The waiter pours Jeff's glass. As he pours mine, I ask if there is any Sprite available, as a mixer. I've never used the word "aghast" in a sentence before, but it's exactly how the waiter looks when I ask him that.

"Ignore him, my son's an idiot," Senior advises the waiter.

When the wine is poured, we clink glasses like gentlemen. There are some conventions which I don't mess with. And like a gentleman, Senior directs the conversation to the subject of Jeff, ostensibly to get whatever he has to say out of the way early in the dinner.

A full, uninterrupted five minutes later…

"…so, really, I'm grateful that the business collapsed. I was a kid. And you can say what you want about the mixed messages from venture firms, how they set you up to fail and get diluted. They did things wrong, but I did things wrong, too. The point is…"

"Oh, there's a point! I was worried…"

"… the point is, the experience I gained, the lessons learned, they're invaluable. I honestly don't know how anyone can even think about leading an enterprise unless they've taken their lumps, just like I'm taking mine now. It's the best education I've ever gotten. Can't even put a price on it."

"I think your investors would price it at about nine-point-four million dollars."

"So, if you ask me, every street-fighting entrepreneur ought to fly too high and take a hard fall, at least once. You need that kind of experience to sculpt real, long-term leadership skills. But that's just my opinion."

"Hear! Hear! Well said, young man. Couldn't agree more. You don't get anywhere in this life without some bumps and bruises along the way. Just you and your bootstraps, that's my line." Says the man who has worked exactly zero days in his entire lifetime. "Could use more people with your mindset at Junior-Senior!"

"I'm really happy to hear you say that, Senior. Because…"

"Now, if you could only get this dingbat to grow up and take some responsibility for the family business. You know, I'm not going to live forever, Jay-Jay." From your lips to God's ears.

"Doing my best, Senior," Jeff sighs.

"I've got a job, Dad. Support myself, hardly touch my trust fund."

"Taking the reins of Junior-Senior, that's what your job is. I'm all for taking a few gap years, Jay-Jay, but we're wasting time here. You've got to learn the business if you're ever going to run the business."

"And it would be easier with a savvy person who he can trust at his side when he's learning it." Jeff shoots for three, and…air ball.

"It's time to wake up, boy. Look, I just stole a hotshot executive producer from one of the big content firms in New York. We're gearing up for expansion. This is the perfect time for you to come into the picture."

"That's really great, Senior. My strengths are geared towards management and strategy, so a strong production person…" This is just sad, now.

"Dad, just give me a little more time to think about it."

"Do I look like an idiot to you?" I'm honestly not sure if he wants me to answer that one. "I've been giving you a little more time to think about it for ten years! Ten years is not a little more time! Ten years is a…it's a…"

"It's a decade?"

"Always the wisecracks. Well, I'll tell you what. You've got until July first. Sew things up however you want, but if you're not ready to step into your God-given role and learn to run Junior-Senior by then, well, I'll need to rethink whether you're the best person to control the family wealth when I'm gone."

Oops. We just sailed into troubled waters.

"I'm your only heir, Dad. What, are you going to give it all to some dog shelter in St. Pete?" I really should dial it back here. I blame momentum. Damn you, Isaac Newton.

"I'll give it to whoever I goddamn please. Four weeks. Your call."

"Sammy and I will talk through it, Senior. We'll come up with a…"

"Fine. July first. In or out. The whole enchilada. Okay, I'll let you know," I say.

"It's a hard stop."

"Yeah, I get it."

What follows is probably the most painfully awkward dinner in the history of mankind. For my dad and me, at least. Jeff, he just keeps on talking, the sad bastard.

PENNY

1. I'm grateful that I didn't have to drink any pee today.
2. I'm grateful for my nightmares last night. Because no matter how awful, they still make me feel like I'm right there with Catelyn, for a little while at least. Like I can hear her voice. Like I can look into her eyes.
3. I'm grateful that Catelyn helped me see why I have to be alive. Why I have to be happy. I'm made of the same stuff as she was. And I'm all that's left of her. So, if I'm not alive and happy, then she really is gone. I get that now. And not only happy. Fearlessly happy. Just like she was. Sob.
4. I'm grateful to be working with a bunch of thirty-something guys who can spend a whole day composing bizzaro haiku poems, and they don't feel even a little weird about it.
5. I'm grateful I ran away because where else would I meet people like this?
6. I'm grateful for Sammy because he made me think today. About art. I've never thought about art before. And even though I'm not sure if I think that pointless stunt they pulled at the deli was actually art, I'm also not sure I don't. But thinking about it makes me happy. Somehow, thinking about it makes me feel more grown up.
7. I'm grateful for Mealy, as usual.

8. I'm grateful for another one-hundred-twenty dollars in my kitty.
9. I'm grateful to have this cozy bed and green bunny to sleep with again tonight.
10. I'm grateful to the universe for taking such good care of me.
11. I'm grateful to myself for being brave and open so the universe could take care of me.

For the first time in I don't know how many nights, morning comes without an accompanying heart attack. That's progress, I think. I buzz through my morning routine and am waiting on the front steps when the guys pull up.

And then. Today's brain-job, I'm not happy about it.

It's like the universe is trying to test me. I'm comfortable with these guys. Can hold my own with strangers when I pretend I'm Catelyn, but that's usually one-on-one. This whole public spectacle thing, though. I don't know.

"Explain it again," I say to Mealy.

"It's a competition. Jeff's secretary, so he doesn't play; he just keeps time."

"Why does he get to sit out?"

"Because someone has to keep time. And Jeff especially sucks at this competition."

"And the point is?"

"You win by holding up the line longest. I'm not sure why that's so hard to understand."

"Go high level, explain it like I'm a five-year-old." Maybe I'm missing something.

"Okay, it breaks down like this. We hit McDonalds on Kennedy at five-thirty. Busy, but not crazy busy. Probably four counter workers, maybe five. Either way, we always leave at least one line alone."

"Here's where you're losing me."

"Okay, you've been to a McDonald's. There are usually, like, five cash registers in front of the kitchen, with like, a counter worker behind each cash register ready to take your order. And lines form in front of each register. Follow?"

"Yes."

"Okay, the objective is to reach the register and hold up the entire line behind you for as long as possible before they ask you to step aside. Whoever holds up their line longest, wins."

"I get the broad concept. But when I get to the register…"

"When you get to the register, Jeff starts the clock. And the winner is, who can hold up their line longest without being asked to step aside. What part don't you understand?"

"How does Jeff track more than one person at the same time?"

"We got an app. That's what you're stuck on?"

"No, it's…to hold up the line, you just, what?"

"That's the brain-job, Canada. Figure out the best strategy to hold-up your line. And the cool thing, it's not about votes. Totally dispassionate. You get the minutes; you get the win."

"Give me just one or two examples. Come on, Mealy. It's my fourth day at the circus."

"No can do, Canada. That would defeat the whole brain-job aspect of this exercise. Just give it some thought and make your best effort. You'll be fine," Mealy drones.

SAMMY

"But you've done it before," Canada says.

"Yes, several times."

"So, you can't just tell me what the winner did last time?"

"No. You got to come up with your own strategy. That's the point of today's brain-job."

"Okay, then. Tell me more about your art stuff."

"I don't know, Canada. It's not like we keep records. Once we've sculpted the experience, our work is done. Keeping track kind of soils the art, if you know what I mean."

"So that thing in the deli yesterday, it was the first time you ever did it?" Canada drones, having sunk way into spindle-painting mode.

"What? Oh, 'That Guy!' No, we've done it a bunch."

"That Guy?"

"Yeah, 'That Guy!' is what we call the deli gig."

"You have a name for it."

"Well, it's not like it's been baptized or anything, but yeah."

"Isn't giving something a name, like, keeping track of it?"

"I honestly never thought about it like that."

"Just give me some examples of other stuff that has names."

"I don't know. Let me think. 'Shopgifting' is one."

"Shoplifting is something you consider art?"

"Shop*gifting*. It's kind of like shoplifting, but the exact opposite."

"Makes sense."

"Really?"

"No, not really. Explain."

"We buy a bunch of grocery bags worth of store-brand canned goods from four or five local supermarkets. We stick them in a cart and walk into, say, a Publix, and restock them."

"You just walk into a store with a cart of full grocery bags?"

"No one cares what you walk *into* a store with, Canada. Unless it's, like, on fire or something."

"And then?"

"And then we restock the stuff and leave. That's shopgifting."

"Like, you're gifting Publix a bunch of canned goods. How's that art?"

"No, we're gifting Publix employees with a surreal experience that causes them to question their perspective on the world they know. Duh."

"How so?"

"Alright, say you work checkout at Publix. In the course of a week or so, you're gonna be failing to ring up cans of Trader Joe's string beans, Winn Dixie fruit cocktail, Target condensed tomato soup, Walmart golden sweet corn…You get the picture?"

"Yeah. Very confusing for the checkout people."

"No. One, maybe three cans…that's confusing. One hundred or two hundred cans, it's impossible not to think bigger picture. That's what we're gifting."

"Bigger picture."

"Who has a greater appreciation for art, dumb people or smart people?"

"I'd have to say smart people."

"Right. So the dumb employees at Publix probably just think, weird, and move along with their days. But the smart employees at Publix, they can't let those loose ends just hang. Okay, they think, it's no accident. Not with this kind of volume and frequency. Someone's messing with us, they think. But who? And why? Exactly what kind of evil genius buys a few hundred dollars-worth of competitor-brand canned goods and restocks them on Publix shelves? And the variety of different store brands, is there some kind of malevolent supermarket syndicate at work here? Are they sending a message? And what's the hell's the message? Or is Publix being punk'd? I guarantee, some employees are searching for hidden cameras, doing their hair and make-up extra nice in case they end up on reality television. But no matter how many ways they slice and dice it, the numbers just don't add up. Smart people, Canada. Although they don't know it, smart people are the biggest appreciators of our art."

"I need to think about this."

"What's to think about, Canada? We've shifted perspective about the normal, ordinary world where certain Publix employees live. How is that not art?"

"Give me another example."

"We go into a pizza place, halfway through eating Beer calls over a waitress, asks her to explain why there's a dead cockroach in his meal."

"Gross, but not even that original."

"That's because you're focused solely on the cockroach. The waitress, however, is considering a proper response to the cockroach, but in context of the fact that they don't serve anything remotely like the plate of Chicken Tikka Masala on rice, which is what's on the table in front of Beer."

"Ah. So how does that one end?"

"Usually with Beer adamantly refusing to pay for his dinner, to which the waitress eventually acquiesces, when she realizes that that particular dish wasn't on the menu in the first place."

"Uh huh. Funny. Not, like, ha-ha funny, but still."

"We once did a variation on that same gig, but Beer ordered something from the menu and then complained about finding a severed finger in his lasagna."

"And?"

"And, meanwhile, he was blatantly ignoring a blood-soaked napkin tightly wrapped around his left hand."

"Ah."

"That one wasn't great."

"How so?"

"Too much prep. And the waitress puked on our table. We like to keep things more cerebral when possible."

"One more. You're on a roll now."

"Holiday times. Christmas, maybe Gasparilla. We scan the neighborhoods for a really ostentatious door wreath…something that totally sticks out. So, when we find a good one, we take it off the door, replace it with a note that says something like, 'Nice décor, bozo! Get one for yourself, too.'"

"That's just mean."

"No, it's art. And what makes it art is that we proceed to hang the wreath on a neighbor's door." Canada takes a moment to think that one through.

"Deep."

"Yeah, I took a stab at that one on a bigger, more corporate stage. Got a couple months court appointed therapy for the effort."

"I heard. More?"

"That's enough for now. Focus on your McDonald's strategy."

"That's exactly the focus I've been trying to avoid."

"Helps if you think of it like a chess problem."

PENNY

We're washing brushes when I finally come up with my brain-job strategy.

I'm going to hang back, watch what the other guys do, and hope for some inspiration. Weak, but it's all I've got.

Roofie's already back from dropping off Juan and Carlos, early exit but with a full day's pay. A high integrity and profoundly sympathetic move by the partners. Those poor guys don't need to be subjected to what's about to happen.

By the time we get to McDonalds, it's like Mealy said. Five registers open, three or four people lined up behind each one. Sammy, Mealy and Beer all make for the shortest lines, indicating to me that there's an advantage to being first-off-the-mark. Probably because it doesn't take long before the counter workers get wise to this fiasco.

Roofie joins the longest of the five lines. I slip in a couple of people behind Mealy, just as Sammy reaches the register. I see Jeff hesitate a few beats, then finally begin timing him.

"Sorry, guys. I've got kind of a big order here." Sammy glances at the line behind him, then looks at the counter worker. Pulls a long grocery receipt from his pocket, studies it a moment. "Okay, so I'm going to need four Whoppers."

"Big Macs."

"Sorry?"

"Whoppers are Burger King. Ours are Big Macs."

"My list says Whoppers."

"Then you'll have to go to Burger King."

"Have you ever had a Whopper?"

"Yes."

"How similar is it to a Big Mac?"

"If you don't say anything, they won't know the difference."

"Excellent. Four Big Macs, then."

"Is that all?"

"Not even close. Next, I'll need, uh, looks like an eight-piece chicken bucket, original recipe, but spicy."

"That's KFC."

"Cool, cool. KFC, MSG, whatever. Prepare it however you guys usually prepare it."

"Kentucky Fried Chicken, the restaurant, is what I mean. We don't serve buckets of chicken here at McDonalds."

"No?"

"No."

"Have you ever considered it?"

"Considered what?"

"Serving buckets of fried chicken, man!"

"I'm not in a position to make that kind of decision. So, just the four Big Macs, then?"

"What would you recommend in lieu of the chicken bucket?"

"The closest we've got is McNuggets."

"What the hell is a McNugget?"

"It's fried chicken, but in nuggets."

"Real chicken?"

"I believe it is."

"I heard a story about these big farms raising headless chickens. All breasts and drumsticks. You guys into that type of nasty stuff?"

"Not as far as I know."

"Okay, let's go with a bucket of nuggets."

"We don't have buckets. You can get a twenty-piece or a forty piece."

"Which would be about the same as a bucket?"

"Depends on how big is the bucket you're talking about."

"It's not for me, actually. It's for my friend, Jeff. He eats a lot, but he never puts on weight. My suspicion, bulimia. You think a forty-piece bucket is about right for a bulimic? Or maybe two twenty-piece buckets, because when he finishes the first one, that empty bucket could come in handy, right?"

"So two twenty-piece McNuggets, then."

"Let's do that, yeah. And three Shamrock shakes."

"Shamrock shakes are only in March."

"No kidding?"

"As I'm standing here."

"Why?"

"St. Patrick's Day."

"Huh. Okay, let's make it three large chocolate Frosties."

"The Frosty is at Wendy's. Look, I'm sorry, sir, but I'm going to have to ask you to step aside and look at our menu..." Here he points at the glaringly obvious menu above his head. "...and coordinate your order in line with what we've actually got here."

"Seriously? Come on, man. One more minute and I'll be done."

"I'm sorry, sir." Sammy walks away from the register, head hung low.

Sweet Jesus, these guys are pros.

Mealy's already standing by Jeff. I missed his performance, but it's clear he didn't come close to Sammy's effort. I look to my left, where Beer is stepping up to the register.

"I want to lodge a complaint."

"Something wrong with your food?"

"No, the food was fine."

"So?"

"It's about your restroom."

"Alright, sir. If you could you just step aside, I'll call the manager."

"Aw, Goddammit! Don't bother."

Huh. I expected more from Beer but guess that could have gone either way. Can definitely beat his time, at least. The woman in front of me walks away from the register, I step up.

"Hi. What can I get for you today?"

"Hey, uh, is James working today?" James is the most common man's name in America. I Googled it once.

"You mean Jimmy?" Phew.

"Yeah."

"He's in back on the fryer."

"Um, can you ask him to come out here, please?" Here's where everything can fall apart.

"Not when he's on the fryer, I can't." Oh, thank God.

"Alright, that's okay. But could you give him a message? It's important." The counter lady eyes me for a few valuable seconds. Somehow, she concludes that I'm legit.

"What you want me to tell him, honey?"

"Can you tell him…oh, this is hard."

"Go ahead, baby."

"Can you tell him, oh God, can you tell him that I'm definitely pregnant." I put on an innocent pout, probably makes me look even younger than fifteen. "And can you tell him that my daddy, he called the police."

I can't help but think counter lady has something going on with Jimmy on the fryer, the way she spins and stomps back into the kitchen.

So I wait, no idea what's going to happen next. And I wait. Seriously, I could take a nap, how long she's gone. I think about calling it, but something about this situation doesn't seem over to me. And after a seriously long interval, this big guy walks out from back of the kitchen with counter lady.

"You…you're not James," I stammer.

"Baby, I never seen this girl in my life! I told you!" Big guy shouts.

"This isn't right. Wait…is there another McDonald's on Kennedy?" I ask, all kinds of innocent.

"Yeah, down by the college," counter lady sighs, hangs her head. Jimmy stomps away.

"Oh. Well, uh, how embarrassing. I'm…"

"Maybe it's time for you to go now, baby."

"Sure," I say, turning from the register, congratulating myself on the clever wrap-up. No harm, no foul.

"And…time!" Jeff shouts. Roofie is standing with the gang. He obviously took his shot and whiffed. Does that mean…?

There is no one standing in my line, and all I can see is that group of idiots smiling at me from the soda dispenser.

And what I'm doing? I'm hopping on one foot. Screwing in the light bulb with my right hand. Strumming the ukulele with my left.

SAMMY

"All I'm saying, it wasn't just luck."

"I never said it was just luck, Canada. I said you were lucky. There's a difference."

"There's an element of luck in all these games, Canada." Mealy, the softie. "Fact that you were lucky takes nothing away from your brilliance of play."

"Can I lay it out for everyone, so we aren't talking about Canada's brilliant game play all evening? So, here's brilliant. The statutory rape pregnancy thing, how your daddy already called the police. Meta impressive."

"Thank you." She's actually blushing. God. So cute it almost makes me feel human.

"Here's luck…no way you could have known someone named Jimmy worked in the kitchen."

"James is the most common male name in the United States. I Googled it."

"You googled it when you were in line?"

"No, my iPhone's broke. I Googled it a few months back."

"So it wasn't strategic. And that's the kind of thing you research before a backpacking trip through the States? Don't answer, you'll only make it weirder. Anyway, luck. Luck that you Googled it, whenever, even more luck that there was some guy named Jimmy in the kitchen."

"Fair," Canada sighs.

"And luck that counter girl didn't just tell Jimmy to get his ass to the register."

"Wrong, Jeff. What's unbelievable luck is counter girl's hooking up with said Jimmy."

"I didn't get that." Jeff.

"There was definitely something going on between those two, right?" Canada.

"Obviously. Why else would she have spent ten minutes in the kitchen instead of just sending ol' Jimbo out front?"

"Yeah, that was an act of God, right there." Canada shakes her head. I really admire a girl who can admit to pure luck. Maybe Canadians are better people than we Americans think.

"Point is, I'm proud of you, Canada."

"Fourth day on the job and she shatters the world record for 'McSlowdown.' We're all proud of you, Canada." Roofie.

"Like Sammy said, it was mostly luck." She's blushing so hard, it's like her eyeballs will pop out. Jesus, is that a tear?

"That world record…not why I'm proud of you, Canada. Like you say, that record is mostly luck. Got to keep it real, right?" I shrug.

"Come on, man. Be nice." Mealy.

"Why I'm proud of you is, we have a code. And I'm pretty sure it was never even explained to you. We leave people questioning their perspective on the world, sure, but we never leave any real damage. The thing about another McDonald's on Kennedy, that just a top-of-head guess?"

"I mean, it's a big street, so I figured…"

"So, luck. But the fact that you didn't just walk away when you'd clearly won the night, before Jimmy and counter girl came back? The fact that you stayed, made sure there was no collateral damage? Made sure they knew it was your mistake. That's code, right there. A code you didn't even know about. You're a natural, Canada. A good person and a real painter. One of us. That's why I'm proud of you. So, how 'bout can we stop talking about this now?"

"Canada!" Roofie raises his pint. The rest of the table does the same. Except Canada.

"Bathroom!" the back of her head squeaks as she darts from the table.

"The hell's that all about?"

"Shut up, Jeff. She probably just got her period. In fact, I'd bet on it."

PENNY

Oh, God, Catelyn. Help. I can't.

Inhale, two, three, sob. I can't. I can't stop. Catelyn, help me pull myself together.

"Kyle Breslin has mommy issues." Ha! Sob, sob, sob.

"Kyle Breslin has mommy issues." In Sharpie, by the toilet paper. Ha! She put his full name. Mean. What was she doing with a Sharpie in the bathroom, anyway? Ha! Sob, sob, sob. Catelyn, how am I supposed to stop? Come on, sister! You always help me with the sad tears. You always make the sad tears go away. You've got to help me. It's got to stop. I've got to go back out there. You never told me. Oh, God, it won't stop, like it's never gonna stop. You never told me how to handle the happy tears.

And I never thought I'd ever have happy tears again.

I think I'll be okay in here for another couple of minutes.

After a couple of minutes, it'll probably stop.

Sob. Just a couple minutes more.

SAMMY

"If Brady ever really retires, they've got at least five years of rebuilding before they can even be a mediocre team. Take yourself back three years, remember what it was like."

"What if they get Aaron Rogers? What if they're trying to be the place where the greatest quarterbacks go to die? It's like *Moneyball*."

"Seriously, dude. It's nothing like *Moneyball*."

"The strategy's different, sure, but what's like *Moneyball*, it's a unique strategy. Attract the older greats who haven't got a ring, short contract deal, one last shot at the Super Bowl before retirement."

"I'm pretty sure Brady has more rings than anyone who ever played the sport. And Rogers has a ring, too."

"Yeah, and you pay those guys enough to play their last years out here in Tampa, you're gonna attract the other retiring greats. Last year, the Bucs were the oldest team in the league, average age."

"You think someone should check on her?" Mealy asides me.

"In the ladies' room."

"She's been gone a while, is all."

"You think one of us, at this table, should go knock on the ladies' room door to check on our underage friend, who is probably employing a tampon as we speak?"

"The period thing is unconfirmed."

"I'm sticking with it."

"No one needs fifteen minutes to take care of woman-issues. Go check."

"You're the one who's worried. You go check."

"'Jerry Springer' for it?" Ugh.

"Jerry Springer," it's like our version of Rock-Paper-Scissors. But instead of Rock, you've got Sleazy Brother. Instead of Paper, you've got Drunk Husband. And instead of Scissors, you've got Cheating Wife.

"Two out of three," I sigh.

"Take care…of yourself…and each other…shoot!" we say simultaneously, timed with the swinging of our fists. Mealy throws an open hand. I throw a middle finger.

"Drunk Husband smacks Cheating Wife!" One for Mealy.

"Take care…of yourself…and each other…shoot!" Mealy throws a closed fist, me a middle finger.

"Cheating Wife screws Sleazy Brother!" We're even. Next one for all the marbles.

"Take care…of yourself…and each other…shoot!" He throws a closed fist, me an open hand.

"Sleazy Brother beats up Drunk Husband!" I lose. But it doesn't even matter, because Canada comes back to the table before I can get up. Actually, it does matter. I hate to lose at anything.

"Where the hell you been?"

"Everything okay?" Mealy is making me look bad, no lie.

"I'm fine. It was nothing. Just, uh, woman stuff." Jeff and Roofie reach for their wallets, each pull out two tens and hand them to me and Beer. "Gross. Seriously, Mealy?"

"No payoff here. I abstained from the bet."

"Sweet…um, thanks."

"Always got your back, Canada. And after your performance today, totally serious, that's a forever thing."

"I got to go to the bathroom again!" she literally flees the table.

This girl might need to see a gynecologist, like, stat.

PENNY

I mean, really?

SAMMY

"Because it's a flawed strategy! You use up all your picks and salary cap for these doorstep retirees, ultimately you end up being the New York Jets."

"Hey! The Jets own the basement because of gross mismanagement. There was nothing even resembling strategy in it. The Buc's strategy, at least it got them a Super Bowl win. And if it can get them another ring, they're better off than most teams, however much it costs. Who cares whatever slump comes forward of it?"

"Jeff, I don't even want to know your opinion on global warming."

"Should someone go check on her?" Mealy asides. Again.

"Seriously, Mealy? She's probably just shooting up or something. Kids these days, right? You don't want to embarrass her, do you?" Truth is, I'm starting to worry about the disappearing Canada, too. But first rule in a foxhole is, never show any panic. Not that we're in a foxhole or anything, but foxhole rules apply pretty generally.

"I don't want to be over-skeptical or anything, but do you really think your judgment is solid in this area?" Mealy asks.

"Absolutely, I do."

"How many people here do you think woke up next to a dead pregnant girl within the last seven days? Here being the American continent, not just Tampa."

"Really."

"Just saying...oh, here she is!"

"I need a beer." Canada looks a little banged up.

Mealy dumps her warm pint, refills it with a fresh dose from a new pitcher.

The Goat is a totally responsible joint, stringent on the whole underage drinking thing. But we're drinking pitchers at an outside table, and we come here with ragged crews all the time. Can't blame the bar in a situation like this. Plus, it's Tampa. So, like anyone really cares. Live and let live, that's what's what around here.

"You good?" Mealy asks, as Canada drains her beer in a style that reminds me of Monday night. I immediately refill it. She drains it as fast. Recognizing a pattern, I fill it a third time out of morbid curiosity. Mealy puts a hand on her drinking wrist. "Go easy, huh?"

"Are you some kind of random-timing alcoholic? The demons come up for air, like, in short bursts or something?" I ask as Canada gently removes Mealy's hand from her wrist, drains her third pint in less than two minutes.

"I'm dealing with some stuff, okay?"

"We're all dealing with stuff, sunshine." I hate when people take their lives too seriously.

"Did your mom die a year-and-a-half ago?"

"Maybe. I haven't seen my mom since I was two." I also hate when my argumentative side gets the edge on my sensitive side. "Are you on probation for any kind of big balloon nonsense? Are you the main suspect in a murder investigation? Step it up, Canada."

"Okay! Did your sister die six months ago? The best person you ever knew? And did she die because of you?!"

"To the first question, I don't know. But it would have had to have been a half-sister, regardless, since I haven't had a single word from my mom in twenty-nine years. To the second question, I can answer that definitively. No. Not unless I was somehow related to Janice." Yuck, thanks for that image.

JOE BARRETT 187

"So you don't know what stuff I'm dealing with, then." Three beers really open this girl up. I wonder what four would do? Mealy stops me from pouring her another.

"You ready to go home, Canada?"

"Yeah." Canada bursts forward and wraps her arms around Mealy like she's skydiving without a parachute. I have no idea what's happening here.

"How 'bout we get the check?" Mealy mumbles through Canada's death-grip embrace.

PENNY

No idea how to count my blessings tonight. The walk from Aunt Sally's place, where they dropped me, I guess I'm grateful it cleared my head some. That beer at the Goat, it wasn't any Miller Genuine Draft. Whatever it was, it was strong. Like, head-spin strong. Like, I dove into Mealy's arms and cried like a baby, strong. That's gonna make tomorrow a little awkward.

Crazy. This all seems so, I don't know, permanent. When was the last time I felt like that? Before mom got sick, probably. Or have I ever felt like that? Even when I spent time with Catelyn, it was like I was being included in her awesome life. It wasn't my awesome life. This feels, like, honest. Like, my honest, awesome life.

And, obviously, I know. Know I'm stowing-away in a back-guestroom belonging to, no idea who. Know I'm fifteen pretending to be nineteen. Know I'm a runaway, on the downlow. Know I'm pretending to be Canadian, for Christ's sake. And these guys. God, I love these guys. Even Beer, I love these guys. But not a one of them even knows my name.

Maybe sometimes you have to be totally dishonest with everyone else…just to figure out what's honest for yourself?

It's like I was born again on that train from Penn Station. Right now, I'm superhero. It feels like I can do anything. I'm the world record holder at McSlowdown for God's sake! I have friends, four days old, sure, but I really love them. The only other people I've ever loved in my life were mom and Catelyn. I never had friends that I loved like these guys, not even close.

And I'm thinking in big concepts about the meaning of art! Not because school tells me to, or because I'm fronting or just trying to fit in. I'm actually thinking about it because of me. Me, no one else. The guys don't care…who I am or what I am. They respect me for what I do. What I contribute. I can paint. I'm an excellent painter, actually. I can think, big concept stuff. I can play, fearlessly happy, in front of total strangers at a fast-food joint. But none of it's for anyone but me, really. And that's why the guys like me. With them, I'm genuine.

Aside from all the lying, I mean.

So, yeah. I know it can't go on forever. But nothing goes on forever. We're all gonna die someday. So, best I can do is enjoy the time I've got. Enjoy every day, every minute of it. No panic, just fearless happiness. Being the real me, disguised as a nineteen-year-old Canadian backpacker, with guys who appreciate the real me. What's next? I'm trusting the universe to take care of all that. And even if it all goes sideways, I'm more than grateful enough for everything I've gotten so far.

But yeah. Maybe I'm especially grateful for killing McSlowdown earlier.

And for Sammy's respect.

And for Mealy, obviously.

And for Catelyn, who showed me the way.

SAMMY

Mealy's brain-job of the day, come up with the best off-color rename of a crayon from the Crayola One-Hundred-Twenty pack. It's a pun, but still kind of clever. Good for a Friday. Introspective. But I'm having trouble getting into a deep painting meditative state because Canada is sulking two stairs above me.

"What?" she asks my stare.

"Is this about your rando drinking problem, or your menstrual stuff?"

"Maybe your period problems are affecting your brain," Jeff says in passing, threading through us, up the stairs, "like, the hormones make you go on those quick booze jags."

"How 'bout I stop you right there, Jeff," I say, "because menstrual cycles, hormones and female psychology is not a rabbit hole that you, specifically, want to go down."

"Could we stop talking about my period, please?"

"No one's used to girls on the job, Canada. Don't take it personally." What, Mealy is like her guardian now?

"You brought it up," I say.

"MENSTRUAL CRIMSON!"

"I said I was in a quiet mood today."

"Between the lines, Canada. It's all we ever read."

"The stuff about your mom and sister?" Mealy asks.

"Not really. Maybe a little embarrassed about my breakdown last night. Crying like that."

"Ha! Seriously?" I interrupt. Canada clearly has no idea who she's painting with. "You think that ranks with embarrassing moments, like, here? Because you cried at the bar? The ego on you."

"It's an ego trip, that I'm a little shy right now?"

"It's an ego trip that you'd think your little crying jag even warrants being shy about! It totally doesn't measure up. I bet we all can give you a crying story that altogether dwarfs yours in terms of humiliation."

"Fine. Whatever. Okay, you first."

"Me, first? Fine. Let me see. Oh, okay. This is from a few years back. I was telling this girl how the cancer had made me sterile…"

"Cancer?"

"Yeah."

"My mom died of cancer."

"Really. That's sad, but this is kind of about me right now."

"WHITE PRIVILEGE!"

"I mean, I didn't know."

"Know what?"

"That you had cancer. Are you, like, in remission or something?"

"What are you even talking about? I never had cancer. What I had was no condom, and I wanted to have sex with this girl, so I was explaining that I was sterile. Can I continue?"

"Ugh, so gross. Go ahead, it's like a train wreck I can't stop watching."

"Don't be judgy, Canada. It's not a good look. So, this girl, I could tell how much of an impact this cancer-sterility story was making. Maybe she had someone die, like you, I don't know. But it was really getting to her…"

"Hold on. Was this one of those girls who, like, imprint on you or whatever?"

"Yeah."

"So why did you have to lie to her at all?"

"It wasn't that she didn't want to have sex with me, it's that she was being pretty damned insistent about not getting pregnant. Maybe she was raised on the Far Right, I don't know."

"And you didn't respect that?"

"I know how to be careful."

"MORALLY GREY!"

"Oh, sure. Careful. And that woman whose murder you're being investigated for, wasn't it you who got her pregnant?"

"Unconfirmed. Look, do you want to hear this story or not?"

"Fine. Go ahead."

"Where was I?"

"This poor girl you wanted to sleep with, she was touched by this gross lie you were telling her…"

"Right! And I could tell it was getting to her, so I kind of leaned into it, you know? Really got deep, not just about the cancer and the sterility, but about never being able to have a kid of my own, who I could, like, raise and love, et cetera. It was so poignant. And the next thing I know, I'm actually bawling. About a story that I was making up right off the top of my head! In front of everybody at the DMV."

"You were having this conversation at the DMV?"

"I know, weird. We were headed to my place after, but I was getting my license renewed and had to wait around anyway, so thought I'd get this conversation out of the way. Two birds, you know?"

"Why didn't you just stop at a CVS and buy condoms on your drive home?"

"Would have been out of my way. The point is, I was sobbing uncontrollably in front of all these strangers, and you know what kind of freak show the DMV is. But afterwards, it didn't bother me in the slightest. Had a happy ending, if you can believe it."

"Meaning you slept with the girl."

"Yeah, I had unprotected sex with her. But no, that's not what I meant."

"What was the happy ending, then?"

"Well, I was crying so much that it really messed up my face for the license photo."

"And that's good because?"

"Because, if I get stopped while driving really drunk, the cop can glance at my license and assume that's the way I always look."

"Shrewd."

"So, that beats your story, easy. Mealy, go."

"I once saw that old Tootsie Pop 'How Many Licks' commercial at this kindergarten, and I started to cry right there in front of all the little kids. Funny how certain commercials can bring back something from your childhood."

"And this was?"

"About two years ago."

"SUICIDE BLUE!"

"And why were you at a kindergarten, first place? Wait, do I even want to know?"

"Easy, Canada. Career Day. My niece asked me to attend, explain our work to the class."

"She asked *you*. A house painter. Didn't she have any living parents?"

"Whoa, harsh. Impressed, Canada. But actually, when you're five-years-old, being a house painter is, like, the coolest job ever. Someone pays you to sit around all day and paint stuff? Kids are all like, sign me up! Anyway, the guy before me, some kind of advertising exec. He showed the commercial at the end of his lame spiel about how ads work. And that's when I started crying, standing off to the side of the ad exec, right there in front of all those kids. No one even clapped for the loser ad exec, he was so boring."

"And you don't think, maybe, they didn't clap because they were weirded out by the sobbing adult at the front of the room?"

"Possible. But even though they mocked me some through my talk, it was obvious they thought my job was way cooler than that corporate schlep."

"And you weren't embarrassed?"

"In front of five-year-olds?"

"See, Canada?" I break in. "And you feel weird about crying at a bar? Everybody cries at bars. Hell, I don't think a night goes by when someone isn't sobbing suicidal in the corner of most bars in Tampa."

"Okay, that's fair. How 'bout Roofie? Does he have a crying story?"

"Roofie cries so much that a story from him wouldn't even matter."

"I don't suppose…Beer?"

"You don't suppose Beer, what?" Beer says from top of the stairs.

"Tell a more humiliating crying story than what Canada did at the bar last night," I supplement.

"Bah. Too easy."

PENNY

"Bah. Too easy."

"You've got one." I say, intrigued. You'd asked me, I'd have bet Beer never cried in his life.

"Sure do," Beer shrugs. "Cried like a baby when I came out to my father."

"I'm sorry, what? Came out to him, like…"

"Told him I was gay."

"And…you were messing with him."

"No." This, I did not see coming. "Why? Do gay people offend you or something, Canada?"

"Of course not. Two of my good friends growing up are gay. I just…" I cannot help but look him up and down.

If anything, I'd think that the whole LGBTQ community would be offended by Beer. He's just not, well, he's not attractive enough. He looks like something a rat wouldn't eat. But also, it's his tone-deaf attitude. Political incorrectness. He reminds me of a nineteen-eighties alcoholic high school football coach, like, from one of those after school specials.

"You just, what?"

"I just, I guess I have a higher opinion of you than I did before. I think I like you more."

"Oh…thanks. You know it's possible to talk and paint that spindle at the same time, right?" See what I mean? Dick.

"So how does that even count, then? Everyone cries when they come out to their parents. It's an emotive event. That's as ordinary as me crying in the bar last night." I decide to step up, not shy away. Like I belong here. Beer's smile lets me know it was the right move.

"I came out to my dad at his Friday poker night. Drinks and cigars with all his cop buddies. And I didn't cry because I was emotional. I cried because he hit me hard enough to break my arm. He had to save some face in front of the boys."

"Jesus," I gasp.

"Different time."

"DIRTY COPPER!"

"How old were you?"

"Twelve, I think. Eleven or twelve. Anyway, I knew it was coming. It's why I came out in front of his buddies. That way I knew he wouldn't hit hard enough to do long-term damage, because room full of cops, right? And I also knew it would make him look bad in front of his friends, so at least I got that."

"You win. I'm done." I focus hard on the spindle, so he doesn't see the tears in my eyes.

"You're not the sole vote here, Canada." Sammy, an eye roll I don't see but know is there.

"LAST RAINFOREST GREEN!" Mealy shouts, murmurs, "That might be a winner."

"They're back!" Roofie, slaloming us like moguls as he darts down the stairs, through the kitchen, out the back door.

"Battle!" Beer yawps. "Just video, nothing aggressive besides Roofie on the hose!"

Collective sigh from Mealy and Sammy.

"Should I ask?"

"Gangland activity." Mealy places his bucket on the stairs, lays his brush across the lip. So I do the same. Sammy's already out the door.

"I wasn't aware there was much of a gang problem in South Tampa." I follow Mealy out the front door, take a quick glance along the oak-lined street of beautiful houses.

"Take out your phone and get as much video as you can."

"My phone's broke." I almost want to turn on my phone to participate in whatever this is. Not even sure why I still carry it with me. Habits are weird.

"Alright, then just stand back. You should be out of range by the door here."

What I see is a small boy, maybe nine. In a baseball cap, Vineyard Vines t-shirt and Crocs, peeing vigorously on Roofie's motorcycle at the end of the driveway. The little guy is actually walking front-to-back, side-to-side, so that he covers as much of the bike as possible in his urine.

He notices me staring from the door and flips me the bird. Meanwhile, all the guys are circling at safe distance, capturing video on their phones.

"Take a picture of my prick and you're going to jail for child pornography!" the little urinator shouts defiantly.

"I'll blur it out! Just get all the video you can!" Beer encourages his troops.

Roofie comes 'round the driveway from back of the house, garden hose on full blast.

"Hose!" the urinator yells.

A golf cart accelerates around the corner, skid-stops in front of the driveway. Four other kids, similar age and attire, the driver maybe a smidge older than the rest. They stand up in the golf cart, begin throwing shiny round things the size of boss marbles at Roofie, who is stopped short by the length of garden hose he's trying to spray the urinator with. Said urinator appears to reach the cart still hose dry, begins pelting Roofie with those red balls like his friends are doing.

"Capture all of it!" Beer shouts, platoon commander under heavy fire, until he gets beamed in the head by one of those red balls, lowers his phone and says, "Ow!"

Roofie, dejected, realizing he's not in range of the golf cart, turns the hose on his bike.

"Think of us on your ride home, Shaggy!" one little bastard howls as they peel away.

"You got to post it, like soon, Beer," Roofie moans, bending to pick up one of the little red balls from the driveway, which he unwraps and pops into his mouth. Similarly, Beer squats, grabs a red ball, unwraps it and puts it in his mouth.

"Godiva. Almost worth it." Beer says.

"Tell me, seriously. Is this one of Sammy's quote-unquote art pieces set up to mess with me?" I ask Mealy, who's walking towards the front door.

"Not everything's about you, Canada!" Sammy shouts, already inside the house.

"Nope, that was the real thing." Mealy walks past me to the stairs, picks up his brush and begins painting. I join him.

"If you wouldn't mind," I drone, once in rhythm with my own brush and spindle.

"Trask Street Boys."

"Please."

"Standard street thugs, been targeting Roofie. Like to pee on his bike."

"Standard street thugs? They're like ten-years-old."

"Standard for around here. Gang activity is defined by the neighborhood."

"YELLOW BASTARD!"

"Why do they pee on Roofie's bike?"

"Just marking their territory, I guess. Consider us outsiders."

"And they call themselves the Trask Street Boys."

"I don't know what they call themselves. We call them the Trask Street Boys."

"Because?"

"Roofie chased them on his bike a couple weeks ago, lost them on Trask Street. Thinks they must have pulled into one of the driveways and shut the garage. He didn't get a chance to rinse down his bike beforehand, smelled like kid-pee the whole rest of the day."

"What were they throwing at you guys?"

"Today? Godiva chocolates. Kids obviously come from monied families. Last week they chucked Burgundy Black Truffles at us. Those things are, like, twenty-five dollars an ounce."

"And you guys fight back by, what, taking video of them?"

"Yeah, I mean, it's not like we're going to physically attack a bunch of rich kids, are we? Beer came up with the idea of capturing video, so we can post it on this Next Door neighborhood network site. Figured it would get back to their parents, who'd be super embarrassed. Enact whatever passes for corporal punishment these days, which is probably not letting them drive the golf cart for a week or something."

"And it didn't work? The site wouldn't let you post the video?"

"Yeah, that. Beer's a bit of a perfectionist. He got all Michael Moore about the whole video thing, won't post it until he's got the right amount of footage from which to edit. Seriously, it's become his *March of the Penguins*. I don't know if we'll ever get it posted. Roofie's pissed, but what can he do?"

"HESTER PYM SCARLET!" Beer. No surprise, deeper than I thought.

"JUDAS SILVER!"

I open my mouth to tell Mealy how bizzaro all that Trask Street Boys stuff is. But bizzaro is so redundant in this circus life that, what's the point?

"We should set a trap for them," I say instead.

"I like the way your mind works, Canada."

SAMMY

Mealy takes the day with LAST RAINFOREST GREEN, but only because it's a crayon that was formerly called Concrete Grey. I argue the win ought to be based on the stand-alone name merit, my SUICIDE BLUE analytically better, sans qualification regarding the actual color. And naturally, Beer then gets all cerebral about his HESTER PYM SCARLET.

So I abandon questioning and we give the glory to Mealy. Then Roofie takes the truck to drop off Juan and Carlos, I hop on Roofie's bike, and all the rest of us head to the Goat. We rarely hit the same pub twice in a row, but this week has been rough, and it's like we all need a place that feels like home. Especially me…with what I've got to talk to my partners about.

When there are three pitchers on an outside table and Beer's sucking on a chicken wing, I dive in. Normally I would reserve this type of talk for partners only, but at this point I don't really care if Canada and Jeff are a part of it. I actually want Jeff to be a part of it, the bastard.

"You got something to say."

"What makes you think?"

"Come on, man." Mealy can read me like a comic strip.

"How 'bout Jeff tells you? It's his grand design."

"What?"

"Shut up, Jeff. Like I was being serious about you talking."

"Again, what?" Jeff, all innocent. How he can look in the mirror, I don't know.

"Okay, guys. Senior gave me the ultimatum."

Mealy and Beer let out a long, slow sigh. Canada keeps her mouth shut. Respect, Canada. Jeff doesn't say a word. YELLOW BASTARD was one of the brain-job answers today, wasn't it?

"When did it happen?" Mealy looks green but is still reassuring. We all knew this was coming, eventually.

"Wednesday night. Bern's. With Eggs Benedict over there."

"Hey, what goes on between you and your dad..."

"Shut up, Jeff." My partners and I, in chorus. Canada looks on, mouth still shut.

"What's the long-and-short?"

"July first or no inheritance. Like, zilch." These guys know my father's net worth.

Silence.

"It's cool, man. It'll all be fine." Mealy looks like he's gonna cry.

"So you put in a few years at Shawshank. Eventually the old man dies, and you come back. No big deal. Don't overthink it." Beer, refusing to accept reality, like the champion he is.

"I can't believe you guys." Jeff, shaking his head. "This is good news. Look, I know change is painful. But this is Sammy's shot. And I'm telling you, it can be big. With me as wingman, we can make Junior-Senior a player of global scale. Believe me, this could be special. Don't hold him back, guys."

"Really!? Like what they've built isn't special enough?!" Canada continues to impress me.

"Relax, little girl. This is adult talk."

"Speak to her like that again, Jeff..." Mealy, all kinds of John Wayne.

"All I'm saying, this isn't just painting houses. Junior-Senior is a serious growth opportunity. You guys really feel good about Sammy painting houses when he can be out conquering the world? Not to mention walking away from an almost nine-figure inheritance."

"How do you know what my father's worth, Jeff?"

"He told me." Of course he did. "How selfish are you guys? Sammy can be something here. Let him spread his wings. It's not like he's irreplaceable. Get another day worker. Hire Canada full time. House painting, it's not that difficult. You'll all be fine. Sammy, on the other hand, might actually get a life."

"Sammy's the only real artist I've ever met, IRL, you weasel!" Thanks, Canada.

"We're drinking beer in what's essentially a Tampa parking lot, right now. We could be at the Four Seasons in Maui. Or at least Sammy and I could be. And when Senior dies, maybe you guys, too. But how can you feel good about being the only thing keeping him from a major next step? YOLO, guys. You can't get in the way of real life."

"YOLO, Jeff." I say.

"That's right."

"Exactly what I was thinking."

"It's cool, man. We're with you regardless." Mealy.

"We know you're stupid, but no reason to let the rest of the world in on our secret." Beer.

"See, that's what I'm talking about. Everyone's still together, just in different places." Jeff.

"Sammy, seriously?" I don't even think Canada knows what we're talking about. Just gets the sense, maybe the company is falling apart. It's been, what? Five days? I so love this girl.

"Yeah, I mean, it's true. You only live once. And we're talking about almost a hundred million when the old man eventually dies. So, it's got me thinking, maybe time to grow up."

"Exactly!" Jeff.

"Reassess my priorities. Take a fresh look at what's really important."

"It's not like you have to break ties with the past, you just can't let them keep you from your future!" Aw, Jeff. I almost feel cruel.

"So, I'm sure about it…one hundred percent. I'm turning Senior down, flat-out. I've still got my trust fund, whatever's been funded so far, at least. And we do okay, financially speaking. And otherwise, I can't imagine my life any different. Like you said, Jeff. YOLO."

Mealy smiles, puts his hand on my right arm. Beer puts his hand on my left. Canada, oddly, throws her arms around my neck and starts to cry. Five days. This girl obviously has issues.

Jeff, on the other hand, looks like someone whose reserve parachute has failed to open.

Roofie walks to our table, asks what he missed.

"You sure, man? This is big. Huge. Want to make sure your head's straight."

"Mealy, dude. I mean, it's been twenty-five years. When did you stop knowing me?"

PENNY

"Should we be worried about him?"

"Who, Jeff? No, why?"

"He's got a look in his eye that kind of screams, mass shooter."

"That's just Jeff. He's fine. Who I'm worried about is Sammy."

"Sammy seems okay."

"A little too okay for someone who just made the decision to walk away from almost a hundred million dollars," Mealy drones.

"Doesn't seem like money means much to Sammy. Looks happy to me."

We're playing a giant knockoff version of Jenga within sight, but not earshot, of the table. Mealy's focused on the game, same way he paints, his semi-hypnotized voice calming me like it does when we're on the job. Sammy, Beer and Jeff over at the table, drinking heavily. Roofie having already departed with a girl who looked very much like Velma from the Scooby-Doo cartoons.

"Happy because he just curb-stomped Jeff's dreams. That won't last. The inheritance thing though, big safety net, and Sammy's never walked the rope without it. Not so easy to shrug-off that kind of game-change."

"You're worried it's gonna make him different?"

"Dunno. Sammy's never had to worry about money, so he's never really had to worry about consequences. I mean, he's the prime suspect in an ongoing murder investigation, and I imagine he sleeps like a toddler on Benadryl. Beer and me, what we earn from the painting company, it's a step up. We came from nothing special. Guess I'm just worried about how it's gonna affect his brain-jobs. His art. How he, you know, looks at the world."

"Give him a little more credit." I pull a stubborn bottom piece. The tower trembles, then stabilizes. I gently place the piece on top of the stack.

"It's just, what we've got is really good, you know? It's possibly the suckiest job in human history, and I'm happy every single day. I don't want anything to mess it up, is all."

"Not to get too hippie on you, but sometimes you just got to let go and trust the universe. My sister used to tell me that all the time. Even when everything looks like it's falling apart, even if you're only a minute away from total collapse, you've just got to keep trusting that the universe is gonna take care of you. She'd tell me that's the secret to being a great traveler."

"Deep, Canada. But I'm not a traveler. Haven't been out of Florida in, like, ten years."

"You are so totally a traveler! All you guys are, at least the way Catelyn meant it. You guys are so brave. Every day, you make your own world. You guys are fearlessly happy. The universe cares about people like you, believe me."

"Catelyn's your sister."

"Mm-hmm."

"The one who…"

"The one who died, yeah."

"She sounds pretty great."

"She was great. She was great, the same way that you guys are great. And she definitely would have told you that the universe doesn't let the sky fall on a group like yours."

"The universe takes care of you?"

"You have no idea."

"Whoa!" Mealy surges out of his trance as the tower collapses.

206 SEMI-GLOSS

"How are you so bad at this?"

"Don't Jenga-shame me, Canada. But, hey. Thanks. For what you said. It helps." Mealy picks up the Jenga pieces, flashes me a smile.

"It's true, if you believe it."

"Okay, I will. Now let's get back to the table and check on those...oh, hell no."

"What?"

"Jesus, if anything is gonna trigger Sammy tonight. It's fine, his back's to the door. We just need to keep him at the table."

"What are you even talking about?"

"The White Whale."

"Explain."

"It's this girl, Fiona. She's like, Sammy's nemesis. The Estella to his Pip. Moriarty to his Holmes. Catwoman to his Batman."

"I know what a nemesis is."

"She's the only woman I've ever known Sammy to lose his mind over, and she doesn't even acknowledge his existence."

"The bartender from that Dog place you went Monday? So he's, like, in love with her?"

"Tilts a little more towards obsessed, but yeah, that ballpark."

"It's cool. We'll keep him occupied."

Mealy and I take our seats at the table, catching the midstream of a Jeff rant...

"...because it's too big of an opportunity!"

"For you, Jeff. Too big of an opportunity for you." Sammy, cool as ice. "For me, not so much."

"For anyone! I've got loads of contacts looking for sponsored content. I flip the switch, Junior-Senior's local car dealership and ambulance-chaser ads turn into world-wide sponsored content campaigns for pharmaceutical and insurance companies. The traditional content market doesn't understand the internet, not yet. We've got an edge, and that edge can turn us into the Amazon of the content industry. Just give me five years, that's all I'm asking."

"Five years."

"Yeah, just five years. Maybe less. Then you'll have your inheritance and probably an extra fifty-million or so that I've made you. After that, you go back to painting just like it never happened."

"Well, if it's only five years. Let me think…yeah, no."

"You're really gonna take this away from me?"

"I thought we were talking about what's best for me."

"You're gonna take this away. Just like Janice. You're an apocalypse, dude."

"What's Janice got to do with any of this?"

"It's your fault she's dead!"

"That has not been even remotely proven. What do you care, anyway?"

"Janice should have been my mine! I'm fifty times the man you are. It doesn't make any sense. You have everything. Everything, laid right out in front of you. And you ruin it all. You're a goddammed plague, Sammy."

"Sounding a little crazy there, Jeff."

"Christ almighty, would you stop calling me Jeff! Dillon! My name is Dillon! Randomly deciding to give me a different name, who the hell even does that? What kind of working environment is that? Call me Dillon, Sammy! You call me Dillon right now!"

"Dillon, okay? Jesus. Really, you gotta calm down, Jeff."

Here, Jeff actually lunges across the table. Sammy slides his chair backwards a foot or two, while Beer calmly grabs two fistfuls of Jeff's shirt-back, hoisting him like luggage off the tabletop, tossing him onto the concrete. Clearly Beer is way, way stronger than he looks.

"We gotta rethink this whole hazing thing." Mealy, shaking his head. "And I really thought Jeff was handling it so well."

"What we gotta do is just man up and not hire any more fallen angels we knew from high school. Nothing we've tried has come close to working. And Roofie doesn't count."

"Maybe you're right."

"Hey, what do you say we do brunch at The Mill, tomorrow? Been a few weeks since we hit that place. They got that, what is it? Sausage Benedict, but like, on a cornbread waffle, right?"

"Cornbread, man. I don't know why regular flour bread even exists."

"Word."

I look at Jeff, hands-and-knees where he hit the ground, face feral. Beer ready to swat him down in response to any sudden moves. This must be what it's like to live in a pack of wolves. It's oddly comforting.

"Okay, Jeff. That's two strikes. Going after my partner with the intent to cause bodily harm, for the second time in the space of a week, is right on the edge of what we'd consider a firing offense. One more and you're out. Now go walk it off. You're done for tonight." Beer, all business.

Jeff says not a word. Just picks himself up, shakes his head, walks towards the parking lot.

"Two strikes?" I ask.

"Jeff went bananas last Friday night, too. Tried to hit Sammy with a bar stool." Mealy takes a pull from his plastic pint.

"Hey, I totally forgot about that."

"You've had a busy week."

"How so?"

"Pregnant dead girl in your bed, murder investigation, walking away from your inheritance."

"Right. Yeah, totally. Maybe that's why brunch has been on my mind all day. You know, since I missed it last week."

"Probably."

"He gonna be okay?" I ask, because someone probably should.

"Jeff? He'll be fine. Just needs to walk it off." Beer sits back down, digs around in a plate of chicken bones and sauce, looking for meat scraps in a way that makes me want to vomit. "Whelp, I think that fills my excitement quota for tonight. We ready?"

"Yeah, we should probably make it an early night if we're hitting The Mill tomorrow. Day drinking takes a lot more out of me than it used to. I'll close out the tab."

"No, no. I got it…" Mealy makes a quick move towards the door, gets tripped up on his chair. By the time he's righted, Sammy is standing stock still in the doorway of the bar.

"Thar' she blows," Sammy whispers, loud enough for me to hear.

"Come on, Ahab. Not tonight. Been a long week."

"Didn't expect to see her in these waters."

"We're doing the Mill tomorrow, remember?"

"I'll get the tab. You guys go on without me."

"You don't have a car."

"I'll get an UBER."

"On a Friday night? That'll take forever."

"Go on with ye, matey. My destiny's thar' a way."

"If you do end up talking to her," I say, getting up from the table, "you might want to reel in the creepy pirate talk."

"Last chance."

"Mealy, it's been a rough day. A little cathartic heart stomping might help me sleep. I'll only be a few minutes, don't worry."

"Want us to wait, then?"

"No, go on. I'll see you guys tomorrow."

SAMMY

"Excuse me, I wonder if you'd do me a solid and let me have your bar spot?"

"Seriously?" Attractive thirty-something. A scan of her eyes makes it clear she wants nothing to do with me. "Why would I do that?"

"I want to stare longingly at that girl over there." I point at Fiona. "Where you're sitting, best spot for it."

"Is that some kind of pickup line?"

"In what unholy universe would that sound like some kind of pickup line?"

"You were here earlier in the week, right? Stood up on a stool, told how if anyone was attracted to you, their life might be in danger?"

"Oh. Sure, that was me. Yeah."

"You know there are places you can get help." Sweet Jesus, she's some kind of social worker. What kind of weird karma am I dealing with today?

"Thanks. Maybe we just start with the bar stool, though. Huh?" She considerately slides off the stool, flashes me a concerned look, and walks to the other side of her friend group.

"Appreciate it," I call after her. I order a Tullamore Dew, neat. Beer chaser. And then I get to work.

Where Fiona's sitting, she'd have to have fish eyes not to see me. But since her eyes are on the front of her face, all she has to do is glance forward and she can't help but look at me. Just take a neutral posture for a second, Fiona, and you're going to be looking directly into my eyes. That's all I need. After that, I'll call an UBER. But she's gonna at least notice me tonight.

Thirty minutes, two whiskeys and three beers later, zilch. It's like I'm some kind of physical manifestation of her blind spot. She's got to be doing this on purpose, right? I slowly climb, stand up on my stool. All eyes in the immediate vicinity look to me. Except for hers. She just continues talking to her friend. Her friend, who is gaping wide-eyed at me. This is like some God-level brain torment.

"Not tonight, Town Crier. Get down, Sammy, or you're gonna have to leave." Bartender Kate. She's a friendly one. I climb down. Anyway, my theory's proven.

"Another round, Kate."

"How 'bout just the beer this time."

"Your circus." I shrug. Fix my gaze on Fiona. Everyone in the bar notices me staring googly eyed at Fiona, except her. I'm actually a little worried Ms. Social Worker might fifty-one fifty me, I keep this up.

Tonight I decided to walk away from almost a hundred-million dollars. To preserve my soul, I guess. Even though my soul probably isn't worth a twentieth of that amount, in food stamps. I stare at Fiona and it's like watching my self-esteem sink into a tar pit of despair.

I'm walking away from almost a hundred-million dollars. Have I lost my mind? There's an aroma of spite about my decision, sure. Spite for my father. Spite for Jeff. Spite for the whole corporate normality that I've been able to sidestep with my high school contracting company. But it's not all spite. Occurs to me that spite isn't even that relevant to the decision, more like an added bonus. The reality is, I don't think I'd be able to live with myself if I were to walk that rainbow path, no matter how big the pot of gold at the end. So maybe it's not so much what you get for selling your soul, but what you avoid by not selling it. Either way, there's something heroic about it. A deep kind of heroism, more I think about it.

So if I'm such a hero, what am I doing on this stool, so blatantly ogling the object of my obsession? I'm no passive-aggressive, non-confrontational mind-gamer. I'm not even asking for Fiona to like me; I just want her to see me. Or…I just want to understand why it is she can't see me. So why don't I just walk over there and ask her? Nothing's physically restraining me.

Today's about life-changing moves. No point in stopping now. On the bright side, could anything in confronting Fiona really make me feel worse than she already makes me feel? Probably not. And that's my battle cry as I walk to the other side of the bar. Probably not!

The guy to Fiona's right steps slowly aside when I sidle up to her. Clearly, he saw me ogling Fiona from across the way, saw me stand on my barstool as a punctuating gesture, and wants none of my crazy tonight. Good. Helpful.

"Fiona."

I get nothing. Not that she can't hear me, because I've obviously made a spectacle of myself over the past forty minutes and, since I made my move, everyone has stopped talking. Everyone is watching me. Except for her.

"Hey, Fiona!!!"

"Jaysus!"

"Sorry, didn't mean to startle you."

"Ah. 'Oweya, Sandy."

At least she knows it's me. Kind of.

"Sammy."

"Roi. Where are yer lads?" Still not looking at me.

"They called it a night."

"An' you're not doin' de same?" Still not looking at me.

"I'm going soon. But I wanted to ask, did I offend you, somehow, over the past couple years or so? Did I do something that made you, I don't know, not like me?"

"Why would yer ask me somethin' like dat? Sorry, oi've got ter go." Still not looking at me. Could this be a past life thing? Or did my ancestors hurt her ancestors in some way I don't know about?

"Wait. Just one minute, okay?" I raise my arm, hold it in front of her shoulder. Not touching her, because God knows what kind of hell that would bust, but in what's clearly a hang-on-a-minute gesture. She settles, sighs, but still doesn't look at me.

"Waaat?!"

I spy, with my little eye, some emotion. Not positive emotion, but still.

"Can I lay my cards on the table?"

"Yer can put yer cards wherever yer want dem, but oi gotta go."

"No. Listen. I've had a planet-sized crush on you for the past two years. To the point where going to Mad Dogs has become some weird sort of self-flagellation for me. I look at you just to feel my heart break, because somehow that's better than not feeling anything at all. And maybe you're just my bad karma. Or maybe the sight of me just makes you sick for whatever reason. But please, I'm like begging you, just tell me what it is that makes you hate me so much. Because it's driving me crazy, and I don't think I can take much more…"

"Oi don't hate yer."

"Okay, that's fine. Right, how can you hate something that doesn't even exist? Just help me out here, and I promise I'll never bother you again. Why don't you see me?"

"Oi clap yer."

"Sorry, I have no idea what that means."

"It means I see you." Suddenly, she sounds human. But she still isn't looking at me.

"Wait, you talk normal?"

"Oi play up de brogue a bit, mostly for tips."

"No way. Are you even from Ireland?"

"T'be sure oi'm from Oirlan', yer eejit. Chucker yer really think Oirish people don't nu 'oy ter blather proper?"

"I'm sorry. Could you…?"

"People from Ireland know how to talk proper, yer dense yank." Still won't look at me. "Jaysus, we watch yer flicks an' television shows.

214 SEMI-GLOSS

I could sound more American than you do, if I wanted." That last sentence, she says it without even a hint of accent. So weird.

"Fine. Not important. I'm just…Fiona, can you please help me out here?" I ask, with more genuine sincerity than maybe I've ever employed in my life. "Think of it as an act of mercy, okay? Just tell me why you don't see me. Just tell me that and I swear, I'll leave you alone forever." I am not leaving here without…

She looks at me.

And her eyes, I swear, are like a Dyson vacuum that sucks the soul clean out of my body.

And her lips, suddenly on mine, just hard enough to still be tender. And I'm not kissing her back, because I am in a sort of full-body paralysis shock. It's a car crash, whole-life-flashing-before-you moment and I feel my knees buckle. I see my mom's face, clear as day, from my two-year-old eyes. I feel tears on my cheeks. Somewhere I hear Beer's voice, faintly asking if I need to borrow a tampon.

"Dat wasn't much av a pogue."

Full body exhale.

"Sorry?"

"You didn't kiss me back."

"Oh."

Here I gently clasp the back of her neck and kiss her like I don't even care if it's a good kiss or not. No fronting, no pre-consideration. I kiss her the way I kiss. Wholly. Genuine. Maybe for the first time in my life, being really me. For seconds, minutes, hours or years, I kiss her. Some eternity later, I decide breathing might be a better idea than passing out.

"That's de stuff," Fiona sighs.

I take a quick look around the Goat. We might as well be dinner theater.

"I'm confused. Can we go somewhere?"

"Sure," she says. "But oi'm not gonna ride yer."

"Proper?"

"We can go somewhere, but I'm not having sex with you."

"Yeah, fine. I just want to talk without feeling like I'm the second act of Circe du Soleil."

"Bleedin' deadly."

I pull out my phone, hit the UBER app.

PENNY

Permanent is never a good perspective. Permanent is not a language the universe speaks. Be okay with it, sis. You're on for the ride, not the stops.

I just want to take a beat, Catelyn. I know this can't last forever. But it's just…you don't understand. You never needed a home. The whole world was your home.

Whatever you see on the surface, underneath you should always imagine the opposite. Almost always, the opposite is its true nature. There's a reason I was away so much.

You were afraid of never feeling at home, so you made sure you never had a home. Just like me. Except you're a traveler. You went out and explored every part of the whole wide world to search for what you needed.

You're younger than I was when I left home. You think I inspire you, Penny? The idea of you is what inspired me. And look at where you are now! We're a circle, you and me. A wheel. But that wheel has got to keep rolling.

I'm not saying I want to build a summer home here, but it's been less than a week. Let me have another. Maybe two. Mealy. Sammy. Beer. Roofie. I feel like these guys are home for me. Let me have it for just a week or two more.

Count your blessings, Penny. The reason you count them every night is that everything might be different tomorrow, and you don't want to forget the good stuff that happened today. Appreciate it, but don't cling to it. The universe is made of ups and downs. Zeros and ones. Yins and Yangs. It's all about riding those waves.

A week more, maybe two. Or forever. I feel like I belong with these guys, Catelyn. Can you honestly tell me that you ever found a place where you felt like you really belonged, and then just rejected it for no reason?

You don't need to reject anything. It's more like, if you love something, set it free. If it comes back, then it's yours forever. If it doesn't, it was never meant to be. Point is, don't be clingy. Let whatever happens happen. And know you'll be okay. Know you'll be better for it.

I don't have the head for this right now, okay, Catelyn? I love you, but I don't have enough fuel in the tank to think about anything but this bed, this house, this job and these friends. At least for a little while more.

We all get tested, kiddo. And usually the big tests come when we're feeling top of the world.

You're the one who always told me to live in the moment, Catelyn. Can you please just let me enjoy this moment, right now?

Then enjoy it. Dance with it. But just don't grasp it too tight.

Okay. Not too tight.

I'm grateful for everything that happened today, full stop.

There's nowhere else in the world that I'd want to be than right here, right now.

Time for sleep.

Amen.

SAMMY

"It just cancelled."

"After foive minutes?"

"What do you want me to say? It's Friday, prime time. You obviously don't have a car."

"Came wi' me friends."

"Who are?"

"Gone."

This logistical dead-zone, I feel like it's slowly killing my whole Fiona-awakening thing. I need alternative solutions.

"Hey, wanna take a walk?"

"Wha?"

"Place where we can talk."

"'Oy far?"

"Less than a mile. And could you dial back the brogue some, just being you and me here?"

"Naw problem. An' a walk wud be killer." I help her up from the curb, don't let go of her hand as we walk across Henderson.

"So, you never answered my question."

"Ah, what question is dat?" I glance over as we walk north on Church Street. Her eyes locked on mine now, sparkling in the dark, make me wonder if I'm dreaming all this.

"How come you never even looked at me before?"

"Oi looked at yer."

"No. You didn't."

"Ye callin' me a squealer, den?"

"I have no idea what you mean."

"Ye callin' me a liar?"

"Oh, okay. Yes. I am."

"Well, that's a bang on way ter start a relationship."

A relationship. It might be the first time I've ever heard that particular phrase without immediately calculating the logistics of a swift and final departure.

"When did you ever look at me before tonight?"

"First time yer and yisser lads came into Mad Dawgs. Oi looked roi into those weird emerald eyes of yers an' tart, aw naw, dis is trouble."

First time I came into Mad Dog's, something about my emerald eyes.

"You liked my eyes."

"Oi nearly full myself, I liked yer eyes."

"So why didn't you, I don't know, talk to me? Or at least be nice to me. Or, at minimum, acknowledge my existence. I felt like a leper around you. For two whole years! What was that all about?"

"Chucker yer not nu anythin' aboyt people from Oirlan'?"

"Proper?"

"Yer don't know nothin' about the Irish."

"That's true. What of it?"

"We're not loike yer yanks, wearin' our hearts on our sleeves, are we?"

"So you're shy?"

"Oi seem shy to yer?"

"Can you just talk like an American?"

"Oi'm not an American."

"Please."

"Nope."

"Why?"

"More fun dis way. Keeps yer on yisser indian joes."

"Indian joes."

Fiona stops, lifts her sandaled left foot, points at her wiggling toes. Her index toe has a little silver ring on it. I feel an almost uncontrollable urge to put it in my mouth. Too soon. Don't judge.

"Rhyming slang." Possibly the stupidest thing to ever come out of the British Isles.

"Too roi."

"Fine. Let's circle back to why you treated me like a festering boil for twenty-four months, if not because you were shy."

"Oi don't know if oi'm comfortable enough witcha ter discuss it yet."

"You don't know if you're…you just stuck your tongue down my throat in front of a bar full of people, who were already staring at me before you did it."

"Told yer oi'm not shy."

"So you liked my eyes, and then just decided not to look at them, or me, for two years. Were you mourning a dead husband? Waiting for a case of herpes to clear up? Didn't want to get together with me until you kicked your heroin habit?" I probably shouldn't be so flippant, in case the reason does happen to be one of those I listed.

"Emoshuns."

"Emotions? Say that again."

"Why?"

"I like the way it sounds when you say it."

"Emoshuns." Here I stop, turn, and kiss her for another fifteen years. Then we keep walking, holding hands.

"What about emotions?"

"Oi'm Oirish. We allerge emoshuns."

"Irish people don't like emotions."

"We hate dem. They scare us ter death. Yer really don't know anythin', chucker yer?"

"And yet you kissed me like that at the Goat, in front of all those people."

"Like oi care what people at that battle cruiser think? I'd dance nip on de bar an' not give a shoite."

"I got most of that, I think. Battle cruiser?"

"Battle cruiser rhymes with boozer. Boozer is another word for pub."

"Dance nip?"

"Means naked." Ouch. Something just broke in me.

"This doesn't make any sense. You're contradicting yourself."

"An' yer being dense."

"So explain it. In English, if possible."

"Oi'm blatherin' English, yer bungalow."

"See, that's not at all helpful."

"Ugh! Oirish hearts are like big conkers, yer clap? Real hard an' protected on de outside, real tender an' timid on de inside. An' when somethin' touches our hearts, it freaks us oyt. We're terrified av ourselves, an' we're terrified av whatever can touch us like dat. Naw one else matters. So, de standard protocol is ter squeeze all those terrifyin' feelings into a wee ball an' bury it pure deep in our stomachs. Chucker yer git dat?"

"If I'm interpreting you correctly, which is anyone's guess, your heart is like a...what's a conker?"

"Loike a chestnut."

"Okay. Your hearts are like big chestnuts. Hard on the outside, tender on the inside."

"That's roi."

"And I'm paraphrasing here, but when something gets through the hard shell and touches the soft center of your chestnut heart, you get all wigged out. With yourself and with whatever touched your heart. But not with anyone else."

"Roi."

"Okay, and this is interesting. So normal practice for you Irish lunatics is to squeeze all these scary feelings into a little ball and then bury that little ball of feelings deep in your stomachs. Did I get that right?"

"Bang on."

"Well, that doesn't sound very healthy. Psychologically speaking, I mean." Listen to me, I almost sound like a real person right now.

"Oi can't recall anyone ever tryin' ter make a really strong case for the psychological strength of de Oirish condition, can you?"

"That's a fair point."

"Well, when yer guys first walked into Mad Dogs an' oi saw yer eyes, it was like lightnin' struck me heart. Oi needed to lock dat shoite down hard. So oi just didn't look at yer anymore."

What are the chances? Seriously, the chances are, like, infinitesimal. The odds of Fiona being one of those weird girls who, like, imprint on me? Like a lottery. But not like a national lottery or anything. More like a church raffle, I guess. But still, long odds. And I am totally overcome with these feelings of empathy right now. For those poor girls I would hook up with until they figured out what a shallow dick I am. That must have plain sucked. Alright, enough introspection. Back to Fiona.

"Why'd you keep calling me Sandy? That was mean, if you actually knew who I was the whole time."

"Yeah, dat was just me bein' a wee spiteful."

"Considerate. So then what happened?"

"Den what happened, what?"

"Den. Ugh. Then, what happed with tonight?"

"Don't know. Yer broke me, oi guess."

"Why was tonight any different, though? I've been making googly eyes at you at least once a week at Mad Dogs for the past two years."

"De truth? You've been gindin' me down the whole time. An' then, at the boozer tonite, oi don't know. There was somethin' different about yer. Oi mean, yer were still an eejit, standin' on de stool like dat. But there was a different energy about yer. An' when yer walked over an' shouted me name like dat, oi jist sort of crumbled."

I kiss her again. Walk her up the driveway.

"Where ye takin' me?"

"We're here." I key in the alarm code.

"Ye breakin' into dis place?"

"Yeah. I know the alarm codes for all these houses. Stop. That's our truck in the driveway, there. We're painting this place. The owners won't be back for another month."

"Ye sure we're allowed?"

"I don't know, maybe I better ask the boss...hmm. Yeah, we're good."

"Oi'm not gonna ride shag witcha. Oi'm not sum bleedin' scrubber, if that's what yer thinkin."

"Where'd that come from? You think I'd sit around staring at you, ignoring me, for two years because I just wanted to have sex with you? Okay, that actually might be something I'd do, but I swear it's not the case here. There's an upstairs guest room we painted early; we can just hang out up there. Really, perfectly safe. Promise."

"Gran' but just so yer know, oi got a cutty knife in me purse."

"Really?"

"Girl's got ter protect herself. Yer got a problem wi' dat?"

"I actually think it's kind of cool." I open the door, she walks into the house.

PENNY

I open my eyes when the house alarm beeps off. My heart immediately starts bouncing against my chest like a basketball. Voices downstairs. The people who own the house? Breathe. Breathe. Breathe slower. Breathe quieter. But breathe. One of the guys, maybe forgot something? That's all it is. There's no reason for them to come up here. I'm safe. I stay quiet, I'll be safe. Breathe slow and quiet. The voices are coming up the stairs. That's okay. Probably left something in one of the rooms we're painting. No reason to come in here.

Sammy. It's Sammy's voice, clearly. And a girl who sounds like a leprechaun. He just left his wallet somewhere. No one's been in this room since I've been squatting here. No reason to come in this room. It was painted before I even got here. Pull yourself together, Penny Sullivan. You will not lose the best situation you've ever been in, just for making a stupid noise! Footsteps in the hallway. I glance at the walk-in closet. No way. Never make it. They'd hear me anyway. Why would they be coming this way? Quietly I pull the comforter up over my head, make myself as flat as possible. And the door to my guestroom opens.

"It's a guestroom, of course there's gonna be a bed. But there's nothing, like, suggestive about it. It's just one of the only clean rooms in the house."

"We can fib down together, but oi'm not gonna sleep witcha."

"Yes, you've made that clear about thirty-seven times. Come here."

They're kissing. I can't see them, but it's obvious. I breathe so slow that my chest barely moves. Minute-to-minute. Live minute-to-minute. Come on, universe. I need a fast miracle here. I believe. I believe. I believe, I believe, I believe. And the two of them collapse onto the bed, directly on top of me.

"Whaaa! What the what!?! Whaaaaaat!" Sammy sounds like he just landed on a live alligator. The leprechaun's scream is so loud and shrill that I'm pretty sure all three of us are going to have some kind of permanent hearing loss.

"Hi, Sammy." I pull the comforter from my head. Green bunny is still in the crook of my neck, and I quickly scooch her into my lap.

"Canada, holy Jesus! What! The! Hell! Are you doing here!?"

"Exactly what de feck did ye think was gonna happen here tonight?!" Leprechaun screams at Sammy, justifiably, I think.

"Not this. Canada, what the hell are you…oh my God. You have got to be kidding me."

"It's a long story."

"How long have you been living here, Canada?"

"Only a little while."

"I thought you were staying with your aunt. We dropped you off at your aunt's place last night. Jesus, do you even have an aunt?"

"Yeah, I have an Aunt Sally. And it's her house you dropped me at. She just…well, she doesn't exactly know I'm here. And she had an alarm system installed, so I…"

"Is anyone gonna tell me what de feck is going on here?"

"Sorry. Fiona, this is Canada. She's a friend. She's part of our crew."

I could cry. Part of their crew. Tears in my eyes when I hear him say that. But I hold it together.

"Yer name is Canada?"

"My name is Penny."

"Your name is Penny?"

"Yeah, Sammy. My name is Penny. Short for Penelope."

"Oi thought yer said yer knew her?"

"I do know her. I just didn't know her name was Penny or whatever. She's from Canada, which is why…"

"I'm actually from New Jersey."

"You're really not helping the situation here, Canada."

"That's it, oi'm out."

"No! Fiona, just wait. I guarantee you, there is *possibly* a very rational explanation for all of this."

"Oh, my God. Is she the White Whale? So cute, Sammy!"

"Am oi de white what ye say?!"

"I'm sorry, I don't know what you mean."

"Could we just shift the focus back to what the hell are you doing squatting at our work site, Canada?"

I can't think of anything to say, and it wouldn't matter if I could. Because I start to cry. Hard. In, like a split second, everything comes up and I'm just bawling like a baby.

"Oh, for the love of Christ."

"Jaysus, she's just a sprog, Sammy. Ye guys, like, abduct her or something? Buy her from a human traffickin' ring to, what? Paint for yer?"

"She's not a sprog, or whatever. She's a college graduate. She's, like, nineteen."

"I'm fifteen," I sob.

"*Okay*, Canada! Is there *any chance*?! That you can stop with these *unexpected revelations*?! While I am trying to *clear my name with Fiona*?! Please, *huh*?!"

"Sorry," I sob.

"Naw, oi'm sorry. Dis is just too weird. Oi'm out."

"Fiona, come on. Seriously. Just give me…"

"I lied to them, Fiona, okay?" I sob. "I told them I graduated university. I told them I was staying at my aunt's house down the street. I snuck into this house because I didn't have anywhere else to stay. None of this is Sammy's fault."

"Okay, see, now that's totally helpful, Canada. Thank you."

"Ye run away from 'um, 'oney?"

"Not sure what you mean," I sob.

"She's asking if you ran away from home."

"Bang on."

"I'm picking it up from context more than anything else. What do you say, Canada? You want to unpack?"

Fiona sits on the bed and hugs me, like a mother would hug a child. This doesn't help my crying jag, but it's so nice. Sammy paces, no intention of hugging or, really, any kind of human contact with the radioactive weirdness that is me. But that's okay. I can tell he cares, in a Sammy kind of way.

So I tell them everything. About my mom. About my dad, the ice-cold bastard. About Catelyn, her travels, and how it was my fault that she died, even though I know it really wasn't. About how I'm all that's left of Catelyn in the world and it's my job to be fearlessly happy because she can't be that anymore. And I cry the whole time. And it's okay. I tell them about Aunt Sally, realizing that she's really all I've got left in this world, aside from these dear, sweet idiots. She's part mom and part Catelyn. And she might love me. Catelyn was her favorite, but she still might love me some. At least more than dad does. And I wonder why I didn't realize that before. Why did I ice her, push her away? First when mom died. Then when Catelyn died. I thought she was pushing me away at the time. But maybe I couldn't handle being around her, when the people I'm attached to always seem to leave me.

"Yer really slept in a feckin tree?"

"Only for one night."

"De barguckers on yer, lassy."

"Thanks," I sob. "I think."

"You drank. Two bottles. Of your own urine."

"I didn't want you guys to drink them."

"Why didn't you just pour them out?"

"First day on the job and I start dumping your beers. How would that have gone over?"

"Fair point. Respect, Canada. Seriously. But if you'd just pointed them out, we could have given them to Jeff, you know."

"Hindsight," I sob.

"Alright, let's pack it up. Your stuff is here somewhere, I assume, Canada?"

"No! Sammy, I can stay here."

"No, Canada. You cannot stay here." Is he going to put me in a shelter? Call the police?

"'Her name is Penny, yer eejit.'"

"No, really! I can. I won't mess anything up. I promise. I…I don't have anywhere else to sleep." Here, the crying starts again. And I thought I was all cried out.

"Stop it. Of course you're gonna crash at my place. We'll round up Mealy and Beer tomorrow, have brunch at The Mill, and figure it out. We'll figure it all out, I promise. You're one of us, Canada. We've got your back."

"Sammy, hang on. I mean, technically I'm a runaway. Like, on the lamb. I crash at your place, you could get in trouble. Legally, I mean. Seriously, just let me stay here. Plausible deniability."

"How do you know about plausible deniability?"

"CSI is on, like, all the time."

"You're not staying here, Canada."

"You're worried about the people who own the house? Like, what if they find out or something?"

"I could give a damn about the people who own the house. You're, what, thirteen or something? You're not squatting alone in an empty house. Come with me, it'll be fine."

"But you could get in trouble."

"Canada, I'm on probation for starting a minor riot and I'm the prime suspect in a murder investigation surrounding a dead pregnant girl in my bed last Friday. Do you really think harboring a teenage runaway is a big thing for me?"

"Hold on. Yer what's all that now?" Fiona flashes Sammy a wooden stare.

"Just a string of random misunderstandings. Let's not get off subject."

"Really, Fiona. He's one of the good ones. All appearances aside."

"Hey."

"Gran', love," Fiona takes a beat and then sighs, "Oi'll trust yer on that."

SAMMY

Canada gathers up her stuff and I lead this motley crew out the door, pack them into our company truck in the driveway.

"Are you still drunk?" Canada, sliding between Fiona and me in the front seat.

"Some, I guess. Why?"

"No reason."

I drive us all to my place. Fiona and I go in with Canada, help get her set up. After five minutes of pointless arguing, Canada agrees to take the bed and let me sleep on the couch in the living room. After five more minutes of pointless arguing, Fiona proceeds to change the sheets on my bed even though I did this myself just last Sunday after the cops took dead-Janice away. Freaking women. Like I've got fleas or something.

When, pointlessly, the bed's made up, Fiona tucks Canada in, like a mom would a toddler. Then she goes over to Canada's backpack and pulls out some limp green rag doll, sticks it under her chin.

"Oi've slept with de same one since oi was two, honey."

"How did you know?"

"Oi saw her witcha at de last place."

Canada hugs Fiona like she's about to be launched into space.

"I didn't brush my teeth," Canada yawns to Fiona.

"'Tis gran' for tonight, love. Yer can brush them extra the-morra."

"Okay." Canada mostly asleep. "I love you, Catelyn."

"Oi love yer, too, me ud flower."

And now there are tears in Fiona's eyes and a sob in her voice. So, absolutely zero chance of any more romance for me tonight. But that's okay. I have a feeling my stock went up, all this Canada stuff.

"Come on, it's almost three a.m. Let me take you home." I whisper.

"Can oi come ter brunch witcha tomorrow?" she whispers back.

"I can't believe I'm saying this, because any other Saturday, brunch with you would be the stuff of dreams. But I think tomorrow it's best just Canada, Mealy, Beer and me. And Roofie, if he shows up. Kind of a company thing, this. Don't take it…"

"Understud, love."

"I'll tell you all about it, I promise." I whisper.

Canada is snoring lightly. Fiona gently cups her cheek, and then we walk out to the truck. She rests her head on my shoulder as I drive her home, but we don't say anything. And that's okay. That's exactly how it should be.

When we get to her place, she cups my cheek just like she did Canada, kisses me sweet on the lips. This is everything I ever wanted out of life. So much more than nearly a hundred million dollars. I tell her I'll call her after brunch tomorrow if, like, I'm not too drunk. Otherwise I'll definitely call her on Sunday, when I can tell her all about our plan vis-à-vis the Canada situation, while she and I get drunk together. She gets out of the truck and my heart goes with her. I watch her unlock the door, wave, go inside. Best night of my life. Weird. But the best night of my life, no equal.

PENNY

I open my eyes when I hear Sammy come back into his condo. I could have stayed passed out for days, but my bladder feels like it's going to explode. I roll out of bed, start walking to the bathroom. Through the cracked bedroom door, I see that it's not Sammy at all who just walked in the door. It's Jeff. And he looks psychotic.

I dart into the closet, keep the door slightly ajar, just as Jeff walks into the bedroom and turns on the light. Like he owns the place. What the hell is he doing? I've got a clear side view, watch him take a bunch of little white plastic thingies out of a brown paper bag. It looks like he's wearing women's Isotoner gloves, like my mom had when I was little. Whatever he's doing, it so obviously is not good. And it is so obvious that he's doing it to Sammy. But the real question is, what am I supposed to do about it? Something ominous about this question.

We all get tested, kiddo. And usually the big tests come when we're feeling top of the world.

Oh, no. I tap my sweatpants, feel my iPhone in the front pocket. No! I don't want this to end, Catelyn. I don't want this to be over. And I'm crying again, but quiet. Because I know what I have to do. It's like the universe is telling me exactly what I have to do. I pull out my iPhone, hesitate for just a second. This is going to end everything. I mean, really end it. And then I turn on the phone. I immediately pull up the camera and start taking video of whatever sinister shit Jeff is pulling right now. Careful, quiet with my sobs.

I try to get comfortable in a squat while I watch Jeff scissor the top off one of the plastic white thingies, dump something into a water bottle that's sitting on Sammy's bedside table. He does this same thing, like, twelve times. Enough times to get boring. Boring enough to remember how badly I have to pee. When he's finished, I video him trying to gather up the empty white thingies in his hands and dropping half of them onto the floor. Is he drunk? He looks drunk. He manages to gather about half of the white thingies in his hands, walks to the bathroom and dumps them in a drawer beneath the sink. Then walks back out and begins to gather up the remaining thingies that he left on the floor.

"Whatcha doing there, Jeff?"

I almost can't help but scream, hold my hand over my mouth and stop breathing. Where the hell did Sammy come from? I didn't even hear him open the door. Jeff gives him a look like a snake, then softens his expression, then falls over in his squat. Yeah, he's definitely drunk. I keep videoing.

"Just picking up your trash." Jeff scrapes the white things from the rug into his palms.

"My trash."

"Part of my job, right?"

"Yeah, I don't remember seeing anything about showing up at my place at three-thirty a.m. in the job description."

"Like you even gave me a job description. Real professionals, you guys."

"Oh, sorry. There's definitely a job description, thought we gave it to you. Paint stuff, follow orders and don't sneak into my condo after three a.m. Where's Canada?" Sammy asks.

"How the hell would I know where Canada is? Probably at her aunt's place, since it's three-thirty in the morning."

"About that. And *you* being *here*."

"I went for a walk. To walk it off, like Beer said. Was in the neighborhood and thought I'd come over to apologize. Saw you drive away when I was walking up to your house. Waited outside for a bit, then thought I'd clean up some while you were gone. Make up for earlier. Who was the girl in the truck?"

"Not important."

"No, that's right. What girl is ever important to the aloof, demiurgic Sammy Junior? Janice certainly wasn't. Not even important enough to live, was she?"

"Dude, that turned quick. And why are you so hung up on this Janice thing, anyway?"

"Because she's dead. Because you killed her, you…cancer!"

"Whoa, Jeff. I'm sensing some serious hostility. But can we not get into this right now? It's been a long night."

"How come you're not drunk?"

"I am drunk, but only slightly. Looks like you had a few."

"More than a few."

"If you came here to make a last ditch shot at Junior-Senior, you're wasting your breath. I don't care about the company or the inheritance. My dad can leave it to Scientology. Or you can have it. I don't care."

"It's like you're reading my mind."

"You a scientologist, Jeff? I know the headquarters is right up the road there."

"Nope. And I'm not here to talk to you about Junior-Senior, either. I've come to grips with that. Never talk to you about Junior-Senior again."

"Really."

"You're not worth it."

"And you're acting a little Norman Bates meets Hannibal Lecter right now, Jeff. Why are you wearing ladies' gloves?"

"Cold hands."

"Whatd'ya got in those chilly hands?"

"Just trash."

"Let me see."

"It's just garbage. No."

"It's my garbage. Let me see."

I video Jeff turning his back. Sammy circles him from behind, trying to get an over-the-shoulder peek at what's in his hands. One of the white thingies drops onto the rug and Sammy picks it up.

"Visine."

"Yeah, I knew you were out. Bought you some."

"It's empty."

"Probably a factory defect. Here. Have a drink of water."

"You didn't happen to put Visine in that water, Jeff?"

"Yeah, I did."

"Really? I wasn't being serious. You actually put Visine in my water? The police told me that drinking that stuff can kill you. Plus, that's a colossal waste of Visine, Jeff."

"Can't kill you, Sammy. Can kill Janice, a girl I actually could have had something serious with. Can kill her unborn baby. But can't seem to kill you."

"Did the doctor change your meds recently, Jeff?"

"You haven't even seen me act psycho yet."

"Hold up, you evil genius. Did you put Visine in my water last Friday night, too?"

"The speed at which your brain works is truly astounding."

I mean, this is kind of exciting and all, but it feels like it's going to drag on all night. And by this point I'm starting to worry about doing permanent damage to my bladder. I have to pee so bad. I quietly look around the closet. Notice Sammy has a pair of hiking boots. I wonder if they're waterproof?

"So it was you who actually killed Janice. Wait, hold up. Why'd you kill Janice, Jeff? Just a second ago you were saying how much you liked her."

"I didn't *mean* to kill Janice, jackass. I meant to kill you."

"Well, that's crossing a line, Jeff. And given how much Visine I use, I doubt it would even have worked. Got a lot of it in my system, probably developed an immunity. Like Iocane powder in *The Princess Bride*."

"Here. Drink this and let's see."

"I'd rather not test the theory. Also, totally not cool, Jeff. You know I missed brunch last Saturday. Had to spend the entire day in the police station."

"Janice and her unborn child had a pretty rough time of it, too. That thought even cross your mind, like ever?"

"How about you let me mourn in my own way, Jeff?"

"Stop calling me, Jeff!"

"Fine, okay, no problem." I wait for it, nearly peeing myself. "Jeff."

"That mouth of yours is going to do you a whole lot of good in a federal penitentiary."

"Why would I go to jail, Jeff? You're the one who killed Janice."

"Really? Where's your proof? What do you think the police are gonna say when you suddenly start blaming me? I think they're gonna look at the facts. You are the one who was getting Janice drunk and screwing her…"

"Janice didn't need my help getting drunk, Jeff. Everyone knows that."

"…you were the one who got her pregnant and didn't want the baby…"

"Unconfirmed! God. And I didn't even know about the baby until after she was dead."

"…her dead body was found in your condo, with a whole mess of empty Visine bottles."

"Yeah, found by me. Who do you think called nine-one-one? Should count for something."

"…and when the toxicology reports come back tomorrow morning, what do you think those tests are going to say regarding cause of death?"

"It feels like you're going somewhere with this, Jeff."

"I'm not going anywhere. You, on the other hand, are going to jail. I wonder how many hardened criminals are gonna imprint on you in the joint, Sammy? But no worries, even if none do, I'm sure you'll still get lots of sex. You're going to wish you had drunk that Visine."

"You're serious right now. I so told the guys that you weren't handling this whole hazing thing as well as they thought. I should make a rule, everyone in the company should just treat everything I say as hard fact from now on. Save us all a mess of trouble."

"You don't even know trouble yet."

"So let me get this straight. Last Friday, you snuck into my house and dosed my water glass with a highly toxic household substance, because you wanted to kill me. When?"

"About the same time as now."

"But I was here with Janice this time last Friday."

"And you were both passed out cold, which is how I expected to find you tonight."

"Creepy, Jeff. Not a good look. So, Janice apparently got thirsty in the night and drank the evil concoction that you'd intended for me."

"That appears to be the case."

"And then you returned a week later to try and kill me again. Why?"

"Why, what? Same reason as last time."

"I mean, why did you try to kill me tonight when you already knew your clever ruse was going to land me in jail? Wasn't that enough?"

"I was pissed off at how you kyboshed my plans with Junior-Senior earlier, okay? It was knee-jerk. I got anger issues. What do you want me to say?"

"A simple apology would be nice. But what I don't get is, how did you think killing me was going to help your situation with Senior in the first place?"

"You mean the first time I tried to kill you, or tonight?"

"The first time, when you killed Janice instead. How was that gonna help you?"

"Are you kidding me? I'm like the son Senior never had. I'm like the son he wanted, but instead got you. He told me himself, maybe a dozen times. I figured with you out of the way, he'd have a vacuum to fill. And I have no doubt he'd bring me on board to fill that vacuum."

"Don't want to burst your bubble, Jeff. But I think you're seriously overestimating my father's integrity."

"Well, I guess we'll see about that. Because when you go to jail for the rest of your life, Senior's going to need someone to step in and be groomed to take the reins. I'll send you a care package at Christmas, though. That about wrap things up?"

"I guess."

"So, you're just gonna let me walk right out of here?"

"If that's all you got, you're free to go."

"Have to admit, I thought this conversation was going to lead to some kind of physical confrontation. But you're gonna be all typical Sammy? No emotion at all, huh?"

"Not my style, Jeff."

Jeff glares, like, frustrated he can't seem to get a rise out of Sammy. Then he shrugs, walks past Sammy and straight out the door. Sammy follows him, closes the front door, and lets out a huge sigh.

"You can come out now, Canada!" Sammy shouts.

I figured as much.

SAMMY

"You can come out now, Canada!" I shout, watching Jeff stroll happily down the sidewalk. He must have parked a block or two away to avoid detection.

"How'd you know I was in there?" Canada, stepping out of the closet.

"Open floor plan. Jeff didn't know you were here, so it was either the closet or under the bed. How much did you get?"

"All of it. From before you even showed up."

"Audio?"

"And video."

"Well, that's convenient. When'd your phone start working again?"

"When I decided I'd rather let however many New Jersey State Police tracking programs are tracing it, find me. Instead of letting Jeff hurt you. I didn't know what Jeff was doing, Sammy. But I knew it was bad right from the start."

"So now our Canada problem has a timer on it."

"Yeah. Not a long one, I imagine."

"It's alright. We'll get it figured."

"Not sure how."

"It'll work out. Hey, uh, Canada. What you did? Turning on your phone like that, when you knew what it would mean to your whole, uh, situation. It might be just about the nicest thing anyone has ever done for me in my entire life. So thanks. I mean it."

"Right back at you, Sammy. Anytime. Seriously, any time at all."

"Same. So, the video. It's safe?"

"My stuff uploads automatically to iCloud. It's in the ether. Safest and most redundant place in the world."

"Okay, turn the phone off and get your stuff."

"Why?"

"We're staying at Fiona's tonight."

"I figure we've got at least twenty-four hours. It's not like I'm a wanted fugitive. Plus, it's New Jersey that's looking for me."

"You come from money, right?"

"Well, not, like, crazy money, but my mom's family…"

"Yeah. Well, if the New Jersey police are tracing your phone, they now know your exact location here in Tampa. And they don't know if you've been abducted or run away, right?"

"I didn't leave a note or anything."

"Right. So how long do you think it will take New Jersey to contact Tampa P.D. and we get some squad cars over here?"

"Uh."

"I'd say we've got about forty-five seconds. Coming?"

We're out the door in thirty. I can swear I hear sirens just a few blocks away as I head the pickup towards Fiona's place.

"Does Fiona know we're coming?"

"No."

"Why not?"

"Because I turned my phone off."

"Why?"

"Because your exact traceable location in Tampa, during your twenty-minute video capture, happened to be my address. The police aren't stupid."

"Why don't we just go to a hotel?"

"Sure. And I can pay with a credit card, show them my I.D.?"

"Then why don't we go to Mealy's? Or Beer's? Scrap that, why don't we go to Mealy's?"

"You got a problem with Fiona, Canada?"

"No, it's just kind of a lot. On the first night in two years that you've ever exchanged words, much less saliva. Don't want to mess things up. This, right here, is a little much for a new relationship."

There's that word again. Relationship. And I feel no compulsion to duck-and-run. Aside from the normal, you know, duck-and-run feelings totally natural to the subject of a police manhunt. But relationship? That word I'm totally fine with. Weird.

"We can't go to Mealy's because I own a registered business with Mealy. Same with Beer. They know where your body was last seen, too big a chance that the police will check there next. We'll see them at The Mill tomorrow. For now, Fiona's the only one nobody can trace me to, here in Tampa. We should both be thanking our lucky goddamned charms that she, heroically, repressed her feelings for me over the past two years."

"That's a half-full attitude. So, we're still going to brunch with those guys tomorrow?"

"Of course we're still going to brunch. Have you ever been to The Mill for brunch? They have this Sausage Benedict thing, on top of a cornbread waffle instead of an English muffin. Oh, God, it's unbelievable. It's going on two weeks since I had a good Saturday brunch."

"I mean, it's safe?"

"Course, it's safe. There are dozens of brunch places in South Tampa. Why would anyone think people in our particular situation are going to be eleven a.m. day-drinking at The Mill? We'll pay cash, totally be fine."

"You're good at this. Have you ever actually been a hunted criminal before?"

"Only theoretically. I've got a big imagination and way too much time to consider these types of absurdities."

"What are you gonna do about Jeff?"

"How do you mean?"

"How do you think I mean? He's walking around out there like you're about to get arrested and thrilled about it. Do you want to send the video to the police or something?"

"Gave that some thought. Let's wait until they come to arrest me when the toxicology report comes in. Show it in person when the time comes."

"Because?"

"More dramatic that way. Oh…but send me a link to that video, will you?"

"No."

"Why?"

"Both our phones are off because we're running from the police because of my stuff, remember?"

"Right. Let's just stick together then. But be ready to turn on your phone and show it when the time comes, okay?"

"You bet! Hey, I know this is some serious shit going on, but are you having any fun right now?"

"Little bit."

"Me too. Crazy. Oh, and BTW, I peed in one of your hiking boots when I was hiding in the closet. Sorry about that." Canada begins to giggle uncontrollably. The girl is an emotional wreck.

"Of course you did. What is it with you and urine, Canada?"

"Honestly, I've never had issues with pee before this past week."

"S'fine. I've only worn these things ever once."

We pull up in front of Fiona's bungalow apartment just as the sun is breaking the horizon to the East. Canada leaves her pack in the truck so as not to further freak Fiona out. We knock on the door and a few minutes later, Fiona opens it.

She looks…I can't do it justice. Raven hair that's just a ball of mess. No make-up, face kind of pudgy with sleep. Eyes like a baby. She looks young. Like she's Canada's age, thirteen or whatever. I mean, don't get me wrong. She's obviously late twenties, this isn't a pedo-type thing.

She's just got this ageless type of youth about her, like you'd think of angels having.

"Ah, fer feck's sake, what's all dis about, now?" Albeit a rough-round-the-edges angel.

"No big deal, just need a safe house for a couple of hours and then we're out of your hair." I kiss her on the lips and she kisses me back, despite being obviously annoyed. She has morning breath and she obviously hasn't showered in the past twenty-four. I could devour her right now. All of her, she smells so earthy. Quit judging me.

"Sammy's not going to jail!" Canada says brightly, walking into the bungalow.

"Roi, well there's feckin dat then."

PENNY

"I'll put on de coffee."

"You're up now, like, for the day?" Sammy asks.

"Sure, oi don't think oi can get back ter sleep nigh."

"That's great, I'm gonna commandeer your bed for a couple of hours. Shouldn't day-drink on less than three hours sleep." Sammy walks straight into the bedroom.

"Yer man is a gobshite. Yer want me to set yer up on de couch, honey?"

"Don't think I can go back to sleep either. It's light outside."

"Yer drink coffee?" Never have. Seems like now would be a good time to start.

"Coffee would be lovely," I say.

"How yer take it?"

"However you take it."

"Oi take mine black as midnight on a moonless night."

"Sounds perfect."

Fiona sets two steaming cups on the kitchen table and sits down.

"Oweya, love?"

"I'm good, I guess."

"Sweetie, then why de feck are ye here?"

"Oh, that. Yeah. I might have mentioned earlier, about Sammy being the prime suspect in a murder investigation?"

"Feck yeah, yer said somethin' about dat. Then yer told me to trust himself."

"Oh, it's cool. Everything's fine. I'd show you the video, but I can't turn on my iPhone or the police would know where we are."

"Ah, well, dat makes me feel worlds better. Sammy's de subject of a police manhunt then? An' yer man thought it would be a grand idea ter come to me apartment?" Fiona gets up from the table.

"Where are you going?"

"To murder him, myself." Funny. Wouldn't be the first time someone's tried that tonight.

"No, no, no, no. Sammy's not the subject of a police manhunt. I am. I had to turn on my phone at his apartment earlier to get video of Jeff trying to kill him."

"Jasus bleedin' Chroist, Sammy only dropped me off two hours ago. When did all dis happen?"

"In the last two hours."

"Oi got to re-think getting involved with dis eejit."

"No, Fiona. Really, he's great. Totally honest, Sammy is one of the best people I've ever met in my life. He's the only one who's helping me right now." Fiona flashes me a sharp, insulted look. "Voluntarily, I mean."

"Sure," Fiona sighs. "He's kind of a grand one, oi guess."

"Fiona, can you do me a quick favor?" Sammy sticks his head out of her bedroom.

"Oi thought yer were sleepin'?"

"I need you to text Mealy and Beer from your phone." Sammy recites two phone numbers for her. "Okay, they'll know it's from me, if you text them this exactly. 'Bedded the ginger. Ending my life immediately. Tell no one until you see the body. Sausage Benedict.' Got that?"

"An exactly why am oi textin' dis?" Fiona says, thumbing her iPhone.

"Just letting them know that there's a situation. They need to turn off their phones now and keep them off until they see me."

"You have a code for that?" I ask, somehow not too surprised.

"Yeah. More like a very basic text lexicon for when there might be eyes on our messages."

"And you needed to create that because?"

"Because nothing. It was a brain-job from a couple years back."

"Yer really think 'tis a grand idea for me to get involved with this gobshite?" Fiona asks me. I nod encouragingly.

"You've got to translate," I say to Sammy. He gives me an exasperated look but sits down. Grabs the coffee from in front of me, takes a sip. Nods his approval of the coffee at Fiona.

"Bedded the ginger means bad things happened. Ending my life immediately means, turn off your phones, now. Tell no one until you see the body means keep the phones off until you see me."

"Sausage Benedict?"

"What I want them to order for me, if they get to The Mill before us."

"What about me?"

"Right. Use Fiona's phone to go online and look at the menu. Then text them, 'the condom broke' and give them your order." Fiona makes a vomit face, hands me her phone.

"Nigh is someone gonna tell me why everyone has to go off their phones?"

Sammy gives Fiona a look, as if she should be able to figure this out on her own. Fiona returns a look that says, "Oh, really? And I thought someday you did want to have sex with me." These two are adorable.

"Phones are off because Canada's on the lam. She had to capture video at my place with her phone so there's no question that the police were able to trace it." Here Sammy gives me a look that says, thank you. I well up.

"She told me. Jeff wus tryin' to murder yer, oi understand?"

"Second attempt, actually. Typical Jeff. Last week he misfired and knocked off this girl I was slee…uh, friends with."

"You're quite de catch, fella. Ye tellin' me that dis Jeff character actually killed someone?"

JOE BARRETT 247

"Yeah, and the police think I did it. Hence, the whole murder investigation fiasco."

"But I hid in the closet and got video of Jeff trying to poison Sammy again! And Jeff's confession about when he killed Janice. It was like the longest, most boring Bond-villain-scene ever."

"Quick thinkin.'"

"My sister's idea, actually."

"Wait, yer sister was there?!"

"No, she's dead. But she still talks to me." Maybe sharing too much?

"Ah, oi get it. So you're off yer nut, too. Go on."

"So Mealy and Beer are my legal business partners. When I disappear, they're the logical next step in terms of who the police might contact. That's why their phones need to be off."

"An' oi just sent them a text."

"So what? They get lots of texts. And yours only said that you had sex with a ginger, were going to kill yourself, don't tell anyone, and mentioned breakfast food. Think we're safe."

"An' exactly how long yer think yer can stay off de grid an' evade de police?"

"Just a few hours more. It's not as if I'm planning to end this story in Bolivia or anything. We just need to get together with Mealy and Beer, come up with a plan. I think strategy better with those guys."

"And me."

"And you, Canada."

"An' me."

"Come on, Fiona. I told you this was a work thing."

"An' oi was grand with dat when yer dropped me aff a few hours ago. Situation changed when oi began harborin' fugitives from the law."

"It's okay, Sammy. I want Fiona to come."

"Mealy and Beer don't even know we're together now."

Fiona and I exchange a look, warm smiles.

"What?" Sammy.

"Sammy's got a girlfriend," I sing-song.

"Grow up, Canada." He's actually blushing.

"Dude, all the time I've known you, would have put money on never seeing you blush!"

"You've known me five days."

"Feels like longer."

"I know, me too. Fiona, look. Canada and I, we're in this. You're still totally in the clear. I'm pretty sure everything's gonna work out fine, but it could still go sideways. There really isn't any reason to loop you into something that so heavily involves the law. Do you even have a green card?"

"Oi've got feckin dual citizenship, yer nit."

"Huh? Well, that makes me feel a little better about sitting at your kitchen table right now, actually. Worried we might get immigration cops involved in this circus. Okay, if Canada's good with it, you're more than welcome to join."

"Deadly."

"So when do we meet those guys?" I ask. Sammy looks at a clock above the stove.

"Five hours."

"What do we do in the meantime?"

"Take the bed, Canada. Fi and I are going to make-out on the couch for a while, maybe get a couple of z's, too."

"Oi've got to brush me teeth, then."

"No," Sammy says, grabbing her arm. "Just how you are, is totally fine."

SAMMY

"This is ridiculous," Beer sighs.

"Like, I have no words." Mealy, eyes closed.

"Stupid is what it is." I exhale. "We're just plain stupid. What were we thinking? How long has it been?"

"Too long. Way too long."

"At least a month." Mealy says. "Here, try this."

"Dude, I got the same thing as you." I glance at Fiona.

"No, this is the perfect bite. I don't know why you split everything up."

I look again at Fiona. She gives me a crooked smile. I guess she'll have to get used to this eventually, anyway. I let Mealy put the bite he's prepared into my mouth, on his own fork.

"Oh, you are too right, man. Did you get extra syrup?"

"No, just did a good sopping for you. Best bite ever, no?"

"How 'bout you mix yours up that way and then we switch plates?"

"Sure."

"And you're sure dat Beer is de only one who's gay among those three?" Fiona asks Canada.

"Was before I saw this," Canada answers. Whatever.

"These guys really like brunch, uh?"

"Apparently. My first time on this crazy train, too."

"'Tis feckin weird is what it is." Fiona says. Beer holds out something called a Brunchwich for me to bite. Then he smears the

250 SEMI-GLOSS

breakfast sandwich in the syrup on my plate and puts it in his mouth. "Oi feel like oi'm watching some weird kind of breakfast porn. Naw judgment. Just dat oi was shiftin' dat guy less than an hour ago."

"Whoa! You were what?" Canada asks.

"Shiftin'. Means snogging. Only kissing."

"We should get another side of duck bacon," I say. Mealy and Beer nod, mouths full to busting.

"Oi thought we were here ter talk about dis girl's problems?"

"Eat first, talk later," Beer grunts. "Why doesn't Canada have a Bloody Mary?"

"Ah…cos she's fifteen?"

"It's fine. I got a smoothie."

Beer grabs Canada's smoothie, reaches down and dumps what's left under the table. Pulls the garnish from his fresh Bloody Mary, pours it into her glass and sets it in front of her. Signals the waitress for another round.

"We got stuff to talk about. Better if you have a few drinks in you."

"Honestly, yer people are worse than de Oirish. An' that's sayin' somethin'."

"We're painters, Fiona. Different set of rules." Mealy, the diplomat.

Canada takes the Bloody Mary that Beer gave her, bottoms it up. Fiona side-eye's her.

"Been a long week."

Mealy sets a fresh one in front of her. She downs it just as fast. Be interesting, what a psychologist would think of Canada's intermittent binge drinking.

I sop the last forkful of Mealy's breakfast artwork in the remaining syrup on my plate, stick it in my mouth and don't chew. Not yet. Just let it hang there as I sit back in ecstasy. There is nothing like a Saturday brunch.

Oh, and there's Jeff! I was wondering when he was gonna show up.

I pretend not to notice when he spots our table, is led to a two-top on the other side of the restaurant, clear view of us. He must have made a reservation, specified where he wanted to sit. Or maybe he knows the hostess or something. Good. This ought to be memorable.

"So, exactly what are *you* doing here, Fiona?" Beer pushes back his seat and holds his belly dreamily.

"Watchin' three grown-ass men having a wank ter waffles and duck rasher."

"Wait…did you guys hook up last night?" Mealy burps.

PENNY

I mean, seriously?

I'm being hunted by the police. Sammy is inches away from getting arrested for poisoning his pregnant ex-shack-job. And we really have to endure a full forty-five minutes of ecstatic brunch porn before anyone even brings this stuff up?

Beer gives me his Bloody Mary in a circumvent, but completely obvious manner. I down it in one. Mealy does the same and I do the same. Not sure if it's liquid courage or out of just plain boredom. After another minute or two, it looks like the guys are finally done rapturing over their food and ready to talk.

"So, exactly what are *you* doing here, Fiona?"

"Watchin' three grown-ass men having a wank ter waffles and duck rasher."

"Wait, did you guys hook up last night?" Mealy burps.

"Later." Sammy says, like he's shy.

"What, ye scundered of me now?"

"I'm pretty sure no one at this table knows what that means, Fi."

"Means you're embarrassed about her." Beer groans, holding his bloated belly.

"I stand corrected. How'd you know that?"

"Was hooking up with that Irish guy, Bennie, couple years back."

"Right, whatever happened to him?"

"Not to be impolite, but we're kind of on borrowed time here," I interrupt.

"She's right. Here's the sitch…" In the space of maybe three minutes, Sammy proceeds to give the table such a concise summary of my situation that I feel short-changed.

"Nobody really believed you were a college graduate, Canada. We just didn't care."

"That's fine, Beer. You guys aren't mad at me?"

"Mad at you about what?"

"Oh, I don't know. Fact that you've been employing a fugitive runaway that most of New Jersey is probably looking for? Fact that I've been squatting at the paint house. Fact that I'm fifteen and lied about being Canadian?"

"That Canada thing does sting a little," Mealy sighs. "Canadians are such all-around nice people. But otherwise, none of it really changes how we feel about you."

"So what are we going to do about it?" Sammy.

"Well, she's gonna get caught. That's inevitable. The police know that she's in Tampa, was at your apartment. Why the hell did you even turn your phone on, anyway?" Beer.

"That will unfold presently." Sammy, finger raised.

"Running's out of the question," Beer continues. "She goes back underground and you're gonna get arrested, Sammy. What'll that be, the third time in a month?"

"My time off the grid is done, I get that." I say.

"What'd I miss?" Roofie, walking up to the table.

"Brunch." Beer grunts.

"You guys are going to keep drinking, though, right?" Roofie flags the waitress for a menu, pulls up a chair. "Why's Jeff sitting at that table over there by himself?"

Everyone, including me, looks where Roofie is pointing. When did he get here? Jeff toasts us with his Mimosa.

"He's here for the floor show." Sammy smiles at Jeff, flips him the bird. Turns back to the table. "I know she's gonna get caught. Add another item to my rap sheet. I'm asking, what do we do when she gets caught?"

"Anyone want to give me the back story?" Roofie.

"No. Be more punctual next time." Beer.

"What about emancipation?" Mealy asks. "Maybe we can adopt her. Like, as a company."

"De three of yer? Oi'm sure child welfare would have no problem witcha thirty-somethings adoptin' a fifteen-year-old lassy."

"Just saying, it might be something we could explore."

"You still have access to Senior's lawyers, Sammy?" Beer.

"I guess, until July first at least. But they're pretty busy trying to untie my own knots right now. Anyway, I'm not sure how lawyers are going to help. You're a minor in Florida until you're eighteen, nothing we can do about it. I researched that a few years back."

"Why?" I ask.

"Tricky dating situation."

"Deadly. Dis is something dat oi really don't want to hear more about."

"Point is, she's going to need some sort of legal guardian. I don't think we'd ever have a shot in hell of qualifying on that front. Jesus, Canada. Take it easy, we'll figure something out."

But I'm not sobbing uncontrollably because I'm worried about what happens after the police find me. This particular breakdown, it's because I look to the door and see Aunt Sally staring back at me. And she looks so much like mommy before she got sick. And she looks so much like Catelyn. And I don't know how I didn't notice it before, or why I shut her out of my life when they died. All I can think, I'm not the only one left that's made of the same stuff as Catelyn. And there's this little part of my brain, like maybe two percent, that isn't overcome by waves of emotion. And this little part of my brain, when the five police officers who arrived with Aunt Sally draw their guns and point them at the guys, this part's saying "pretty sure those cops think this girl was abducted."

Aunt Sally runs to me and I meet her halfway, collapse into her arms. Feeling like I never thought I'd feel again, like mommy hugging me. Like Catelyn hugging me. I'm so sorry! I'm so sorry for staying away from you. I just didn't know what to do when mom and Catelyn died. I felt so guilty. I don't say any of this, but it's what's in my head. Through so many tears and sobs, I barely notice the police officers, guns pointed, surrounding the brunch table.

"Okay, how 'bout we just take a beat here, fellas?"

SAMMY

"Okay, how 'bout we just take a beat here, fellas?"

I know this is going to work out okay, eventually. But with Canada in catatonic sobs, hugging that cute forty-something lady, my first priority is making sure no one makes any sudden moves and eats a bullet here. My hands splayed above my head, I say, "This is all me! These guys here, had no prior knowledge or anything to do with any of this!"

"Pure noble," Fiona gives me a nod.

"Hands behind your back." These officers are not messing around. I do as I'm told.

"Samuel Junior, you are under arrest for the murder of one Janice Pirelli. You have the right to remain silent. Anything you say can…"

"Hey! Detective Barney Miller!" What are the chances?

"It's Detective O'Hare."

"Sorry. Has anyone ever told you that you look like…"

"Yes, I've heard it before. Mostly from you, about fifty times last Saturday."

"Should shave the mustache, if it bothers you."

"Mr. Junior…"

"Just call me Sammy. Come on, Detective, we know each other. All those hours at the station a week ago."

"Okay, Sammy, I'll humor you. The toxicology reports came back positive for death by poisoning. Specifically…"

"Large quantities of Visine. I know!"

"I find your enthusiasm to be remarkably ill-suited to the moment. And, just stabbing in the dark here, I'm assuming you had no idea that you were harboring a runaway for whom there was a seven-state manhunt in progress."

"Wrong! I knew that, too. But I only figured it out about ten hours ago."

"You're obviously planning to use the insanity defense."

"Nope. Clear as day, up here." I try to point at my head, but my hands are cuffed behind me. I catch Jeff's eye across the room and he's smiling ear-to-ear. I almost feel bad.

"Well, you're still under arrest. Sorry, Sammy. If it helps, I'll gladly testify that you're certifiable." Detective O'Hare shakes his head sadly. He totally likes me, I can tell.

"Hey, Canada! I don't want to interrupt your catharsis or anything, but…!"

The police officer grabs my behind-the-back handcuffs and starts dragging me towards the door.

"Wait!" Canada shouts, finally pulling herself away from the sobbing embrace.

"No, seriously. Take your time, Canada. I'm only being hauled into custody here."

Canada darts over, her iPhone already out.

"Just watch this!" She hits the button to turn on her iPhone, points it at Detective O'Hare's face.

Then hits the button again.

And again.

"Dammit, does anybody have a charger?"

Thankfully, Canada's outburst has Detective O'Hare curious, so he delays my trip to the big house and lets Canada log-into her iCloud account from one of the police iPads. While she's doing this, Jeff and I lock eyes.

Everyone at our table crowds the iPad to watch Canada's ad hoc documentary. I, on the other hand, am watching Jeff's expression devolve from maniacal glee, to consternation, and finally to trepidation. At this last stage, I raise my eyebrows and round my mouth into a surprised "O."

Two minutes into the video, the guns are out again. But this time, they're not pointed at me.

I honestly feel bad when they drag Jeff away in cuffs, cursing me with the type of rage particular to true sociopaths. Think back on the weeks of psychological abuse we heaped on him. Especially me. We wanted to break him. Guess we can check that box. But I figure none of us really considered that we might break him in the wrong direction. Huh. Well, lesson learned, I guess. No point in beating myself up over it.

Canada, crying like a baby, drops her whole story to O'Hare, the other cops and the lady who actually is her Aunt Sally, house down the street from the job site. Seems Jeff informed the police that I'd be brunching at The Mill, which dovetailed nicely with their dragnet for a missing girl, launched about seven hours prior in cooperation with New Jersey law enforcement. Detective O'Hare has an officer pull my cuffs, apologizes in a very formal and detailed sort of way, halfway meaning it, halfway worried about a lawsuit.

Like I'd ever sue Tampa. I love this town.

PENNY

I'm crying so hard during my whole confession thing, it's a wonder the police can understand a word I'm saying. Even the detective guy with the nineteen-seventies porn mustache tears up some. Because I don't just keep to the pertinent facts. I can't help but weave in my mom and Catelyn and how my dad didn't want me in the first place and still doesn't want me now. And the only person sobbing harder than I am through it all is Aunt Sally. I just can't believe I never realized how she's so much like mom and Catelyn.

After the police uncuff Sammy and drag Jeff out of the restaurant, screaming like a psychopath, I'm left standing in front Aunt Sally and the rest of my crew. While the detective guy is apologizing to a bored-looking Sammy on behalf of the entire judicial system, I hug Roofie, hug Fiona, hug Mealy especially hard. And then Beer extends his hand for me to shake. He's such a dick.

When Sammy's done with the detective, I bolt onto him the way you hug someone you love who you might never see again. I hug him like he's mom. Hug him like he's Catelyn.

"Easy, Canada. You don't want to give Fi the wrong idea."

"I don't want to leave. I want to stay with you guys." I'm ruining his shirt with my tears and snot.

"Then don't leave. Stick around. You know you're one of us."

"I think they're gonna make me go."

260 SEMI-GLOSS

"I mean, you've run away before. And we'll always be here. You know you've always got a spot on our crew." He hugs me back now. Same way I'm hugging him. "And Canada. Thanks, okay? Really. Wasn't for you turning on your phone, I'd be prepping, bride-like, for about six hundred hardened inmates in federal penitentiary. I shrug stuff off, but I know that, okay? Remember, I know that. And if there's anything you ever need, you've got my marker."

"Okay." I have no idea what a marker is, but don't want to ruin the moment.

"Ready, honey?" Aunt Sally, looking at me like she's found the Lost Ark. So full of mom and Catelyn, I feel ashamed that I pushed her away. "Come on, we can talk at my house."

"I need to get my stuff."

"We'll drive it over ter yer later, me ud flower."

"Okay, thanks." I give the guys a wave as Aunt Sally takes my hand, leads me out of The Mill and into her Range Rover.

"Am I in a lot of trouble?" I slide into the front seat. Aunt Sally turns on the car, then grabs my hand, holds it tight. Drops her head onto the steering wheel, sobbing. So, naturally, I dissolve into tears again. Figure I've got maybe three or four years of bottled-up emotion in me, will probably be at least eighteen before I've cried it all out. "I'm so sorry, okay? I didn't mean to…"

"You can't, Penn. God, you can't do this to me, Penny. Not after Gwen and Cat." Gwendoline, my mom, her sister. Cat, what she called Catelyn. "Don't you realize? You're all I have left. The last seven days almost killed me, I was so worried. I didn't know if you were kidnapped or…or dead. Penny, why didn't you call me if you were having trouble? We could have figured something out. You didn't need to run away. You just can't do that to my heart, it's too broke already."

"I didn't know. I mean, you liked Catelyn better. She was your favorite. And then when I killed her…" I'm crying way too hard to continue. Aunt Sally pulls me into a hug while the car idles, my head in the crook of her neck, just like how I sleep with green bunny.

"You didn't kill your sister, Penn. You can't think that."

"I know," I sob, "but I still feel like it's my fault."

"What happened to Catelyn was a freak accident, Penn. It was so not your fault."

"I just need to blame someone, and the only one I can think of to blame is me. And I can't even imagine that you and Dad don't blame me. Or you, at least. Dad doesn't blame anyone for anything because you'd have to have feelings in order to blame. Why is he not here, even?! The police find his missing daughter after a whole week, and he doesn't even show up!"

"Penn, I was with your dad for most of last week. Well, at the house, I mean. Honey, I don't think your dad is…I think he's unwell. His head is just, I'm not sure how to say, it's like there's nothing there anymore. Like he's turned off. I think, when your mom got sick and died, he just broke. Never got fixed. I'm sorry to be so blunt, but…"

"But he has a daughter he's supposed to love! I'm here. He doesn't care about me at all!"

"I don't think he cares about anything these days, honey. I don't think he can. Maybe someday he'll get better, but that's on him. Don't think there's anything you can do about it."

"He tried to ship me off to boarding school in Buffalo. I came here instead. I don't want to go to Buffalo, Aunt Sally! I don't want to be anywhere." I take a breath, try to control my sobs. "No, that's not true. I want to be here. I have friends here. Real friends. And I know how to paint. I'm good at it. Really good."

"Penn, we can make that work, honey," she sobs, looks at me almost excited, like she really wants me to be with her. "We can make that work."

"Sorry I'm not Catelyn," I sniffle.

"I don't want you to be Catelyn, Penn. I want you. Catelyn reminded me of my big sister, my hero. Just like Catelyn was your hero."

"How'd you know that?"

"Anyone who ever saw you two together knew that. But Penn…you remind me of myself. When I was younger. I should have told you. I've always felt connected to you. And I've always loved you, even when I was bad at showing it. But I'm gonna make it up, I promise."

"I guess we both lost our heroes." I use the heel of my hand to wipe my eyes.

"I don't know," Aunt Sally sob-laughs. "Catelyn was pretty fearless, but she never pulled a stunt like you just did."

And I think…yeah, that's true.

And I think, Catelyn really will be in this world as long as I'm in it.

And that makes me feel good.

SAMMY

SAY MY NAME!
How I hit rock bottom and found myself a drill.

"We're gonna finish up these spindles by break-down tonight. I thought it was gonna take us another three or four days, at least. We'll be done with this whole place by Friday."

"We had Juan and Carlos," Mealy drones.

"And me!"

"And you, Canada." Mealy breaks his focus just long enough to give her a crooked smile.

"Don't condescend. I'm almost at pace with you and Sammy."

"No, Canada. You're not. But you're doing a good job for someone who started painting only a week ago." These young painters think they can go from the farm leagues straight to the majors, without putting in the years. Got to keep their egos in check.

Today's brain-job is a natural. Best title and subtitle for a biography of Jeff's life.

"We have another job lined up after this, right?"

"Canada, we have jobs lined up through the end of the year."

"Good. Around here?"

CLEAR EYES, DARK SOUL!
The spectacularly botched Visine murders.

"Few blocks away."

"Good."

"How was sleeping in a real bed?" I ask.

"I slept in a real bed when I was squatting upstairs. How was sleeping at Aunt Sally's? Past two nights were the best sleep I've had in probably five years."

We did some pretty hard day-drinking after Canada left The Mill on Saturday. Lot of adrenaline to dilute. But the party broke up around four p.m. and Fi ended up spending the night at my place. No sex, because she's not "bleedin spare arse," whatever that means. But I'm good with it. Realize lust hasn't been much of a friend to me the past few years, so figure I might want to try the love route, instead. And given the fact that I've finally harpooned the White Whale, seems as good a time to start as any. Not that I've told Fiona I love her or anything. Way too soon for that nonsense. But we did spend all day Sunday together, too. Except for my court-mandated therapy session with Dr. Carter. Fi waited in a Starbucks across the street for that. Only three more sessions and I'm a free man.

NOT MY DADDY ISSUES!
The day-to-day challenges of seeking approval from another man's father.

"So you're really gonna hang around Tampa for a while?" Beer stomps down the stairs.

"That a problem?" Canada drones.

"You gonna make it a problem?"

"My dad didn't care. He was going to ship me off to boarding school in Buffalo, anyway. Probably happy that I'm staying down here with Aunt Sally."

"Because you're with family," Mealy says.

"Because he won't have to pay for room and board." Canada cuts the bottom of her spindle, looks at Beer. "I'm done. Can I go cut trim in the master bedroom?"

"I don't care. Just don't touch the rollers."

"Why?"

"Man's work."

"Oh, I am so rolling the master." Canada darts upstairs.

"Clever," Mealy hums. Only a truly inexperienced painter would prefer the drudgery of rolling walls to skill-work like cutting trim.

"Reverse psychology." Beer taps his forehead. "Nice having a greenhorn on the job again. Their minds are like putty."

ONLY A PENIS!
What makes me just like Steve Jobs.

PENNY

I can't help but slip into the upstairs guest room for a few minutes. Feels like years ago, was it really only eight days? I pull the tarp, lie down on the bed. Try to imagine myself here, just like this, last Sunday night.

But a whole universe happened between then and now. Utterly hopeless to ecstatically happy, with the biggest adventure of my life filling up the middle. I think about how bleak everything seemed early on. How I almost turned on my phone at Aunt Sally's place and none of this would have even happened. None of it, if I gave up then.

Think about how hopeless people should just hang on a little longer, even if it's by a fingernail. Because you never know.

But that's not right.

Because you do know.

If you can just keep believing.

SAMMY

"Last session, Cynthia."

"And yet, I still need to remind you to call me Dr. Carter. Some university should do a study on you."

"I'm going to miss our playful banter, too." I sigh.

"So tell me."

"Only if you admit that you're not asking because it's your job. I want to hear you say that you're personally curious about my life."

"It's been an interesting story; I'll admit that much."

I gave Cynthia the full rundown a couple of sessions ago. The whole Jeff fiasco, Canada's sad tale, me and Fiona, how I decided to buck my inheritance and commit to my current lifestyle, no safety net. She really warmed back up to me when she found out I was no longer the prime suspect in a homicide investigation.

Past two sessions, she's been bingeing me like Netflix. But I get the feeling she might be digging my life ironically, the same way you'd watch a show like *Riverdale*. Whatever, as long as she's digging it.

"Where do you want to start?"

"How about with you and Fiona?"

"All good. Seriously, it's like a real human relationship. We have some sticky areas, but we work through them."

"Like what?"

"Oh, I don't know, hygiene maybe?"

"Hygiene. You mean personal hygiene? Like you don't shower enough?"

"It's Fiona. Told you, she's Irish. Like, off the boat."

"She doesn't shower enough."

"Actually, my point of contention is that she showers too often. I like her to smell a little more, say, earthy than her daily ablutions indulge. It's weird, I've never had a thing about body odor before, but something about Fiona's scent really gets me going. Hey, Cynthia, that's psychology! You want to talk about it?"

"Dr. Carter. And no. That is not a rabbit hole I want to peek into on your last session."

"Fair."

"How's Penny doing?"

"Who? Oh, Canada. Still working with us, really developing as a painter. She might have a future in it. Don't see her ever mastering ladder work, but she's a champ with the floor stuff. I think she cuts better than Roofie, actually."

"I mean, aside from her abilities as a painter."

"Oh, right. Good. She's good. Her aunt pulled strings so she could take some last-minute entrance exams for prep schools down here. Turns out, Canada's super smart. She starts at Berkeley Prep in the fall."

"Berkeley Prep, huh? That's, like, a really excellent school. Maybe the best in Tampa."

"Sure is. For her, at least. She didn't get into Tampa Prep."

"Uh-huh."

"I actually picked her up there, at Berkeley, after her last interviews. Got a nickel tour from the AP Psych professor. Bit of a country club, ask me. Psychologist lady was kind of a hottie, though."

"Always relevant."

"Just, you don't see that too much, in your profession."

She drops her shoulders, stares.

"No offense, Cynthia. You've got an inner beauty that can't help but shine through."

"Dr. Carter. And shut up."

"So, anyway, things are all kinds of rosy for Canada these days."

"Good. Seems like a sweet girl, overdue for a run of good luck. Anything new on the homicides?"

"Nope. Jeff's being held without bail. The video evidence is pretty tight, so don't see any way that's going to end without him behind bars or in some high-security loony bin."

"Prefer the term Psychiatric Hospital, these days. Dealing with any residual feelings?"

"I mean, I'm still kind of proud of myself for the brilliant trickery I employed to coordinate Jeff's arrest and my exculpation."

"Interesting, given Penny was the one who had the brains to capture video."

"Yeah, but I'm talking about everything after that. The whole set up. It was very dramatic."

"Okay. But what I'm really asking is, have you had any residual feelings about Janice? Have you addressed that part of the equation?"

"I mean, it's a shame. But I'm okay with it. Try not to let that kind of stuff get under my skin, you know?"

"Stuff like waking up next to a dead pregnant woman."

"Like I said, I really didn't know her. Other than physically. And it's life. Right, Cynthia? You got to just roll with it."

"Dr. Carter. And it's not everyone's life, thank God. So, moving on, work's okay?"

"Yeah, work's good. Just finishing up another gig in Beach Park, then we start on a really nice place over on Davis Island. Big white house, blue shutters and trim, right on the bay. Near where Tom Brady lives."

"Sounds nice."

"Yeah, owner did well in private equity and that type of thing. But he's actually a good guy, makes him kind of a unicorn in that field. Like most smart people, doesn't know the first thing about the time and effort involved in a full interior paint job, though. So we'll do okay, money-wise."

"Good. That's good. Okay, well, we've still got a little time. Why don't you talk to me about Senior? What you're feeling."

"Deep hatred and resentment, no change on that front for the past thirty-odd years. What else do you want to know?"

"You're still planning to walk away from the money."

"Yup."

"You make peace with that?"

"Cynthia, I don't think I'll ever really be able to make peace with walking away from that much money. But it's the right thing to do."

"Dr. Carter. And good, I'm proud of you."

"Thanks. So that just about does it, huh?"

"Guess I can let you out a few minutes early, last session and all."

"Been a pleasure, Cynthia."

"Dr. Car…it doesn't matter, you're not even a patient anymore. Wish you luck, Sammy. Hope we don't meet again."

"Kinda rude thing to say."

"You know what I mean."

I go in for a hug, but Cynthia wants none of that, so I settle for a firm handshake.

Driving back to my condo, I feel good. Sure, there's some trepidation. I assume that's normal when you're on the verge of relative poverty. But I've got a good job. Got the guys. Got Fiona. And Canada's sticking around. So, yeah. I feel good.

And this good feeling lasts right up until I turn the corner and see my condo.

Because this cannot be good.

That black SUV in the driveway, it's a lawyer car. One of Senior's. I pull up next to it. Rodney, Senior's chief legal, gets out to meet me.

"Jesus, Rodney. I've got another week before I have to answer my dad's ultimatum."

"Sam, I'm not here about the ultimatum. It's about your father."

"What about him?" I'm getting a weird vibe.

"I'm sorry I have to be the one to tell you this…Senior, he…passed away this morning."

Whoa. Senior passed away. I take a few seconds to process this. It seems so out-of-nowhere, but I guess a lot of deaths are like that. Senior's dead. I know I'm supposed to feel something…

"Well, thank God for that. How'd it happen?"

"Heart attack."

"Was he having sex with a twenty-year-old? That's how he always wanted to go out."

"Was the Goop Group thing that did it."

"The Goop Group thing?" I ponder a second. Just how could my father's only cash cow program have anything to do with his death? It's syndicated everywhere, so it's not like all the channels would cancel at once.

"You don't know? It's all over the internet."

"Apparently not on any porn sites."

"Google it. Some kind of corporate sabotage, we think. Not good."

"I'll check it out. Whoa."

"You okay, Sam?"

"Sure, it's just, you had me nervous for a minute there."

"What?"

"Your whole, I don't know, body language thing when you got out of the car. It made me feel like you were going to give me some really bad news or something."

"I never tire witnessing the joy of filial love."

"Come on, Rodney. You didn't like him either. The bastard was all set to disinherit me."

"You were going to turn him down?"

"Sure was. Wait, did he already change his will?" My heart drops.

"Yes."

My face collapses. And there it is. A near nine-digit inheritance, dust in the wind.

"But the company is still yours." What's that now?

"I don't give a damn about the company, Rodney. What about his assets?" Not to sound shallow, but we're talking about almost a hundred million here.

"The assets also go to you." I nod, taking it in. Maybe the old man wasn't such a bastard after all. "For now."

"For now? What the hell does that even mean, Rodney?"

"Like I said, Senior did make changes to his will. He added…certain stipulations." Rodney looks grave, but I think he's actually enjoying this.

"Stipulations."

"Given some sensitive aspects as regards the business, we've pushed the reading to tomorrow, before the wake and funeral next week."

"Of course the bastard added stipulations."

"It'll all be clear tomorrow at the reading. Four o'clock, our offices. And, hey. Condolences on your loss, Sam."

I get this weird feeling that last sentence wasn't about my father at all.

HIGH-GLOSS
FORTY-EIGHT HOURS EARLIER...

TASHA

"I know, I'm late." I walk into the conference room, unabashed. Six weeks and I'm already unofficially running this whole damn company, so they can cut me slack. When it comes to content, production unofficially runs everything. Unofficially as in, all the work and none of the credit. I should have gone to beauty school.

Senior raises his palm towards me in a halting gesture, nods at Clifford to continue whatever nonsense he was spouting.

Clifford Phelps, Creative Director at Junior-Senior, shoots me an exasperated look. As if my showing up late was a personal assault. In my short tenure as SVP Production, Clifford and I have already developed the type of hostile working relationship that typically takes years to evolve.

"Okay, like I was saying, the new opening starts with an image of the sun on clear blue."

"Just like the old opening," Senior nods.

"Right, just like the old opening," Clifford continues, talking over the video. "But then we pull the shot back and see that it's really a reflection of the sun in the kaleidoscope of Blue Goop's eye. And as we continue to pull back and pan right, we see Blue Goop staring peacefully at the sky on a warm summer day. It's all very Zen."

"I like it," Senior says.

"Yeah, one small comment." They look at me, I swear, like I just broke wind.

"I know you're still working out how things work out around here, *Natasha*," Clifford pauses the video, rolls his eyes. "But you're really just in charge of the execution…not the creative."

"I understand my role, *Clifford*. How long is this sequence you're talking about?"

"Twelve seconds. The opening credits roll underneath, just like the old sequence."

"You've got Blue Goop staring straight at the sun for twelve seconds? Does anyone else have a problem with this?"

The room is silent.

"We're talking about a little kid show here. A demographic that is very prone to replicating the behavior of our characters. Anyone?"

"I got it!" Dixie chirps suddenly. "We don't want little kids to go outside and stare directly at the sun!"

"That's a gold star for you, Dixie," I say. "We don't want little kids to go outside and stare directly at the sun for extended seconds. Because they could go blind, *Clifford*."

Clifford gives me a murder stare. Senior tilts his head, drums his fingers on the conference table for a few seconds.

"Girl's got a point, Clifford."

It's the nineteen-seventies here at Junior-Senior. Because where else would a thirty-four-year-old senior executive, me, be referred to as "the girl" in a business meeting? I should say something, but I don't. Don't have the bandwidth to open up another battlefront, especially with the owner. A self-aggrandizing old man who loves *The Goop Group* almost as much as he loves his pathetic, trying-way-too-hard-to-be-forever-young self. So I let it slide.

"I really don't think…" Clifford stammers.

"Just use the old opening. No one cares about a new opening for *The Goop Group*, anyway. Well, that about wraps things up then, and I've got a tee time." Senior claps his hands, ending all discussion.

"We'll get sorted and make it happen, Senior," Clifford all kinds of suck-up. Although since we've just decided to use the same opening credit sequence that we've used for the past ten seasons, I'm not sure exactly what he needs to get sorted and make happen.

"Stick around a minute, Clifford." I say, as Senior walks out of the conference room without any acknowledgement of Dixie or myself. "We need to discuss your crew changes for the Grantford Dealership commercials."

"I don't know what makes you think you can pull rank on me," Clifford peeves, as Dixie leaves the conference room. "You're not my boss, you know."

"I never said I was your boss, *Clifford*. But I have a job here. And a pretty basic part of that job is making sure we don't lose money on the work we do."

I hand him a crew sheet. He doesn't look at it.

"You realize people judge us by our work, right? Look at the big picture. We put out sub-par work, we don't get new clients. Period," Clifford whines.

"Let's walk through the crew, shall we?"

"Fine." Clifford curls his upper lip, shrugs.

"Okay, great. Grantford is a regional car dealership with a package deal for one commercial per quarter at an all-in fixed price, right?"

"I've been working with Grantford for ten years, Natasha. I know the deal."

"So, right, we've got mostly local talent. Hair-and-makeup at a three-hundred-dollar day-rate." Which means they come from an upscale Swann Avenue retail salon. "Actors, aside from Grantford family, at a two-hundred-fifty day-rate." Which means local community theater folk. "Stylists, same. Gaffers, our own staff. Location, free because we're shooting at the dealership, that's good. And, oh, what's this? A twelve-thousand-dollar day-rate, plus travel expenses, for the videographer. Are you out of your mind?"

"Chris Freeman is an artist."

"First of all, I've worked with Chris on a number of occasions, and he's a pretentious dick. Secondly, we're not flying in a camera guy from New York for this low-budget project just so you can pad your resume with the fact that you worked with the great Chris Freeman. Because, thirdly, we would be operating at a loss of over thirty percent if we were to go forward with this absurd plan. The hell were you thinking?"

"Sometimes you've got to be willing to take a loss for greater gain down the road." Clifford doesn't look at me. "We don't invest in our projects, which is exactly why we don't get new clients."

"No. Exactly why we don't get new clients is because we're based in Tampa, *Clifford*."

Sourcing content from Tampa is like sourcing technology services from Mobile, Alabama. The only reason Junior-Senior has survived for the past twenty-years is because we have the infrastructure necessary to produce *The Goop Group*, which we can also employ to produce bottom-feeder content like local car dealership and ambulance-chaser commercials at super competitive rates.

"The whole shoot is composed of three-figure talent. So how exactly does a five-figure videographer raise the tide?"

Clifford opens his mouth. Then shuts it. Because there is no suitable response. In lieu of, he dramatically throws up his arms, stomps out of the room.

I have a three-year-old niece who does the exact same thing when she doesn't get her way. I need to clear my head.

I walk back to the post-production room. Though, for *The Goop Group*, it's the pre-production, content creation, and post-production room, because almost the entire show is computer generated imagery. This essentially makes it Thanial's own giant office.

"Tasha."

"Thanial."

Nathanial Tracey. To everyone else, he's Nathanial. One of those mom's basement creative tech guys who goes by full name only. Not Nate. Not even Nathan. It's always Nathanial. Except with me.

"Play the reel. I need it."

"Comin' up. Hey, Jocko! Take five." Thanial's post-production lackey doesn't need asking twice. He grabs a pack of Marlboro Reds and makes for the roof.

"Anything new?"

"I show you Tomas de Torquemada?"

"Spanish Inquisition. Was wondering why I hadn't seen that pop up yet."

Thanial, chief animator and editor of *The Goop Group* adventures and related content over the past fifteen years, has a side gig. For his own, and now my, personal enjoyment he has been working on a magnum opus reel featuring Goop Group characters enacting the most depraved scenes in human history. No joke, I'm talking Nazi goose-stepping rallies, Holodomor, Jack-the-Ripper, Marque de Sade, holocaust concentration camps, Rwanda, John Wayne Gacy…and dozens more. The content makes me cringe, but balances nicely with my violent hatred for what is probably the worst program ever created. We should be in jail for producing it.

"Booze?" Thanial produces a handle of Jameson's from his bottom desk drawer.

"Christ, yeah."

He pours heavy into two legit whiskey sipping glasses from the same drawer. No paper cups for Thanial. Guy's got class. He hits play on the reel.

"This is the new stuff. I roll the scenes FIFO." First in, first out. An inventory management term, but Thanial's not shy about adopting the right words to describe his creative process.

"This is utterly disgusting." I drain my whiskey, Thanial refills the glass. "But it's like I can't look away."

I watch Red Goop slowly lower a naked young lady by rope onto a Judas Cradle. So gross. Thank God this is animated. In other scenes, he sometimes mixes CGI and live action. Still, it's going to visit me in my dreams, and not in a good way.

Why we get off watching this kill-porn? Why did Thanial abbreviate his name for only me, just like my own abbreviated name?

In solidarity, is why. Because we both believe that *The Goop Group* is straight-up evil. Part of the problem. We feel dirty about making money because of the show. Dirtier even than we feel just working at Junior-Senior.

"We got to release this for broadcast someday," I say, as Thanial fills my glass again. It's two in the afternoon.

"Ha! Only in the context of a suicide pact."

"Deal. Hey, have you uploaded tomorrow's content to the broadcast server?"

"Just reruns, got till three. Oh, this is good. Have you seen Vlad the Impaler? Purple Goop's finest moment, I think."

"Saw it last week. How 'bout one more?"

"How 'bout you buy the next bottle, then?" he fills my glass.

"I'll buy the next case."

"Oh, shit. Got to take this." Thanial looks at his iPhone.

"Take it then."

Thanial picks up the call, paces the room for a minute or two, speaking in a low voice.

"Hey, Tasha. I got to bolt."

"Everything okay?"

"Yeah, sure. Okay, no. It's my mom. She's in the hospital."

"You told me your mom was dead."

"Fine. It's my LSD guy, okay?"

"You have an LSD guy? You, like, dose regularly?"

"Daily. How exactly do you think I create *The Goop Group*?"

"No judgment. Everything okay?"

"There's a chance he's in hostage negotiations with Tampa P.D. in Ybor City."

"A chance?"

"Yeah. More likely than not he's in a pillow fort in his bedroom, but he gave me an actual Ybor address this time, so I need to check it out."

"Fair."

"Hey, can you upload tomorrow's files to the broadcast server for me?"

"Sure, no problem." I pour a little more Jameson's into my glass.

"You know the naming conventions? The right folders?"

"Thanial, I run production at this joint. It's fine. Go save your acid guy."

"You're sure?"

"What could possibly go wrong?" Just a hint of slur in my voice.

ACKNOWLEDGEMENTS

When I mentioned to my son that I was planning to write a book about house painting, he asked if I'd ever considered writing a novel about something even remotely interesting.

My son is kind of a dick.

But he had a point. House painting may be the most mind-numbingly boring work on this planet, so how could a novel *about* house painting possibly appeal to any kind of readership? It's like writing a novel called "Managed Care" – you lose roughly ninety percent of potential readers just because the title is so boring. Sigh.

But here *you* are at the end of the book! And assuming you're not one of those people who immediately skips to the end of a book just to read the acknowledgements, I want to thank you for reading it. Seriously, you might be the only person in the world who's read this book, so I want to thank *you* specifically.

Other people to thank... My aforementioned son, whom I conscripted on many an afternoon to riff for hours on brain jobs and urban art projects when he should probably have been doing his homework. Thanks, Joe – I honestly couldn't have written this book without you and every day I'm grateful for your amazing creativity and fantastic sense of humor. Love you, bud.

And of course my lovely wife, Michelle. Thanks for your patience, love and support throughout the writing of this book and life in general.

I have a daughter, too. But she refuses to read any of my books before I die, so I'm thanking her in my post-mortem future. I hope you liked them, Sophie! You'll always be the quiet inspiration for any story I write.

Thanks also to my regular first readers: Kate McGinty, Aimee Barrett, Joe and Maris Barrett. Reading a pre-edited draft of a manuscript is painful and I totally appreciate your time and effort. And special thanks to two new early readers – my buddy John Kirtley, one of the smartest and most well-read guys I know (why he reads my books is beyond me) and Breeze Giannasio, a brilliant interior designer (seriously, Google her) with some amazing writing chops of her own. Thanks so much to all of you!

Thanks also to my editor, Rob Carr, who always makes my books better. It's a low bar, so not much of a compliment, but still he's great.

And finally, thanks to Reagan Rothe and the team at Black Rose for their questionable judgement in publishing this thing.

ABOUT THE AUTHOR

Joe Barrett, award-winning author of *Managed Care* and *Unplugged*, has been a #1 best-seller in multiple Amazon paid categories (Kindle and Book) in the United States, United Kingdom, Canadian and Australian markets.

Prior to an early retirement, he spent twenty-five years as chief executive of entrepreneurial organizations ranging from private, venture-funded companies to large publicly-listed multinational corporations. None of which was much fun.

Joe writes and lives in South Tampa with his wife, two kids and a rat in a dog-suit.

NOTE FROM THE AUTHOR

Word-of-mouth is crucial for any author to succeed. If you enjoyed *Semi-Gloss*, please leave a review online—anywhere you are able. Even if it's just a sentence or two. It would make all the difference and would be very much appreciated.

Thanks!
Joe Barrett

We hope you enjoyed reading this title from:

BLACK ROSE writing™

www.blackrosewriting.com

Subscribe to our mailing list – *The Rosevine* – and receive **FREE** books, daily deals, and stay current with news about upcoming releases and our hottest authors.
Scan the QR code below to sign up.

Already a subscriber? Please accept a sincere thank you for being a fan of Black Rose Writing authors.

View other Black Rose Writing titles at www.blackrosewriting.com/books and use promo code **PRINT** to receive a **20% discount** when purchasing.

Made in the USA
Las Vegas, NV
27 January 2024